Don't Change A
THING

Don't Change A
THING

WILLIAM LOWRY

authorHOUSE®

AuthorHouse™ UK Ltd.
1663 Liberty Drive
Bloomington, IN 47403 USA
www.authorhouse.co.uk
Phone: 0800.197.4150

Published by AuthorHouse 05/20/2014

ISBN: 978-1-4969-7813-4 (sc)
ISBN: 978-1-4969-7814-1 (e)

TABLE OF CONTENTS

Foreword

If we were to review our own life span, we could probably recognise a number of people who have crossed our path as friends, relatives, workmates or maybe casual acquaintances, or even someone you have seen at a distance, who have stuck out as being different for whatever reason, and it could be that they just looked different, dressed differently, or maybe just spoke differently, which caused us to put to them in a category of "not one of us" for whatever that might mean.

One of the "stand-outs" is Tourette's Syndrome, a neurological condition that has the individual making involuntary noises and tics.

This may cause undue concern to anyone in close proximity and embarrassment to the person concerned.

However that person is only different from a sociological perspective, and is normal in every other way as demonstrated by a young man named Marc Elliot, a Washington University graduate and now a gifted public speaker educating people on this subject of being different with Tourette's Syndrome.

Savants readily fall into this categorisation of "not one of us".

Their brilliance in a particular field, whether it be drawing like Stephen Wiltshire, music like Leslie Lemke, complex calendar calculations by Orlando Serrell, or the exceptional mathematical and language abilities of Daniel Temmet makes them special.

Let's not forget Kim Peek famously portrayed in the "Rain Man"

They were different.

Those with Asperger's Syndrome are another group of "stand outs".

Dr Hans Asperger nick named his young patients as "little professors".

Most of the major advances, in science and art, have been made by people with Aspergers, from Mozart to Einstein.

Generic traits or learned skills is yet to be formally determined.

They were different.

However it does seem to me that there is the possibility that a "smidgen" of these characteristics could appear in anyone of us to varying degrees.

Martin O'Leary is a case in point, which separates him from the ordinary.

While none of these 'syndromes' are deeply imbedded in his make-up, his life is anything but mainstream, which may account for the complexities of his journey.

A "smidgen" perchance? Maybe, *but he is different.*

"DON'T CHANGE A THING"

WILLIAM LOWRY. AUTHOR. 2014

Chapter 1

The Journey Begins

The stillness of the early morning air was disturbed by the rumbling garbage trucks as they went about their necessary tasks of maintaining the city's cleanliness. The noise echoed through the narrow back streets of the sleeping city heralding for some, the start of a new spring day.

Martin O'Leary resented this intrusion that interrupted a blissful sleep, which over a long period of time had almost eluded him, and but for this fleeting time, allowed him to bathe in the intoxication of fantasy and freedom, and thus deliver him from the nightmare of a tortured mind.

He yawned lustily and rolled out of bed, and sat on the edge of the mattress trying to gather his thoughts before launching himself into the day. With one almighty heave he stood unsteadily, as if drunk, but Martin was sober, as he was on a self imposed "dry". He'd been a bit liverish and needed to go on the wagon.

Stretching as though reaching for the ceiling Martin promptly kicked the bedside table in his move toward the bay window. A sharp pain shot from his right little toe, followed by a howl and umpteen curses that would have awakened his neighbours if not the dead. Hopping about, shouting obscenities and blaspheming vigorously he finally consoled his little toe by putting the other foot on top and stayed in that pose until the pain subsided.

Finally he made his way to the window and looked out on the beginnings of a beautiful spring day. The sight was such that already Martin was putting the bad start behind him and determined to take the best out of what this day had to offer.

Sundays had become a ritual. He would visit his favourite coffee shop, have a nice breakfast and pass a few pleasantries with his old friend Bernard the owner of the establishment; admire the ever fascinating opera house and of course the pretty girls as they passed by, and curse the fact that he was no longer young and could only look . . . . "For who would be interested in a worn out old bugger with no future," He would say under his breath, and after reading all the Sunday papers Martin would make the same observation, as he always did, "what a load of crap these bastards write . . . no wonder the public is still as confused as ever with all these lies and dodgy feather-bedding politicians".

And then he would throw down the papers in total disgust, followed by a series of expletives, and profane his own weakness in having read them.

Bernard would cast a watchful eye in Martin's direction and once satisfied that this was a passing indiscretion, would continue with his other customers, assuring them not to be concerned about the harmless eccentricity from their neighbour.

Once having got all that off his chest Martin could now settle in to enjoying what he liked to do best.

The study of human nature had always fascinated him.

Watching people's expressions, their body language and conversation. In many ways it could have been interpreted as trying to find answers to his own complex make up, and at the same time relishing his own deep interest in what made people tick. It was a form of behavioural science, watching the foibles and strengths of his fellowman.

A curiosity, that had been with him since childhood, and had continued into his adult life. It had helped him he thought, to have the ability to read people and understand where they were coming from. But there were times when he thought this was all delusional, a figment of his imagination. "Who knows what's going on, particularly when you're dealing with women."

Martin was quick to qualify this thought. He was not a misogynist in any way, as he loved women; it was just that they were unique, and on a different playing field, and played by foreign rules, that mortal men could not keep up with.

But then, that's the challenge he enjoyed.

God, he thought, must have had a wonderful time making them.

'Just dreaming . . . . just dreaming' he would conclude to himself, and even though the opera house forecourt was full of hustle and bustle on a Sunday morning, there was a certain contemplative aspect to the whole collage of humanity, against a backdrop of the most beautiful harbour in the world.

What a fantastic place this was. The sinecure of all things cultural.

Chapter 2

The Holder Of The Keys

As Martin basked in the ambience of this place, which he often referred to as his "little touch of heaven", his attention was drawn to a family occupying the next cubicle, where the children were holding court on matters wide and varied as kids are want to do.

He was particularly drawn to their manner of speech, which had an accent of culture and not the common idiom. They were polite to one another, and if they reached a point of disagreement, there were no ugly overtones that so many resort to in getting their point across.

He turned himself around in an attempt to get a better view of this group, and noted that there were two children, a boy, and a girl, who was as pretty as a picture, and from what he could see they were with an elderly gentleman, who Martin presumed must have been the Grandfather as the children referred to him as Opa.

The girl it would seem was the apple of his eye, for she pulled his ears, fiddled with his moustache and adjusted his tie, all to his obvious delight, and took pride of place on the old man's knee.

She had acquired the feminine genotype so successfully that already, even at this tender age of maybe seven, it was clear she could already take a man's heart and mould it into submission.

Eventually the boy, who Martin guessed was about five years old, got the opportunity to get the old mans attention by saying "please Opa can you tell us the story again of how the little boy helped you to escape from prison camp". There was a pregnant pause, while the old man considered his response, which eventually came with a "you don't want to hear that story again" which drew an immediate chorus of "yes we do . . . . Please Opa, please".

Opa steadied himself as though he was being asked to walk a plank that stretched out over a ravine. He cleared his throat and took a pose as though he was looking into the distance beyond the horizon. The children were suddenly silent as they waited upon his first words.

Martin was captivated by this turn of events and found he was, as the children, hanging on for the moment that the old gentleman would start his story.

He began with the measured tones of recounting an epic event that had to be told precisely and with a sense of reverence. "Children your Opa will never forget these times, and I hope that you will always remember them too for they are of times which speak about the worst and the best of mankind, and no matter who we are, we are all God's children, and this little boy was certainly so, if not an angel.

I remember the day it all began as if it were yesterday.

Saturday the sixth of October 1939. It was the Sabbath, and the Germans knew that if they came early enough they could gather up all the Jews, dressed in their best clothes, before they set off for Synagogue.

Our house was in a cul-de-sac of a small village with a country atmosphere, on the outskirts of Warsaw and all seven of the houses, with the exception of one, was occupied by fellow Jews.

It was an enclave of sorts with the exception of the one family made up of this little boy, his mother and father who were Australians.

The father was an Engineer at the Power Station and his wife, a beautiful lady, was an artist.

They had arrived only two months prior and had settled into our little group just nicely.

On this particular Saturday, the old man gesticulated with his hands, the father was preparing to go on an early morning hike in the woods, which were near by.

He had bought with him to Poland, from England, a specially made duffel coat, which had been designed for mountain climbing in the snow country.

It had a huge hood, and enough room to carry a rucksack under cover.

However he had made up a harness, in its place, so that he could take his boy with him. They were inseparable.

The day was cold, as the temperature was quite low and the air frosty.

Then . . . unexpectedly, the early morning was shattered with the ear piercing wail of the SS armoured cars and trucks as they screeched into our private sanctuary electrifying the air with their sirens, followed by swarms of soldiers discharging themselves from the vehicles, banging on doors and barking orders, along with their dogs, in an insane manner that made our hearts stop momentarily, followed by a rush of adrenalin that almost, and in many cases left us paralysed".

By this time the old man became more animated as the memories flooded back, and the children sat wide eyed and engrossed as if hearing the story for the first time. But this was a repeat rendition.

Martin was in a state shock as he got caught up in the story.

His mind was racing at a dizzying pace. Something was happening. He felt his heart rate leap.

The old man interrupted his narrative by saying to the small boy who had now climbed onto his knee, "really Jacob do you want to hear this story as you are so young". The boy's response was quick, "but Opa, Martie was my age wasn't he?"

Opa looked at him wistfully saying, "Indeed he was, in deed he was." There was a more sombre tone in his voice now and he lifted Jacob onto his other knee for balance, before continuing, saying "now where was I? Oh yes, we were all eventually dragged out onto the street with women and children separated from the men, and I can still see Martin's father, Declan, arguing and remonstrating vigorously with the soldiers, that he was an Australian citizen and was entitled to diplomatic immunity.

They in turn would only reply "we know who you are" and roughly shoved him along with the other men up into the waiting truck.

It was pandemonium and in this fracas Martin went undetected as he clung to Declans back, in his harness like a small possum, out of sight under the cover of the duffel coat hood.

Declan had planned to go on their early morning hike when the raid was made."

"I can still hear Declan whisper to Martin," lay close to my back and don't make a noise."

Martin at the next table nearly erupted over the unfolding story and could not contain himself any longer, and abruptly got out of his chair and approached the group in the other cubicle standing momentarily before them, stumbling out an apology for the interruption.

The children looked at him with wide concerned eyes, almost expecting some form of abuse, while the old man looked at him with a look that said he'd been through this scenario before, and his hold on the children became a little firmer, to give them the reassurance that 'everything's OK.'

Martin on the other hand was searching the old man's face for some form of recognition.

Finally in a quavering voice, very nearly unintelligible, "excuse me Sir, I could not help overhearing your conversation, may I ask, are you Samuel Rosenberg?"

An almost defensive response came back with a more noticeable European accent saying, "who wants to know?"

"As I said, I overheard your story to the children" . . . Martin faltered again, slightly choking as he felt his chin start to quiver with emotion, and he momentarily steadied himself before taking a deep breath "and from what I heard, I think I maybe the Martin in your story. You see my name is Martin O'Leary, and my father was Declan, and the man I remember was Samuel Rosenberg."

The old mans jaw dropped, as did all the children, as he stared at Martin in disbelief, and for a space of time, which seemed endless, not a word was spoken.

A moment of shock.

The children got down off their Grandfathers knee and sat on their chairs, and stared in stunned silence.

As the light of truth finally dawned, the old man stood to his feet and the flood gates open with both men reaching out to one another vigorously hugging and unashamedly sobbing tears that come from the heart. The old man crying out "Martie, Martie my Martin." Then they would take turns of standing back and looking at each other, noting the passage of time, until the emotions subsided sufficiently for them to sit down to reclaim a form of normality.

"See my children this is Martin, the Martin of my story of escape. Now Jacob you have come face to face with the boy who is now a man, who saved your Opa so many years ago. God is good", the old man said proudly, and with a great deal of excitement.

Martin started to protest these accolades, but the children, and in particular Jacob who now looked at Martin with childish adulation, and his old friend would hear none of it.

Ruth, the beautiful little grand daughter, in wonderment, could not take her eyes off Martin.

All this hugging, crying, and shouts of joy and jubilation drew the attention of other diners as well as 'mine host' Bernard who came to see what the commotion was all about.

Sam began to tell him, but realised the disturbance had effected the rest of the patrons, and so moving into a more suitable spot, he lifted up one hand to indicate that he was about to address them, "friends I do apologise to you for any disruption that may have been caused to you at this breakfast time, but my explanation is simple and brief. More than fifty years ago I was in a Nazi prison camp only moments from extermination and this man you see before you, and he gestured to Martin, as a young child save my life and I was able to escape the gas chamber. So as you can imagine meeting him again for the first time after so many years has caused my heart to overflow with joy unspeakable".

Chokingly he continued, "please forgive me for interrupting your morning".

And with that he gave a short bow and returned to his table, but before he could sit down the place erupted with applause, shouts and whistles.

Sam looked slightly bemused, but acknowledged their generosity with a smile and a wave.

Bernard rallied around and appeared with ice cream for the children and brandies for Sam and Martin.

After a period of excited questions and answers, laughing and tear shedding, Sam finally drew an agreement from Martin to come to his house to meet the rest of his family, and the next day was set for 4PM.

Martin made his way home that day with mixed emotions, that went from total unbelief to almost uncontrolled exhilaration. There would be no sleep to night.

Martin lay on his couch studying the patterns on the ceiling, much like you do when looking up to the clouds and seeing if there are any identifiable shapes that may give more meaning to life from such a vast canvas.

The cornice around the perimeter of the room had a pattern which resembled, after staring at it long enough, of a row of old fashioned door keys, that could fit any number of doors and the first key looked as though it had just been rehung for it seemed to be moving.

Was today the first key that opened a door ever so slightly to Martin's life?

A life he had up until this day kept under wraps in the deep recesses of his mind? Hidden from the world, his family and friends for the best part of his life.

He had been a man of secrets.

The wonderment of this day's events thrilled him and at the same time opened up a pocket of apprehension and concern.

Rubbing his eyes as though to clear the vision Martin allowed himself to drift into a slumber.

It had all been too much.

Chapter 3

More Keys-More Doors

Monday was much the same as the previous day except for the increased hum that goes with a working day, traffic and people all moving, all making their own peculiar noise, everyone in a hurry.

It reminded Martin of ants scooting along the pavement, all of them with a job to do and seemingly with so little time to do it in. Martin's view from the bay window had been his look out on life, but now this limited vision was about to change and this thought of change was opening a backdoor and the face of fear stood at that entrance. It was not so much the fear of the unknown but the fear of what is known, that had been suppressed for convenience; the sweeping aside of obstacles and unfinished business that had never been satisfactorily dealt with.

Bloody hell he thought, why am I doing this to myself. I'll give old Sam a miss. This could open up a can of worms.

A known expression floated in and out of his mind "you have nothing to fear except fear it's self"

A bloody lot of good that is he thought, as he braced himself.

The day was moving quickly and Martin's decision making went back and forth like a shuttle-cock, until at last he concluded "I can't do this to the poor old bugger".

He then wrestled with what he should wear, which was not a great challenge as his wardrobe was quite meagre by any standards, as his line of work placed few demands on dress, and so the debate came down to "will I, wont I wear a tie" with the latter coming up trumps.

He approached the front door of what he noted to be an up market house, situated in a tree lined street in the better part of the Eastern Suburbs and he then automatically check his watch.

He had been a stickler throughout his life for punctuality and he could hear in his thoughts," at the third stroke it will be four o'clock." He pressed the door bell and at the same time spotted the Mezuzah nestled in the top right hand corner of the door jam signifying the blessing over the house.

The door was promptly opened and there stood Sam, expansive in his gesture of welcome and with his arm around Martin guided him to the lounge room to meet the family gathering, all eagerly waiting to meet the little boy, now the man, who has been the subject of a story of escape, told many times over.

"This is my wife Anna, and immediately Martin was taken aback as she appeared much younger than he had expected, and this is my first born Samuel, my eldest daughter Rossannah and Samuel's wife Sarah, who is the mother of my grandchildren whom you have already met, Jacob and Ruth" Martin was immediately sent into a spin. First with Anna and then with Rossannah, who as he remembered was Sam's only child. Maybe he had his facts wrong, after all it was more than fifty years ago, but then Rossannah looked no more than forty, if that. How could this be?

Too many questions for a befuddled brain. Leave it Martin, he thought and was saved from any continuing confusion by an offer of a whiskey, which he gratefully received and which he proceeded to drink too quickly, gulping it down as if it was his last.

Questions came thick and fast as they do when friends meet for the first time, like where do you live, what do you do, are you married, any children, have you travelled and so on. Not questions of idle curiosity but of genuine interest that made Martin feel accepted as they all hung on his response, and almost sat in awe of his presence especially the children and Jacob in particular.

This looked as if it was going to be a long night so Martin, as he usually did, in a situation like this, thought it was a good time to move the focus off himself and gently started to probe the siblings.

"What kind of work do you do Samuel"

"I'm in computer software engineering, with a small group of colleagues and we service the banking and finance industry."

"A challenging occupation, Martin said, it must keep you abreast of what's going on in the market place". Samuel's response was guarded and cagey Martin thought when he replied "we only supply the software and support and don't get involved in the other areas."

"How about you Rossannah, what do you do?"

"Oh, I'm a lawyer with Bristol, Brown and Braithwaite in the city. I'm a partner, she replied rather coyly and anticipating Martin's next question, I do corporate incorporation structure."

"How fascinating, that sounds like a very busy job, and one that has a fair bit of pressure attached to it."

"We have our moments," she replied demurely. Martin liked her modest style and noticed her attention toward him when he spoke and reminisced with her father. She was sizing him up. He knew it, but felt comfortable with her interest.

He was about to turn his attention to the little ones who had been firing the odd question now and again, like "how do you still remember our Opa, and were you born in Poland and are you Jewish and if not, why not."

Sam looking on and observing the family interchange was absolutely pleased at how things were panning out, but was slightly concerned with his son Samuel's stiffness. However he put it off as just his *'nature'*. But when the smaller ones posed their questions he attempted to interpose saying "now, now children I don't think you should be asking Martin those things."

But Martin gestured with his hand saying," it's quite alright, fair questions deserve fair answers.

He started by saying "your brain and mine, pointing to his head, is an incredible organ capable of storing a great amount of information, and the things you have learnt and remembered up until now, you will still be able to remember all that information when you are old like me or your Opa. When I was your age Jacob, your Opa used to read me stories, and tell me about where he worked at the Railway Station and things like that.

I could hear his voice in a crowd, and even though I could not see him, I would know it was him just by the way he spoke, and the special sound of his voice. I think I was able to do that because I loved him. He was like my second father.

And no, I was not born in Poland but here in Sydney Australia and not far from here.

As for being Jewish I can't claim that either. Being Jewish is a very special privilege for which only a select number of people qualify, and I missed out".

Before there could be any follow up questions Sam stood up and said "lets go and eat shall we"

Anna and the girls had been flitting back and forth between kitchen and dining room and the aromas that followed heralded a feast that Martin had not been exposed to for as far back as he could remember.

His mouth salivated with the thought of what would accompany the smell.

His greatest expectations had been fulfilled, the meal was definitely mouth watering and complemented with some of the finest wine that bought back memories of better days.

The children were absolutely fascinated by their guest and constantly intrigued by the notion that he was such a close friend, even almost family, to their grandfather, which had him intervene on a number of occasions to halt their interrogation. However Martin was somewhat amused by all this attention until Sam's eldest son, in a slightly arrogant tone said, "and what do you do for a living Martin?"

Sam seemed a touch mortified by the way this question was posed and sought to close it off until Martin, after a moments hesitation, while staring down his inquisitor, and then looking at his old friend said quite softly, "it's OK I don't mind, and looking back at Samuel, said, I'm a missing persons investigator".

"Were you investigating my father before you found him?" A stunned tone filled the room, and Martin quietly replied, "I sense some hostility here Samuel but the answer is no. The memory of your father comes from a period of my life which for many reasons I have repressed up until now, but our meeting was by chance, or some might say by divine providence, although I don't subscribe to that theory myself, it has bought to me a joy I had not expected to experience in my life again. If my being here offends you, then I'm sorry, but I have come with nothing other than good will, and I intend to take with me a love for your father and good memories of yesteryear.

That I will not apologise for."

Samuel realised he had overstepped the mark, as all the family eyes were on him in amazement, and he moved toward Martin with hand outstretched, offering an apology for his unfounded rudeness and appeared genuinely remorseful of his actions as he approached his father and all present with humility.

"I take no offence", Martin said magnanimously, and stood to give the young man a hug and a pat on the back.

Calm was restored to the gathering with the children continuing to ask their questions, until Rossannah asked "what type of missing persons do you trace."

"It varies. Some are Corporate, white collar crime types, family members who have disappeared or missing, beneficiary recipients, and the like."

"How intriguing, that sounds real challenging, you must give me your card." Martin awkwardly started to search his wallet in just about every pocket to no avail and sheepishly said "I don't often get asked for cards, it's not a thing you do in this business it's generally word of mouth, but I'll get one to you".

Finally Sam stood up and said "Anna my darling, that was a beautiful meal and you and your able assistants have out done yourselves for our special guest, and I'm now going to introduce Martin to my study. Do you think you could organise a pot of coffee for us and I will see if Martin likes my cognac."

This statement was taken by the family to mean that Sam was going to have a private time with Martin and the rest of the family should busy themselves with other tasks.

Martin stepped into the study and was immediately taken by the number of books that adorned the walls. This was some serious library, he thought, and quickly turned his mind as to who would use such an array of books.

Was Sam a professor or a literary giant of some kind.

A researcher maybe?.

The leathery mustiness of the books captured his state of awed admiration and respect, which was interrupted by Anna, when she brought the coffee in with some special Jewish cookies, she whispered before leaving the study. Martin had come to a conclusion that this was some special place and it was as if he was on hallowed ground.

Before he could comment on his surroundings, Sam was fussing about, offering the coffee, and asking the polite questions that we all say such as, "do you take milk and sugar? You must have one of these cookies Martin they are Anna's specialty. Sit down, sit down" he gestured Martin to a chair and proceeded to look at Martin as though he was his prodigal son.

The study was furnished with a large mahogany desk, resplendent with carvings that signified it was substantial and expensive, but not ostentatious.

An executive chair sat prominently behind the desk, and out front were two large expansive leather chairs, that were inviting enough to sleep on.

Martin took in the surroundings, and gesturing,

Looked at Sam and said "Wow", who responded by saying "this is where I do my best work".

"Man oh man this must be some kind of work" Martin said incredulously, "I've never seen a study like it before . . . . it's great".

After serving a superb tasting coffee, Sam said "I guess you are wondering what I do here.

Let me start by telling you what happened after we fled the prison camp.

Maybe you don't remember, but after I left you and your Father at Warsaw, I went through an experience that altered my way of thinking.

The depravation and suffering that I saw people go through, determined in my mind that if I ever got out of that mess I would do everything in my power to help people get their lives back together again. When Anna and I arrived in Australia I wondered how I would achieve this. My academic training was as an engineer and in those days it was hard to get a job in that profession especially for a migrant or as we were known in those days a "refugee".

My qualifications came under scrutiny, especially as a German national, you see I was born in Germany and went to University in Berlin, but was forced to move to Poland by the Nazis for being a Jew, and the only employment that I could get there was as a Station Master. Life is full of ironies Martin as even though I could not get employment in this country as an Engineer, because of my suspect qualifications; I was accepted into University under a further education scheme unhindered, and was given a series of credits in recognition of my German qualifications, and subjects taken.

I soon realised that I would not be able to fulfil my commitment to assist those who were traumatised by their war time physical and mental illnesses by pursuing engineering, so I decided to do medicine under a scholarship programme which was open to refugees from war torn countries.

After qualifying I worked in the hospital system for five years and this experience taught me that the greater illness for these poor people who had escaped the death camps and other forms of deprivation was in mental health, and thus I went on to complete an extension degree in psychiatry, and have continued to work in that field ever since."

Some of the pieces started to fall into place for Martin as he again looked around the study and could see that this was a place of considerable learning as well as a 'safe' place for those who came here.

Martin was in the process of making complementary comments on Sam's achievements and his dedication to those who may have suffered through no fault of their own except for being Jews, when Sam cut to the chase.

"Martin, he said, I don't know how you are travelling but my guess is that you may be carrying some scars from your own experiences of that time, and because you were so young with so much responsibility, time more than likely has not healed the trauma of those events and I want to say to you as someone who has always felt that he owed you a debt and never thought I would be able to repay you in any way. Martin as well, as being a "de facto father" to you, by your own words, I would consider it a privilege to assist you in sorting things out should you feel the need".

Martin felt numb by this head on approach and did not know how he should respond to such an offer.

He sat in silence trying to determine whether he had been ambushed into this situation . . . . Should he be insulted at the insinuation that he was in need of help from a shrink.

He was tempted to jump up and storm off. His old pride had been pricked, he felt vulnerable and in a sense deflated by what Sam had said, but somewhere in the background of his life's training, a voice was saying don't be rash, be still and wait for the defining moment when men are separated from the boy, because of the judgements they make.

He acted upon this prompting and sat, which seemed endless in time, and allowed the full impact of what Sam had said, seep into his conscious mind before looking up and saying "that has hit me right between the eyes"

"I'm sorry if I have offended you, but I had to wrestle with what I was going to say myself, knowing that it may be taken the wrong way and destroy a relationship which I dearly wanted to foster.

You see Martin sometimes you have to take risks if you want to be a real friend, and I don't know for sure that you need any assistance, but because I have such feelings for you as a friend, and as my de facto son, I could not let this time pass without chancing this risk, because you may walk out of here tonight and never return and I would not have been able to live with myself.

Not being able to return the complement for you saving my life so many years ago, it was not an option".

Martin was mystified as to what he had done to be adulated in such a way. As he looked into Sam's face he was able to discern that he was agonising over the situation.

Finally he said "OK Sam you could be onto something here. I've felt for a long time that some of the machinery was out of whack, but I never put it down to Treblinka. My life has been a bit of a rollercoaster, and up until recently, 'John Jameson' was my only comforter and confessor".

Relief flooded the study and then without warning both men started to laugh and laugh and only drew to a close when Sam got up and went to Martin's chair and putting his hands on his shoulders and giving a squeeze said, "Martin I am so glad and blessed that you have come back into my life and made an old man happy beyond belief and bridged a gap that I thought would never happen"

"So Sam where do we go from here. I want you to know up front that I am not a wealthy man and although I've always paid my way, extended sessions could stretch my means,"

Sam had a look of shock horror and said "my dear boy this is not a billing situation, this is between father and son and I would not have it any other way . . . . please don't mention this subject again because I would hate you to think that I am touting for business.

I'm an old man so the sooner we get together for this adventure the better. We can arrange things to fit in with your schedule OK?"

A glass of cognac sealed the deal.

Chapter 4

Finding The Key That Fits

It was mutually agreed that once per week would be a suitable arrangement and that Monday at ten am would start the week off and would have the most beneficial effects for both parties. Sam showed Martin a side entrance to his office so that a form of confidentiality and privacy could be preserved.

Monday saw Martin sitting in the big comfortable chair, and after the usual formalities of greetings and hand shakes, the pair sat to face each other which gave Martin the opportunity to study the old man's face and try to fathom what the lines and creases meant, along with the shape of the nose and mouth as well as the chin, which Martin had always believed could reveal a lot about the character of the person you were dealing with.

He applied these principles in his own work, in summing up people, in an attempt to establish what made them tick.

He saw the valleys of concern etched in the brow and the crow's feet around the eyes and the bags of sleepless nights that are often distinguishable beneath the eyes. The creases that come from a ready smile of happiness or concern were all there and were now looking at him, caring for him, reaching out to him, deep from within the well of the "milk of human kindness".

Momentarily he felt a serge of emotion spring from somewhere deep in his own being, which he had to stifle for fear that it would bring a big tear and thus make his manliness suspect. He choked it back, because everyone knows that big boys don't cry.

A childhood induction.

Sam's gentle voice invoked a return to the matters at hand by saying, "where would you feel most comfortable about starting our discussion today Martin?"

Martin paused momentarily and said "I guess the beginning would be a good place to start and unravel the twisted threads of my life, but before the age of three there is very little recollection."

"Well let's make a start there and see where that leads us, and we can build on that as time goes by. Now I want you to relax just as you would do at home and if you feel more comfortable with your eyes closed as you recall these memories go right ahead and please feel free to say anything you want as they come back. I want to assure you of the strict confidentiality between us as we proceed along this journey.

I'm going to play, with your permission, some soothing background music for us both to help the thoughts flow and together we will enter into a new dimension of life which I'm sure will be mutually beneficial.

Now I want you to find some incident that is clear to you as a small boy, that stands out, not for any particular reason, but because it's easy to remember."

The background music quickly took effect and Martin followed Sam's instructions and soon found a comfort in his mind that allowed him to drift back in time as a three year old. It was amazing as he felt he was actually there, but as a spectator, playing on the back veranda of his parents' home in a quiet Sydney suburb.

Martin began by saying, "I heard father come in all excited with some news that seemed to make my mother happy as well. I could hear my father saying "there were some risks, because Europe was being intimidated by Hitler. However England was insisting Hitler would not have the temerity to attack Poland, an ally of Great Britain.

No it could never happen". But what ever they were talking about was only to be for three months, so the likelihood of anything happening in that time was remote. All this meant nothing to my three year old ears and many of the words I could not understand, but I sensed a kind of three year olds' joy, as my parents were talking with such enthusiasm because up until then, every day was gloomy with shortages of food, and what there was had a yucky taste like boiled tripe, and mutton that was tough and meat that my father use to always say 'this is horse meat'. Times were difficult in those days with hand-me-down clothes and no shoes, except if you wore the ones with soles made from a tyre rubber.

Men were out of work and there seemed to be a constant stream of them coming to the door for hand outs and food.

The Great Depression took a toll on everyone, and most were almost starving".

Declan, Martin's father was an Mechanical Engineer with a British company based in Australia and was fortunate enough to get three days work a week on a roster system, such as one week on and one week off. So in many ways the family was better off than most.

There had been talk that an Engineer would be required to oversee the installation of one of their turbines at a power generating plant in Poland and as Declan was the most experienced in this field, speculation was that he would get the nod and now it had happened. Hence the excitement that Martin had heard but not clearly understood.

"My earliest recollections of this time, Martin started, centred around the dinner table with my parent deciding on the fate of the children.

I had two other brothers older that me by eight and ten years, and as I did not get on with them for any number of reasons I was not unhappy when my father announced that they would be going to a boarding school, the Head Master of which had been a childhood friend of my father, having grown up together in Ireland, and I would accompany my parents to Poland. It all sounded like a grand adventure.

Soon afterwards we were boarding an aircraft at Rose Bay on Sydney Harbour known in those days as a flying boat. There was considerable excitement about this as I discovered much later that we were some of the earliest passengers to use this method of transport to go overseas. In a way we were pioneers, full of apprehension, which also included the pilots, who were very interested in how I would manage the flight. However I was given a window seat and did not have a problem, much to everyone's delight. "Oh isn't he a brave boy" followed by all sorts of treats which my mother insisted were spoiling me.

I think the trip took three days and finally we arrived in London and was met by a "senior partner" and then off to an hotel where we all slept in one room. My father went for 'Senior Officials' talks and instructions, and mother and I went on a shopping spree as it seems the company had given my father a hefty advance, and mother was not about to waste any time in fitting herself out with new clothes for Poland.

I have a photograph of them taken at this time in London and they were certainly a hansom couple.

I can still remember people, particularly other men complementing my father on his beautiful wife."

"Yes she was certainly a beauty with a great presence about her, Sam said. You've done well to recall so much of that period. Just take your time and let the thoughts drift back from memory lane."

"I can remember arriving at Warsaw Station by train and seeing all the people rushing about and the noise of everything, but where we boarded the train has eluded me, and then the next memory is arriving at our little hamlet of . . . what was it called Sam? As Martin struggled to remember . . . . something Spor . . . "Sporad" Sam interposed. Yes that was it, Sporad. We all eagerly investigated the house which the Power Company had provided, and their representative who met us, telling my parents that the owner, a senior executive of theirs had taken leave and was on holidays in the US for three months and that we were to make ourselves at home and use everything that was at our disposal.

I recall my mother saying that she thought this was a bit odd staying in some one else's home without meeting them first, but my father suggested we relax and take advantage of this beautiful home and enjoy the time we have there. It was certainly big Sam, as you well know, with many rooms, which meant that I had my own room for the first time and a bath room so big that even my parents felt a little intimidated by the size, with it's tiled walls and extra size bath with a shower fixture that my father marvelled at the engineering and novelty of it's operation. However we soon became accustomed to it's grandeur and experienced a great deal of pleasure from the new fangled gadgets it offered although I was too young to fully grasp what was going on.

However I will tell you of an incident later on that exposed me to an entirely unexpected new stage of my junior education".

"Did you feel a sense of insecurity, or 'butterfly fear or maybe a disconnection at this time that you weren't able to tell anybody about?"

"My earliest recollections of what happened next, was I think the following morning my father made his way to the Power Plant, for an appointment which must have been organised on the day we arrived, because I remember my father being in deep conversation with the 'representative' and saying he would be ready next morning first thing.

I recall a sense of abandonment as Mother was a late riser, and I found myself peering through the wrought iron front gate with my favourite and only friend 'Teddy'.

I hung on to the gate as kids do and watched a little girl whom I thought was my own age playing hop-scotch. After a while she looked up and saw me watching and spoke to me in a language I did not understand, which I now realise was Polish. All I could say was, 'my name's Martin and this is my friend Teddy'.

She in turn stopped what she was doing on the hop-scotch court and came over to have a closer look at this strange child who kept repeating, 'my name's Martin and this is my friend Teddy'. Her small face came up close to mine, and she looked at me quizzically and as I said hello she responded 'are you English', and this I understood and said, I'm Australian'. But the way it came out must have sounded like Austrian, as she quickly turned and ran back inside her house shouting 'Mamma Mamma'.

Then Mamma came out to see what the fuss was about and I was encouraged to walk partly across the road, looking very timid and when this lovely lady who happened to be your wife approached.

I again came out with 'my names Martin and this my friend Teddy'. She smiled warmly and said in very clear English 'hello Martin you must be our new neighbour from Australia'. She bent down and picked me up for a cuddle and I remember kissing her on the cheek as she said "I think we are going to be very good friends Martin".

I felt a bond that day that I'd not experienced before even with my own mother. Not that I knew what a bond was, except it felt good and warm. The mere fact that I clung to her now strikes me as being very odd for such a small child. But there it was and I never felt anything but love for her and from her for the short time that we lived at Sporad.

Rossannah as I found out shortly, immediately took to me, when she saw her mother's approval and we became as you know the best of friends, 'little brother and big sister'.

The Australian, Austrian thing was quickly sorted out and Rossie took my hand and really never let it go until we parted on that terrible day.

Sam I must ask you about Anna and Rossannah . . ."

"I know what you are going to ask, Sam said, but let us leave that for the moment and I will explain all as we move through our sharing. Let's continue with your story so that there is no interruption to the memory flow".

"Fair enough, well where was I? Oh yes, Rosie taught me how to play hop scotch that day with endless amounts of patience until I got it right and the skill stayed with me down to my own daughter, when I would tell her, a beautiful girl in a far away land had taught me how to hop scotch.

Your wife Anna became firm friends with my mother and they talk for ages about art which was mothers' passion, and how she was an art critic and curator, and how the troubled times of the world had interfered with her career and so the conversation would go and as I look back it must have driven Anna insane listening to such inane, self serving babble. But she would smile generously, looking interested and at the same time be ever vigilant as to where Rosie and I were".

Martin opened his eyes ever so slightly and caught a glimpse of Sam taking a deep swallow and squeezing his eyes shut, as no doubt he was feeling the pain of this memory. Martin paused momentarily, which prompted Sam to say "Please continue I'm listening".

"My fear of life, or what ever it was at that time ended because of Anna and Rossie.

I was a scared little boy. They showed me a love, care, and trust which enabled me to face the later hardships of life with courage and determination, which I am sure would have not come to me any other way.

Anna was the mother I needed at that time who understood my longing for affection and certainty.

My teacher, and my calmer of ripples in my small pond.

The one who would kiss me good night and I would sleep with perfect peace.

Rossies' memory still haunts me to this day. Oh how I loved that little girl. I don't know if this is possible or not but I was in love with Rossie Sam as a three year old, and still am with her memory.

I'm sorry to have said that Sam, please forgive me if that sounds self serving and offensive."

And at that very moment Sam could not contain his emotion any longer and let out this deep groan, which caused Martin to open his eyes to see rivers of tears flowing down his old friends face which simultaneously had the same effect on his own emotions and they both sobbed almost uncontrollably.

Sam was the first to recover, and placing his hand on Martin's head said "I think we have found the cord in both our lives.

Let's see if we can trace the threads that bind that bind us in this inextricable way".

Martin began by saying, "you remember all those days and nights that I had to lie in that filthy bunk and not make a noise so as not to be detected, I used to imagine that Rosie was there with me, and we would whisper to one another and tell stories like we did when I slept over at your house. Weird stories of monster and ghosts as well as imagining what we were going to be when we grew up. That's what kept me going all through those times when I had to be quiet and be still, as the guards came around to make their inspections, poking the beds with their sticks, looking for anything hidden, Rosie was there and stopped me from being frightened.

I'm sure of it. Not only as a child, but on many occasions as an adult. She taught me how to cry in silence and keep my grief from the world right up until today.

She has always been a part of my life"

"Mine too, and I hear her voice as well. Sophocles was right when he wrote *'One word, frees us all of the weight and pain of life'*: "*That word is love*"

"Let's take a break for today and start again next Monday. I don't know about you but this has completely drained me, but it is cathartic".

Martin concurred.

For rest of the week Martin was experiencing troublesome old memories as they flashed back and forth, but he felt in many ways that the fog or haze as he often expressed it, which generally accompanied these events, seemed to have lifted to some degree and in a way that he had not expected and he was looking forward to the next week and the encounter with Sam.

He also had a call, which came right out of left field for an investigation assignment, which offered some diversity from his own situation.

An insurance company briefed him on a 'suspect disappearance' of a senior executive who was implicated in a serious fraud.

The Police were no longer prepared to pursue the case because of extenuating circumstances that appeared to take it from a criminal case to a civil matter.

Martin had come highly recommended from Bristol, Brown and Braithwaite.

The intervening week helped to keep his mind occupied with matters outside his own dilemma, while he assembled the information that was made available about this executive supposedly on the run. Martin's job was to find him.

He would prepare an assessment of the case, which would also set a fee bench mark, and wait for further instructions before proceeding.

This was not his typical approach to such an assignment, as generally he would front up to the company, haggle over pros and cons, come to an arrangement on projected fees, insisting on an upfront payment followed by weekly instalments paid into his bank account until the job was finished and then a lump sum payment. No mucking about. No paper work. No hassles, no fuss.

That was his way of doing business.

But this assignment was different. He had come recommended by Rossannah's legal firm and this had put a completely different spin on matters, which made him feel ill at ease, because there could be no stuff-ups on this case.

This was not the way Martin liked to work.

He had always operated on a word of mouth referral system where someone who had used his services and knew his style and manner and were satisfied with the way he produced results, paid him well and were happy to pass his name on to a prospect.

The Rossannah-Sam connection worried him as it meant he had to be on his toes and best behaviour in his dealings.

In his work, Martin was his own man, and if someone was playing hard ball and trying to be a smart-arse, he would happily tell them to "fuck off'" and stop wasting his time.

It wasn't necessarily that he was a hard bastard, but more that he didn't suffer fools gladly.

He determined that he would have to set the record straight with Rossannah before closing this deal. With that thought settled Martin felt at ease again.

He phoned Rossannah and invited her out for a drink.

They met at a cosy wine bar where Martin had a passing friendship with the barman and chose a table out of the mid-week crush and straight up Martin became aware of Rossannah's charming manner and that look that most men appreciate when their eyes meet, but for Martin it put him on edge and defensive, and under different circumstances he would have been all over it and trying to score if that was the game.

With out much ado after pleasantries, he tackled the perceived problem at hand, took a deep breath and began by saying," Rossannah I wanted to talk to you on two fronts that have me a little flummoxed at present and I want to resolve them before things get out of hand."

Rossannah drew her head back like someone ready to take a hit, and with a bemused look on her face, waiting for the unexpected. "Is there a problem?"

"Well yes, Martin said, and I'll tackle the most sensitive one first and that is, your attention or intentions toward me. I may be kidding myself but I sense a growing chemistry developing, and if that is the case then I must ask you to rethink your emotions.

If I'm out of line here please say so and if you like, slap my face for being such an arrogant presumptuous prick. But if I'm correct please let me say that I'm not right for you on many levels and only unhappiness for you can come out of such a relationship. The last thing I want to do is hurt you in any way, or to diminish my new found friendship with your father for God knows I would rather kill myself than hurt him."

Rossannah sat motionless for a moment, mastering what she was feeling, and one giant tear rolled down her face and her chin quivered ever so slightly, but she kept a steady eye on Martin, and he felt like a little boy again when he realises that he may have overstepped the mark, and his mind screamed 'Christ, you bloody fool you have just crushed a delicate flower to satisfy your own self righteousness, you arrogant bastard!'

As this internal self berating finished, Rossannah reached across the table and gently held Martin's hand and said "I respect your honesty, and you are right that I am developing feelings toward you, but I do respect your position and I know now how you feel, and I will not do any thing that will make our family relationship uncomfortable for you.

My heart is hurting, as I see so many qualities in you that I desire. But as all Jews know, hurting is a passing phase and in time rejoicing will come".

Martin was relieved as well as troubled when he held her hand in his, and kissed it saying, "we can still be friends." She smiled bravely, but he was lying and he knew it. They raised their glasses as if in a toast, they clinked and the first swallow of wine was like the first day of spring, or the first night in the sack with someone for whom you had strong feelings and as you entered that place where only lovers go your body vibrates with total ecstasy.

And then it was just like it was 'back to business' with Rossannah asking what was the other matter. Martin was taken aback by this strength of character and started with a nervous cough, to relate to his normal modus operandi, stressing that his main concern was not to embarrass her in her professional capacity.

After being assured that there was no problem in that department Martin's mind was now at ease except for the Rossannah question.

His balls were twitching and that was not a good sign.

Chapter 5

Another Key And A Memory Door To Treblinka

"Let's start today with a relaxing technique, that can open up the inner sanctum ourselves, to the free flowing of thoughts, memories and emotions.

Close your eyes and focus on the very top of your head where you imagine your crown to be and you say in your mind "relax", imagining and seeing that word flowing freely over your head as a balm, poured by an unseen hand, and starting to run down through your hair.

You can feel it touching every nerve centre in your head, in your brain from front to back, down your neck, around your ears, through the aches and pain of your shoulders, slowly now, into your chest, down into your abdomen into your groin, all the way through your legs, and as it flows, it's bringing incredible calming and a sense of peace, in this semi hypnotic state.

Martin this is our key word for future sessions "RELAX", and every time I say it to you, you will experience this sensation as it flows from the top of your head to the soles of your feet.

Sam's rich and gentle baritone voice continued.

Keep imagining this experience as it continues to flow all the way down your body, all over those parts that ache or have been injured, and take the healing that is flowing with "relax". Take your time and don't miss any member of your body, and when you finally come to your feet and you feel that total peace that "relax" brings, gently open your eyes, as we can go on to further explore our memories and open up a new page".

Martin probably for the first time in his life was totally absorbed with the experience, so that when he finally opened his eyes he had to virtually pinch himself.

"OK Martin, how was your week and what impact did our last discussions have on you."

"It's like I've had a nuclear track in my brain, with new feelings and memories racing around that I have not experienced for a long time.

It's like a 'southerly' breeze has blown up and for the first time in aeons there is a cleansing and a strange sensation, that I'm going to like it, even though there is an apprehensive twinge surrounding the whole happening.

Sam sat back and looked "fatherly" at him and said, "you are on the verge of a remarkable journey Martin and I am privileged to be going along for the ride".

"There are a number of things that are coming back to me of our time in Treblinka that I am still trying to reconcile and understand and make sense of, that seem to be out of character particularly with my father.

You will remember how close he and I were and how he would hold me and protect me and tell me that I was his 'little prince' and would never let anything happen to me, which gave me a powerful sense of security even under those terrible circumstances.

But all that changed after we returned home.

In the camp he seemed to be so strong and caring, even to the other prisoners who were not coping that well, he would spend ages calming their fears and re-assuring them to the point that they all thought he was some kind of saviour or guru.

You remember he started singing at nights and getting the other inmates to join in as a way of taking their mind off all the horrid circumstances, and lifting their souls to a level way above the difficult nature of that incarceration.

The guards initially warned him to stop making a noise. ("Shut up you pig", I think it was, Sam interposed,) Until some senior officer heard his voice and was so taken by it, that he rebuked the guards and admonished them in no uncertain terms for their ignorance and lack of culture.

The Officer would make requests of certain classical pieces and would stand just outside the barrack seemingly enthralled by his marvellous singing voice.

My father even went to the trouble of learning, under your tutelage, Hebrew songs, which would bring some to tears.

What ever happened, we did not have the guards screaming abuse after that officer's intervention.

He must have been one of the very few *human beings* in the German Army.

My Grandmother use to say in her sweet Irish brogue, 'to be sure he could charm the angles with that voice'.

You remember that horrendous day Sam, when I was discovered hiding on the top bunk after it would seem that another inmate had cracked under the pressure of day after day anxieties, and thought that he would get some privileges from the guards by dobbing us in, only to find that it unleashed a reign of terror for himself as well as everyone else, which finally lead to us all being herded to the showers, a situation that almost everyone understood was the "final solution".

My father, after we were stripped naked was over in a corner consoling that man by trying to convince him that it was not his fault and hugging him like a brother until Colonel Kurt Von Kramer came in. You would remember that day Sam. You remember it Sam?" Martin said insistently.

Sam nodded his head solemnly.

"Fear was in the air as everyone trembled and stared into a vacuum of hopeless expectation.

That's a day which has been etched on my mind. I was a child for Christ sake. Oh God!"

Sam reach over consolingly, already his face was reflecting the memory. Martin paused momentarily, and continued haltingly. He could not have stopped, even if he had want to.

"There I was in my birthday suite clinging on to your leg, shivering with trepidation, and in comes the epitome of conceit; swaggering through the dregs of humanity, inspecting the conquests of doom, riding crop under his arm, a cap with a rakish tilt on his head and with an expression of contempt on his face until he stands before you and me.

He inspects this unexpected form of humanity, as here was a Jew with an obviously uncircumcised Arian child clinging to his leg.

"What is the meaning of this?" he screams at the accompanying guard, who scrambles an answer,

"We found the child hiding in barrack 4 with this man. The child only speaks English Herr Commandant".

And the most amazing thing happens. He bends down so that he is face to face with me and prodding me with his riding crop, he is keen to test out the theory that I only speak English, he says, "do you know who I am?"

I stare at him for what seemed like an eternity, and I am re-assured by your tight hold of my shoulder, and eventually I recognise through all his pomp and regalia an alarming revelation, and I look up into his eyes saying, "you're my Uncle Kurt. I reached out to give him an embrace, and he lets out with a "Whaaaaaaat", as he jerks himself into an upright stance.

That wail bought the attention of the other guards as well as my father to the scene, who quickly came to see what the commotion was all about.

Father anxiously said "what's going on" and at the same time trying to be protective of us both, he looks into the face of our tormentor, and with a startled look of horror says "oh my God, is that you Kurt? This seemingly officious officer utters, "Declan, what the hell are you doing here". He then wheels around and starts screaming at the guards demanding to know why are these people here.

"You and the boy are to come with me right away". And as we all started to move in the direction being pointed, he looks at you Sam with a contempt that only a Nazi could muster, and says, "not you".

This scene was all too graphic for Sam and the tears started to roll again as he said, "this is where you, as a small child became my fiercest defender and it is a time I will never forget. As Declan started to follow, you clung to my leg with such a grip and called out with a determined shrill voice of defiance "No I'm not going without Uncle Sam. Daddy don't leave Uncle Sam here, I wont go without him".

Declan stopped and looked back and unhesitatingly said "Kurt if Sam stays so do I. I will not leave without him".

Kurt Von Kramer braced himself momentarily and then with withering looks to all his German colleagues, agreed for the trio to follow him.

We left that place of human degradation, and marched across the parade ground, draped in blankets to cover our nakedness to a building that was the Colonels headquarters, and accommodation."

"You know Martin our arrival at Treblinka also had a divine hand in there somewhere, Sam started, because when we arrived at the station the whole atmosphere was convivial with everything recently decorated, flowers growing in pots and one could be forgiven if it was thought this was a place of harmonious detention, as the Germans had said.

It had a telephone box right on the platform along side a Post Office, but in reality it was an immediate march to the death chambers that hid behind this facade.

We were all bunched up on the platform being inspected like cattle, and there was a young fellow moving through the throng asking for everyone's shoe laces.

He was wearing the yellow Star of David on his ragged coat and as he got near I recognised him as one of my employees at the Warsaw Railway Station.

As I crouched down to undo our shoe laces, I spoke to him in yiddish undertones, saying Sol, what are you doing here?"

"I'm here the same as you, and if you get asked your occupation, tell them you are a civil engineer. They want civil engineers, the rest here will go to you know where.

I can't stop Station Master as they are watching me as well".

"Thank you and good bye my friend.

In due course the question was put to us, and both Declan and I said we were civil engineers and we were separated along with others into another group.

The rest went one way and we were left in a land of limbo, not knowing what lay ahead of us.

Declan kept whispering to you that everything was going to be OK and to just hold on tight.

How you did that I'll never know.

Just when the order was given for us to move out to who knows where, the greatest thunderclap ever, erupted followed by a torrential down pour of a magnitude I have ever witnessed, drenching everyone in such a manner that no one was spared including the guards and to such an extent the orders were changed and we were all herded into the barracks which were to remained our place of dwelling.

Declan believed God had something to do with this as the confusion that followed enabled him to claim the upper deck of the three tiered bed structure so that you could be hidden.

He took his duffle coat off and spread it over you for warmth, covered it with straw to hide you, and to make sure the guards didn't take it.

Those things have been etched into our psyche, never to be forgotten but to be forgiven Martin".

Chapter 6

The Foot Thorn

The catharsis that followed the recall of events was incredible for both men as the sensation of that poignant moment was relived physically and emotionally.

It was some time, seemingly ages before either could speak as they lay there in their respective recliners.

Martin cleared his throat in an attempt to say something, when Sam without saying a word got up and with hand raised in a manner that indicated 'be still', walked to his wall cabinet, selected his finest cut crystal glasses and poured two large award winning brandy's and returned to the recliner and said "Martin my boy this calls for a stabilizer".

They touched glasses and contemplatively drank their brandy in *silentium*.

Who knows how much time passed. It seemed unimportant. The anaesthetic of the brandy was doing it's job and the atmosphere of that study was akin to a place of worship.

A presence prevailed that neither man wanted to break.

The following Monday, as Martin eased himself into the recliner couch, Sam looked at him as though studying a manuscript, and after settling himself quietly said "RELAX" and waited for the elixir of the subconscious to do it's job, and then said "I would expect that you have had a week in renaissance?" and waited while Martin gathered his thoughts and mulled over choosing his words for a response.

Slowly Martin began in a manner that would suggest a recapture of that whole time frame.

"My father had a mantra in those days which he would repeat to me quite often, when I would ask him the 'why' question that children are prone to do when they don't understand some of the reasons of life, which often don't make sense to a child's mind, and he would come out with this saying, "Martin, the good you do will come back to you" which would cover for an answer, and it was not until I had grown much older that I was able to join this up with what we so often call 'karma'.

Strangely enough Uncle Reg had the same saying.

You will remember the incident, when Kurt use to work at the Power Station and was dismissed due to his excessive drinking on the job, and my father went into bat for him, to try and get the Directors to reverse their decision, but they would have none of it as they'd had enough of his crass ways and inflammatory remarks toward them. They were Jews, and tired of Kurt's anti Semitic behaviour. Father even threatened to resign, protesting that they were not cognizant of other factors in Kurt's life, which he could not divulge, as he regarded that information as too confidential to reveal, which was, that Kurt's wife had up and left him high and dry, clearing out his bank account, pawning what ever possessions he had, even his clothing, leaving him destitute and deeply depressed.

That's when Father enlisted your help Sam, asking you to find some way of getting Kurt back to Berlin where he had relatives who could help him out.

I've pulled all these pieces together Sam, only from past conversations I'd had with my father, which were few and far between, as he was a reluctant conversationalists, particularly about this time of our lives."

Sam looked into the distance as he toyed with his mustache, and then saying,

"I remember, your mother was not too happy when Declan invited Kurt to come and stay at your house as she did not like the man and thought he had an 'evil' streak in him.

I still see Declan reasoning with her,

'Elizabeth there's good in all of us. We all get a thorn in our foot from time to time, which needs to be pulled out.

You can't turn your back on a man when he's down.

Anyway you will be going to London in the next few days so I will handle him on my own. It won't be a problem. 'Sam has come up with a plan,' and he looked expectantly at me to lay out the plan.

I said to your Mother, it's not a real plan but an idea that I might be able to arrange for him to use my entitlement cabin, which I am aloud to use at no cost for my holiday trips, and I think I could arrange a Berlin ticket.

Your mother protested, "You should not sacrifice your entitlements for such an ugly despicable man who would not know how to say thank you".

However as you know, your father's persuasive ways settled the argument, and Kurt moved in, with your mother barely able to conceal her contempt.

Kurt seemingly did not appear to notice and was happy to be in a family environment.

You on the other hand were too young to understand the impact of this situation and far too young to hate, and as a consequence worked your way into this man's heart with love and attention which he had probably never experienced before in his life, and he responded with uncharacteristic fondness for you as though you were his own child.

Your father observed on one occasion, that Kurt was telling you what a grand little boy you were, and as you looked up into his face the beginnings of a tear began to form in his eye, and you climbed onto his lap and with a big hug said 'I love you uncle Kurt' and kissed him on the lips. Kurt was so moved by this action that he held you sobbing 'I always wanted a little son like you Martin, Oh my God.

After a time he regained composure, and excused himself for the night.

Did I do something wrong father? You said, "No, Declan answered, you just opened a sad mans heart".

Sam and Martin looked at each other trying not to let the darkness of the past dominate the present.

"Martin how are you holding up with the revelations so far. I mean, is this bringing more shadows into your consciousness, or is there a sense that some of the cobwebs are being cleared away by exposure."

"It's as a head ache that is slowly receding and revealing a clearer picture of the day.

Not unlike a bad hang-over on the mend."

"That's good. These things and re-experiences are the foundation stones that are gradually laying the ground work for which we can build on, to make sense of the labyrinth of complex pathways of our lives.

Remember Martin, you are helping me, in as much as I am helping you. This combined effort will enrich our lives!"

Sam said this with triumph in his voice, and Martin felt an exhilaration which had not stirred in his being for a long time.

The thorn had been removed.

Chapter 7

The Great Escape

The foursome entered the building that nestled behind a small grove of trees, discretely sheltered from the harsh barracks, the shower rooms and of course the "final solution," the cremation block.

As they ascended the wooden staircase to the first floor office and the Colonels quarters, the Colonel continued to make obscene remarks about Jews to the point that on their arrival, Declan had taken as much of this nonsense as he was prepared.

He faced Kurt off and just as he was to continue his diatribe, Declan exploded and all his usual calm controlled exterior contorted into a rage of in your face finger pointing and shouting rebuke, which took all by surprise, especially the Colonel, who's pompous exterior suddenly lost it's confidence.

"Now look here Kurt I don't give a fuck if you send us all back to the showers for extermination, but I am not going to die knowing that I let you slander a decent man, (as he pointed back at Sam), who made it possible for you to be where you are today when you were down and out, despised by everyone including your own people, who sneered at you because your wife had left you and sold you out completely, and you were a drunk with not a "penny" to his name. Who in the hell do you think made it possible for you to travel back to Berlin first class in your own private cabin dressed like a successful executive in a fine wool British Great Coat with 200 American dollars in the pocket, not your worthless German marks, thus enabling you to be greeted by your so-called friends, who then thought that they had made a grave mistake about your perceived status, so that you could be restored to your social and nepotistic connections. That's how you got to where you are today! And this is the way you respond to his non-self seeking generosity by tipping shit on him at every turn with your perniciousness. I'm sorry but I am just not prepared to let you get away with it."

Declan turned to Sam, and picked Martin up in his arms, looking depleted said, "I'm sorry I just could not let this pass. It's a matter of principle. If you don't have principle, life is just not worth living".

A stunned silence prevail momentarily, while the three captives expected a hasty return to the showers. Declan turned to face his captor to receive an expected "depart from me for I know thee not."

Kurt had leant back on his desk and he removed his cap and in so doing looked at Declan, with an expression of total dumbfoundedness, and instead of delivering an expected rebuke said, "Declan I am truly sorry for this offence, and to you too Sam and to my little Martin", as he touched Martin's cheek. Do you need anything my little man?' to which Martin replied, in a childlike manner, "I want my Teddy that the man took." Kurt choke a little and then regained his composure, as he turned to one of his SS men saying, "you heard the boy".

A thought had ran through Kurt's mind from Sunday School days, 'greater love hath no man that he lay down his life for his friend'. His respect for Declan was replenished that day.

The thorn was remembered.

Then as if nothing had happened Kurt immediately started to organise their departure. First everyone was to have a hot shower.

What an experience. Three months since the last one. Declan was well aware of the thin ice he had created with his outburst and encouraged all to make it as quick as possible.

To their surprise when they re-entered the room a full set of clothes were laid out for Sam and Declan, as they were about the same size and as Kurt pointed out his measurements were similar. Martin had no problem pulling on a full set of tweed trousers and a big woolly jumper, and there on top was his Teddy.

A hot meal had been organised with typical German efficiency and as they all sat at the table Kurt outlined the plan.

A motor bike and side car was the only spare vehicle available, it was fitted with two long range fuel tanks and the side car was big enough to take a passenger and Martin.

As they were finishing the last of their meal, which Sam had quietly cautioned not to eat too fast or too much, because their meagre diet in the camp would have shrunk their stomachs and they may get ill.

Better to put it in a bag and take it with them.

Kurt produced their documentation, which all looked very official, and said he had arranged for them to go to Vienna and meet up with a contact of his who would arrange for a British aircraft to fly them to London.

Declan was absolutely amazed at how quickly this had been organised.

Kurt said his contact in Vienna owed him a favour and was happy to help.

"Some big favour Kurt". Declan prompted. He looked a bit embarrassed at the question, but with a slight smile on his face and an apology to Sam said "my friend had been accused of being a Jew, and as this friend was my second cousin I was able to testify to his bloodline credentials. And so the favour". With raised hands in a gesture of QED.

"Your documentation states that you are surveyors for future autobans and that you are operating under the direct orders of the Fuherer. This should get you through any check point.

However if anything goes wrong, and this matter is traced back to me, I will have to say that you escaped with the help of other inmates. I'm sorry but this is the only way it can be.

Addressing Sam, Kurt told him he had ordered changes to his name to minimise the risk of being discovered. Herr Samuel Von Rosen.

Quickly now, you must be on your way, the BMW bike is down stairs all loaded with equipment, surveying gear, maps, food to keep you going, a woollen travel rug and here, two sheep skin flying jackets, unmarked, and leather helmets. Kurt gave Declan a knowing nod and a wink, shaking hands Declan said "under different circumstance I think we could have been good friends." Kurt stepped back and came to attention and gave Declan a military salute.

Wheeling around with an out stretched hand to Sam said, "I know this is not US dollars, but it's the best I could do at short notice".

All was made ready with the guards. Declan cranked over the bike with a sense of déjà vu, as he had been an avid motor cyclist back in Australia. The feel of such a machine was sensational.

They headed out through the gates and no one looked back.

Sam checked the map and the journey looked as though it was a trip through the country, back toward Warsaw. The wind was chilled and it whistled past as they sped on their way. Not much was said, but after a time and many kilometres behind them, they decided to pull up and get the real sense of their freedom, which was so charged, with so many mixed emotions of what had happened to them, as was it just a dream?

They all needed to relieve themselves and after that to try out the fare that Kurt had arranged for them. Sandwiches, the left over's from their meal, and coffee in a thermos flask and a juice for Martin.

As they packed up and prepared to go, Sam said to Declan on the side, "I've been thinking it over. I will leave you when we get to Warsaw as I want to find Anna and Rossie. You and Martin go on to Vienna." Declan was a bit perplexed but understood Sam's need to find his family.

When they arrived at the outskirts of the city Sam alighted and with tearful hugs and kisses told Declan he knew of a passage where he could get to the Jewish Ghetto without being detected. "You wont believe what Kurt put in my pocket, as he carefully showed Declan a lugar and the money that had been handed over. The money and the lugar he tried to give to Declan, who would not have any of it. More back slapping and hugs and Sam was gone.

The thorn had been extricated.

It was now just Declan and Martin, and they pushed on to their destination almost without incident, except for one young boarder guard who tried to throw his weight about, but he was no match for Declan, who spoke perfect high German.

Declan had gained a great deal more confidence after his run-in with Kurt, and realised that shouting was the edge, and he soon had the young soldier on the back-foot and apologising for his indiscretion.

Martin was immensely proud of Declan that day as he snuggled under his warm rug at the bottom of the sidecar.

Other formalities passed very quickly when they arrived in Vienna, as it seemed their contact there was as nervous as a cat, and hurriedly escorted them to an airfield where a two engine plane was waiting, piloted by a very friendly English gentleman, handle bar mustache and all.

Once in the air he introduced himself and was very chatty, enquiring after Declan's status, who immediately adopted an attitude of suspicion with all the questioning, and decided to ask a few questions himself with overtones in the nature of "what the bloody hell are you doing working with the Germans"?

The pilot looked around and with a cheeky grin and a chuckle said "Oh I see old boy you think I'm cavorting around with Hitler and his mates. Well I suppose I am in a way, but not in the way you think. You see those plates under your feet, if you pull them back you will see what I mean."

Declan pulled the plates back which revealed a bank of highly sophisticated looking cameras.

"You see old man I'm a representative for a British firm that makes military hardware, and the old Hun thinks that I can supply them with some of our secrets.

I've been coming over here for years and got to know these chaps quite well and they are under the impression, that with a few drinks on board, I'm a soft touch, and therefore allow me to fly in and out on a regular basis.

I took the matter up with the Ministry of War and they thought it was a great opportunity to play the double game.

So here I am. I fought these bastards in the last war and it gives me great pleasure to think I'm getting one back on them at their dirty game."

"I was told that you are a surveyor".

Declan was more confident now after the pilots disclosure, and apologised for his suspicion. He recounted the circumstances of how they got caught up in the prison camp and their ultimate escape.

"That's OK old boy, I would have been thinking the same in your shoes."

"I'm not a surveyor, I'm a mechanical engineer."

"Great work old chap you are just the man I need. You see that camera on the right, (Declan looked and identified it), some how it has got out of focus, probably a bump when I landed.

I tried to fix it my self but I'm no engineer. Could you have a look at it and see what can be done? My job for the Ministry is to take photo's of any new developments and now I'm stymied for this run.

If you could have a look at it for me and get it going, we'll take another swoop round and take some shots."

Declan got down on his hands and knees and examined the camera and could clearly see that the mounting had been interfered with, throwing the focus of the bank of cameras completely out of action. He called the pilot for a screw-driver and a hammer, and got Martin to fetch them for him. Martin felt important that he was entrusted with such a mission, and watched enthusiastically as Declan went about rectifying the problem.

Job done and the pilot took a wide swoop over an area that was significant to him, clicking the camera all the way, and once completed praised Declan for his skill, and said it would not go unnoticed at the War Ministry.

All the excitement over, both Declan and Martin were exhausted from the great escape events. They slept soundly throughout the flight, and were woken up by the pilot with a cheery "we're here lads."

Things went rather quickly for the O'Leary family back in London even though there was the never ending interrogations of the 'why's and where for's,' forms to complete for the bureaucrats, they soon found themselves on a DC3 plane after a further few short British formalities, delivered with a final stern seriousness, of "keep all this under your hat". Wink, wink, nudge, nudge.

The inquisition would have been longer, but it seemed the Home Office had bigger fish to fry and the only memories Martin had, was the long trip, with only one stopover before reaching Australia.

Chapter 8

Another Door Is Opened

Another week has past, and Martin was starting to feel the effects the meetings with Sam were having on his day to day life.

His general demeanour had taken an upward climb, as he felt less burdensome, even cheery at times, that had him, of all things whistling.

A character trait that had left him many moons ago.

"My God what's going on?" he said to himself as this realisation became evident.

Even the walls in his small apartment seemed to take on a different appeal when he drew the curtains back and let the light come in.

It was like a new adventure in his commonplace living, which had not been there before.

The shadows had bought him comfort in the past.

And lo and behold he was even cleaning the place up.

Tidiness was never his long suite. It was always easier to walk around the mess until he got desperate, and then call in a cleaner.

Embarrassed, he would say some else had lived there, or he had let the place and this is the way they had left it.

As he and Sam gave each other a Father and son greeting at the start of their next session Martin felt boyish about his newfound revelations, but he could not help himself in telling Sam the good news to which

Sam responded in an infused joyfulness, congratulating Martin on his progress.

"Martin you can't have this all on your own as I too have been going over our get-togethers and I can not remember having such satisfaction in all my career as has happened with us.

My boy you will never know my transformation . . . and we have only just begun. Praise be to God".

"Sam I am keen to hear what happened to you after you left us just outside of Warsaw"

Sam raised himself in his chair so as to look Martin in the eye and momentarily gathered his recollections before recounting the events of that time.

"You will recall that before we got to the city precincts of Warsaw, we stopped to have some supper.

Martin nodded to this memory. Your father and I had a quiet talk about the events that should follow and I put it to him the line of action that I wanted to take, and that was, that I should leave our little group on two bases of reasoning; one being that me being Jewish would jeopardize the whole groups chances if we were detained by some road block guard, and the second was that I needed to find out what had happened to my family, Anna and my little Rossannah.

Of course your father and I disputed over this decision but eventually he saw the logic of it all.

We separated a short distance outside of the city at a place that I had discovered when I first arrived in Poland.

It was a location that the Catholic monks had shown me after I had expressed a deep interest in the architecture of the cathedral and it's history.

It was after a number of visits, when discussing the history of the monasteries origins, that the head monk revealed to me in confidence, a hidden tunnel, and showed me the entrance in the cathedral and took me on a tour, which I was amazed to find that the tunnel had a number of branches all designed to confuse pursuers in the event of an escape.

The correct route had markings that were indistinguishable to the uninitiated as to where the outside entrances were located, and how to gain entry.

He pointed out that the tunnel was originally built, maybe two or three hundred years previously, as an escape route in the event of a purge of the church, and the clergy had to make a quick exit.

At the time I was absolutely fascinated that the old monks of so many hundreds of years before had had the engineering skills and the mastery of intrigue to conceive such a project, which was ultimately to my benefit.

One of the exit points was right near where I got off and said my farewells to you and Declan.

This was how I entered the city to begin my quest.

I was well known to the monks, as the position of Station Master carried some respectability and standing in the community.

They were very helpful, and with the full knowledge that if they were caught harbouring a Jew, some serious explaining would have to be done.

They knew where the main Jewish Ghetto was and the safest way for me to get there.

After a hearty meal with the rest of the Monks, some food in my bag, a flask of wine and many prayers of good will, I was able to make my way to the leaders group.

However I will never forget the kindness of the monks and their courage, and just before I set out the head monk spoke to me in a secretive manner, giving me a warning to be on the lookout for some spies who had infiltrated the ghetto group. Keep your own counsel he warned.

After some weeks of enquiring through the various channels of information and the Ghetto Management system, I finally discovered that Anna and Rossannah had perished at two separate but co-joined camps at Auschwitz.

They were in two separate blocks divided by a barbed wire fence.

What anxiety they went through by being able to see one another on either side of the fence, but not able to touch or embrace, only call out words of encouragement, silently crying for one another, I will never know but only surmise the extent of their broken hearts.

Oh my heart aches every time I remember these events."

Sam began to cry softly, and Martin followed suite just imagining the circumstances.

The two men took time out for this cathartic moment.

Sam continued "I was told that their suffering was not longstanding as they had contracted dysentery in the cattle trucks on the way to Auschwitz, and not long after were struck down with typhoid, a deadly killer under those appalling conditions.

My poor girls, taken so early in their lives."

This statement caused further grieving for both men.

Martin reflected on his own circumstances, which paled into insignificances by comparison.

Once some decorum was re established Sam, with the fatherly gesture of a counsellor, said "how are you holding up Martin?"

"I find this whole experience heart breaking, but at the same time in some queer way liberating. A sense of closure, like some door being closed on that part of my life. The little Martin in me can now move on without that dark shadow. Do you know what I mean Sam?"

Sam nodded with full acknowledgment of the trial they had been through. "Yes my boy, I understand completely and even though this is a sombre time I believe there is a light at the end of the tunnel."

"What happened next after you got that shocking news."

"The ghetto freedom fighters wanted me to join their cause and in my moment of great despair and need for revenge, I entered their group and proceeded to hatch a variety of plots in an attempt to plan and gain freedom and at the same time inflict as much damage as possible on our oppressors.

In groups like this where the majority of participants are emotional insurgents with little or no military training, you can imagine that opinions run thick and fast with some wild imaginings and very little conclusive strategies, aided and abetted by the covert spies who moved in the shadows of deception, that after a couple of months I decided this was not for me and if I was going to be killed by the enemy, who was better armed, better trained and who out-numbered us, then I'd like to think that I had a better chance of formulating some schemes of my own rather than be in the hands of well intention rebels who were working on notions and not sound strategies.

After a series of debates over my intentions I finally received the blessings of the group, and after securing a rifle and ammunition, a hunting knife, some meagre rations, a blanket and the lugar your father insisted I keep, I started on my journey of liberation, and my intended destination was Czechoslovakia, although I did not reveal this to the group, but nominated another destination so as to foil any attempts by the spies to undermine my progress, by saying I still had contacts at the Railway.

I made my way back to the Monks as a shadowy figure of the night with my heart pounding and holding my breath at every noise until I arrived at the Priory door, and luckily the Abbot himself greeted me in whispered tones of welcome.

After he had heard my tales of woe, he immediately dropped into prayer thanking God for sending me back to them, and to enlighten the way we should proceed.

After a period of silence and meditation the conclusion was that my escape route should be the tunnel, clearly marked on a map that was prepared for me. It was not the tunnel that I had come in through, but one of the branches I had seen previously.

It was quite long, maybe two and a half kilometres, which had an exit on a farm. The only way I had of identifying this was that I had to virtually count my steps, as prescribed by the monks, so as to not miss the access to this exit, or otherwise I could go on until a dead end, and may become exhausted and disorientated and who knows what might have happened.

But these clever tunnel builders of centuries past had built a round pier that looked like a support for the roof. However hidden behind it was a narrow entrance to an equally narrow staircase that opened into a large barn, which housed the cattle and fowls, for warmth and shelter.

I appeared as quietly as possible, with a few chooks clucking and some of the cattle stirred in their stalls.

I had hardly gained my breath when I felt the tongs of a pitch fork on my neck, and the rattling of the barn door being opened.

In came a portly gentleman and whispered loudly in Polish, "It's alright my friends, he is one of us."

My friends I soon discovered were six rag-tag individuals all trying to escape the 'German blight'.

How the monks were able to inform this farmer so quickly of my arrival I will never know.

However he was quickly down to business with the first instruction being that 'we do not say, use or exchange our names. You can stay for three days. You will be fed and any necessary clothing will be provided within limits, and then you must make your own way out of this "safe house" with a pledge not to mention this farm to anyone, and with that we all swore an oath.

The barn door opened again and a young boy of about fifteen came in with a tray generously laden with foodstuffs and hot coffee.

I shook the farmers hand and thanked him for his fearlessness in allowing me to stay, and got some directions on the safest way to Czechoslovakia.

"Czechoslovakia, he whispered urgently into my ear, don't you know the Germans are ravishing that place right now"? I admitted I didn't know, but said I had a friend there whom I went to university with, and he is the only one I knew who would put me up.

He turned to the young boy and whispered something in his ear and he disappeared instantly.

The farmer looked at me shaking his head and said "you poor boy"

The young lad reappeared and handed something to his father.

Sam turned in his chair and retrieved an object from his desk, which he passed to me.

I could see that it was an oval bronze box with a hook on the end that you could hang on your trouser belt or something else of that nature, and at his bidding, I opened it to discover it was a compass.

"You'll need this" the farmer said to me. And he was right.

"Now I want you to have it Martin, not because I think you will need it in the same way as I did, but as a physical link between you and me"

No protest on Martins part was ever countenance by Sam and in that moment of this transaction Martin knew this was a father and son thing.

Sam continued on the telling of his journey.

The farmer took me to one side after giving me the compass and continued in hushed tones,

"About two kilometres through these woods, heading due south you will come to a railway line which you should follow to your right until you come to a junction. Take the left arm and follow it for about five kilometres where there will be a siding that is used for topping up the water on the train. They generally stop for about twenty minutes which should give you enough time to find a spot in a carriage, preferably at the back, so if you need to escape in a hurry you will have a better chance of doing so. This train will take you to the boarder. Go on your own, and good luck."

With that he abruptly turned and left with the young lad at his heels

I left the very next day as my fellow "guests" were trying to hatch a plan, which excluded me, for which I was grateful.

The farmer's directions were correct in every detail and I followed his instructions with the help of the compass and in due course arrived at the rail siding he mentioned.

This was all too easy, the train arrived and I found a stock carriage, Made myself comfortable and regularly checked my bearings via the compass and visuals that I could make through the open vent slits at the top of the carriage as the train made it's way to my expected destination.

After about three hours of uneventful 'clickity clack' of the wheels, the train suddenly started to break heavily to a stop and I could hear the yelling of soldiers barking out orders to the train driver.

They were familiar voices of Germans doing their usual routine of intimidation.

Now was the time to leave and as I gently slid the door open I could see that they were on the other side and so I slid down the embankment, hoping not to be noticed, and at that precise moment the train driver blew the whistle which bought a barrage of rebuke from the soldiers, but was a perfect cover for me.

No sooner had I found myself a hiding place, a volley of machine gun fire was riddling the train, and no doubt the soldiers as well, except for one who was making his way down the train inspecting the carriages, when he came to the one that I had been in, and as the bullets rained down, he leapt in to that carriage and exited the same way as I had done, sliding down the embankment and almost on top of me, saw me crouching in my spot, and thinking that I must have been one of his attackers, pointed his weapon at me, but before he could pull the trigger, I had already had my hand gun out, and as an automatic reflex I shot him.

The train took off and the next thing I knew there were two armed rag bag looking combatants, not Germans, standing over me surveying the situation. Seeing that I had shot the German soldier, a grin came over their faces and they started shouting for their leader.

He eventually appeared; a middle aged man, bearded and seemingly battle hardened, and obviously in-charge.

"Get up" he bawled at me and immediately I felt this is it, I'm in for it, what ever that may be.

I was unceremoniously marched backup past the rail siding into the forest behind, into a dense area of bush and trees where there was a small clearing with several tents and a make-shift shed.

Someone tied my hands behind my back, and I thought I'm done for now.

A bullet to the head would be the kindest way to go.

A strange sensation came over me as I realised I was not terrified but in the face of this calamity I was calm and without fear. I could not believe it of my self and as the commandant started to interrogate me I was able to look him in the eye.

His language was Russian and even though I was unable to speak it at that time I did recognise some of the words, and responded in Polish.

"A Pole eh, he stated with a wisp of a smile, what is your business here? Trying to spy on us? Are you a traitor to your country? Did you think killing that German soldier would throw us off who you really are? I should shoot you now like a dog, for trying to infiltrate our position. Who are you".

This type of interrogation went on and on until I finally broke.

"You call yourself freedom fighters yet you are willing to take my freedom without compunction. Yet I am just as much a freedom fighter as you. I'm fighting for my freedom and I don't have any armed bandits to back me up. Don't tell me about freedom. I lost mine when the Nazi's gathered me up like rubbish, threw me into a concentration death camp, and I escaped with the help of friends and went back to the cuckoo's nest in Warsaw only to learn that my wife and daughter had died in Auschwitz!

Don't tell me about your fight for freedom". I blurted this all out in frustration and anger and waited for my stern rebuke which I had expected would come from the end of a rifle butt.

My interrogator turned his head aside and cried out in Yiddish, "please God forgive me"

I was absolutely astounded. The man was a fellow Jew.

"Cut him free" he ordered and he embraced me and cried, "I am so sorry my brother I thought you were a German".

"I am. I was born in Berlin, went to University there but being a Jew I was forced to find work elsewhere and finally landed in Warsaw as the Station Master even though my degree is in engineering."

The day was getting late and he announced to his fellow comrades that I was one of them and to get the supper going and make provision for our new cognate in arms.

We talked into the night and I was so relieved to be in the company of such men that I disgorged my whole tale from woe to go and even having to repeat it several times for the benefit the others, translating from the Yiddish to German Polish and even English so that nothing was lost. The empathy that I got from that group was beyond my wildest expectations.

Let's get some sleep my brothers as the hour is late and we have much to do in the coming days, and we will talk more tomorrow. There was a night 'look-out' roster of three hours on and three hours off. I volunteered to take a shift but all agreed that I should have the night off.

The next morning started at day break and one of the men went out to scout around the area to see if they had the 'all clear'. Mulling over the previous nights activities I became a little concerned that I may have given up too much of my self and my circumstances, and it was as if the "Colonel", as he was called could read my mind and started out by saying that when he translated my Yiddish story he deliberately left out the word Jew because as he said this is your first lesson of association with any group, even though the existing group was made up of three Jews and three others of varying denominations, his firm instruction was "do not trust anyone" as every man he believed, had his weak point where he would give up another to save his own skin, and Jews were vulnerable beyond all others. We only use first names because of this and you will only be known as Sam.

"To you my brother and no one else, understand me, I am Dr Vladim Smirnov. They know I am a doctor but always refer to me as "colonel". I tell you these things because in my heart of hearts I trust you and I believe you are guileless. I have changed my surname, because of past events when my brother who was also a doctor was murdered for no other reason than he was a Jew. I advise you to do the same until this madness comes to an end".

These were sobering thoughts, but wise ones and I took all of his advice on board.

That bond and friendship lasted until the end of the war.

Their mission he told me, as partisans, was to cause as much disruption to the enemy as possible, by blowing up bridges, rail lines, roads, cutting communication lines, killing as many German soldiers or Nazi civilian supporters or sympathizers as possible. Of course I have my medical duties to perform on the sick and wounded, and maybe I could use your help in that area".

"I'm an engineer and have no medical training outside of a first aid course. I can't see how I would be too helpful".

"We'll see, but I think you will do just fine. Trust me Sam.

I went on to tell him that my main goal was to get to my friend in Ostrava, Czechoslovakia, my old university pal, the pharmacist.

The colonel's eyes widened and he excitedly said "we're heading that way our selves. That town is the one we have a contact there as well and I'm running low on medical supplies and many procedures are carried out without appropriate medication.

I told him his name was Joseph Stern, and instantly he took hold of his head in both hands saying "I don't believe this! God has certainly bought us together Sam, for this is the same man that I have to make contact with, and he's a personal friend of yours. Amazing!"

As the days went by we collaborated together on many things from philosophy to religion, politics and music, many of which we had a good level of agreement.

The colonel taught me many tactics of guerrilla fighting, surveillance, and armaments a long with a host of other survival methods. It was a thorough training program that has held me in good stead for many years. I in turn gave him the benefits of my engineering knowledge. We formed a great partnership.

An unexpected skill set developed when the colonel was called upon to repair some of the bodies of comrades and others. On the first occasion of this experience a young man was bought in with a very severe stomach wound, caused by canon fire and a large piece of shrapnel had torn into his stomach. He looked at me and calmly said "I'm going to need some assistance on this one so wash your hands and just do as I say. Do you think you can do it?

I nodded with some trepidation and to my surprise discovered I was more than up to the task, than I expected, so much so that the colonel turned to me after a successful completion of the procedure, and said "are you sure you have not done this thing before?"

I took that as a compliment. After a long period of time together, he commented that I should have done medicine instead of engineering.

It's interesting how providence guides your steps in life.

"Is this getting all too much for you Martin? I seem to have been talking about myself endlessly?

"Don't stop Sam as I'm absolutely enthralled with this story, and I want to hear it through to the end".

Martin was entranced.

"In that case we better have a brandy to cleans the palate and I must tell Anna another place for dinner. No, no don't think of protesting!" And with that he spoke to Anna on the intercom, "One more place for dinner my love."

"Now where was I? Oh yes", the Colonel was familiar with Ostrava and pointed out that the mission to make contact with Joseph Stern was fraught with danger as the Nazi's were brutalising the place, hunting down and killing any dissidents, especially known Jews.

The mayor was a highly placed Nazi and was making it his speciality to go after Jews, as he believed that it would win him some patronage from the Fuehrer.

After long discussions and planning it was decided that I should be the one to go and collect the pharmaceutical contraband, as I spoke the local language, and was a personal friend of Joseph's which would make it easier for identification, and should make for a less difficult transition.

I can tell you Martin that I have never been so scared in all my life going into that town.

I was unarmed and endeavouring to look as jaunty as possible.

At the same time I did not want to bring attention to myself.

Trying to look like a local is not easy, but I knew I had to find my old university pal, whom I had not seen since we graduated.

He was about five years older than me and in those days letter writing was the only way we stayed in touch with an occasional telephone call.

But for all that we considered ourselves close, and exchanged family photo's and the like.

My haversack and weapon was hidden at the front gate of a farm we had been staying, living in the barn with the animals.

It was cosy at night, and safe.

It was a short stay as we were moving west searching out enemy vantage points that we could destroy.

The Colonel had given me my instructions, what to look for and the directions and that I would be identified by my cap which had a broad green stripe, and that I should whistle the Czech National anthem quietly so as to not attract unwanted attention, except that of our contact.

Nonchalantly I was walking down a narrow back street expecting to spot a pharmacy, and just as I was passing a corner book store, a young girl appeared at the door, gave me a signal to come over, and as this was somewhat different from the original plan I hesitated, until she sharply said "block head, over here".

I entered that place thinking 'this is a trap, and the Colonel would not be pleased with this'.

The girl quickly closed the door and in hushed tones said "you're with the Colonel aren't you."

"Who are you I asked?"

"I am Anna Stern"

I held her at arms length and recognised her from photos Joseph had sent.

"Anna I'm Sam Rosenberg your fathers friend, where is he?

"The Germans shot him yesterday when they found out he was supplying drugs to the Colonel. I have been hiding in this bookstore as the owners have run away. My father gave me the package you have come for and I can take you to it now."

"Anna you poor darling what a terrible thing to happen to you" and I held her in my arms until she bought us back to the business at hand, saying "we must hurry as the Germans have been searching for me and I think one of the neighbours has reported me, so there is no time to waste".

We scurried out through a back door, into and alley, in through another house, out the back door and to a wood shed. Anna reached in and retrieved a package. I questioned what she was going to do from now on and she hesitatingly admitted she had no real plan except to keep hiding from the Germans.

"That's not going to happen Anna, you are coming with me and I'm going to look after you. It wont be easy but we will find a way."

"And there you have it Martin that's how my lovely Anna and I met. She was fourteen and I was twenty nine."

Martin rolled back in his chair, mouth open and stunned by this revelation.

"Of course Anna was just like a little sister to me and I was very protective, but she had a maturity well beyond her years and a wisdom that regularly confounded me.

By the time she was seventeen we were in love and the Colonel, with the powers invested in him, so he said, conducted a wedding ceremony, which was the beginning of a wonderful new life and happiness totally unexpected, considering the start we both had.

We continued to fight together with the Colonel and his band of merry men until we were invited by the Russian Army in their push for Poland to join them as Medics and truck drivers.

We eventually became part of the liberation of Auschwitz, a scene that still haunts me today. But remarkable things came out of that experience, one being, to see where my first Anna, and dear little Rossie met their end, and while I was examining the barracks they were housed in and trying to imagine what they went through, considerably more than us Martin, I must add, by comparison, and as stood there, aghast at this human hell hole, a seemingly little old lady dressed in prison rags,(I found out later that she was in her early thirties) came up to me and said "are you Rosenberg"?

Naturally I was stunned that she knew my name, and I asked her how, and she said that Rossannah had said to her that her father would come back for her.

"I'm too late" I wailed. She shook her head, and out of a small tattered bag she was carrying she gave me two cigar tins, the type that was carried by the guards.

"Rossannah asked me to give these to you"

I opened them and found two letters written in pencil.

I asked this lady, "how can I ever thank you for minding these for me?"

Her big sunken eyes looked up at me brimming with tears, "you have given me all the thanks that I need. You were too late for your beautiful little daughter, but not for me. I am free at last. Thank you."

"I left that place a broken man, and only God knows where I would have been had it not been for my Anna of now."

There are times in your life, Martin quietly reflected, when your heart aches with such profoundness that you can never imagine that you will ever be the same. This was one of those times and he knew that his old friend Sam, in retracing these steps was opening up past events, which ultimately bought him some succour, which he now wanted to pass on to him.

Martin saw Anna in a new light that day, with a new respect.

He wanted some of the strengths she possessed.

Sam held the cigar boxes in his hands reverently, telling Martin that one of these was for him and that from the day he had received them he had not read the contents of the letter addressed "To my Darling Martin" out of respect to Rossannah, and for the full expectation he had, that Martin would come into his life again.

Martin took the cigar case and held it to his heart, and without opening it lay back in his chair, closed his eyes and felt the spirit of Rossie once more.

Great gushes of tears poured forth as he felt a renewal take hold of his whole being.

The spirit of Rosie swept through his every fibre, artery, heart and brain function.

Sam said at a later time, a deep groaning, issued from the very innermost core of Martin's being, that went on for so long, that eventually he left the room to confide in Anna as to what was happening.

They had spent the intervening time in quiet prayer, and waited.

So much time had passed that Sam thought it appropriate to check on the situation in case of any some untoward circumstances.

As he quietly opened the door to his study he caught a glimpse of Martin holding the letter to his lips, then with deep respect, carefully folding the paper and placing it back in the cigar case.

Martin lay there, and sank deep into a world he had not been before. It was as though, he recalled later that he was lying on sea shore, of a deserted tropical island, with a gentle breeze caressing his face and ruffling his hair. The lapping balmy waters bought a sense of cleansing to his body as it washed over his skin.

Old anxieties, fears and torturous memories passed out through the pores and washed away.

Free at last, he thought.

Just like that poor wretched woman, who faithfully carried Rossannah's cigar tins for all the time she was in that camp of horrors, was able to walk out through the gates of Auschwitz.

Martin felt the same about the prison walls he had built around himself over all those years. The gates were open. Free at last.

As Martin entered the dining room, he went to Anna and gave her a big hug saying, "thank you, thank you, thank you,

Anna was not too sure what that was all about, but as she looked into Martins' face, she noted a distinct softness in his demeanour.

Holding his face momentarily between her hands said, "You are more than welcome my son".

Sensing there were profound changes in Martin, Sam insisted that he stay that night.

It was a precaution in case Martin might have some reversals.

Before they sat down to eat, there was a moment of quiet reflection and togetherness in the spirit, and it was in this time that Martin said,

"Henry Jackson Van Dyke wrote a piece which to me seems very appropriate to our circumstance, it is also imbedded in my heart.

'Time is too slow for those who wait,

Too swift for those who fear,

Too long for those who grieve,

Too short for those who rejoice,

But for those who love, time is eternity.

Chapter 9

The Picture Gets Bigger

M artin had taken some time to absorb the new dimensions of his life but was fully aware that there were other abstruse factors that needed to be dealt with, if he was to obtain total freedom from the demons that were lurking in the shadows of his subconscious, darting to the surface from time to time, daring him to uncover the other hidden factors of "WHY"

The neurons were still circling in Martins mind when he elected to leave Sam's place in the early morning to walk back to his apartment. It was only about four kilometres or so and it would be head clearing exercise.

He cut through the Botanical Gardens and was abruptly halted in his tracks as the combined perfumes of the flowers bombarded his old factory senses, and for the first time in living memory, he was smelling "the roses" so to speak.

Joy filled his heart and he knew he was ready for any eventuality that awaited him.

At his next scheduled meeting, Martin and Sam went over the triumphs of past sessions and ticked a number of "boxes".

Sam leaned back and looking directly at Martin saying, "there's more to this Martin, and I want you to start and recount your life after you returned from Poland and how you felt toward your parents, and your siblings and they to you.

I want you to go deep into your emotions, thoughts, feelings as a child and progress through your age change, trying to remember the things that made you strong and the things that made you weak or vulnerable."

It's important Martin, and I don't want to miss any unturned stone which could rob you of the healing which has begun.

"Now relax, just relax", and as this magical neurological experience took hold, Martin began his new journey by saying,

"When we first came back from Poland there was a short time of normality, but it was not long before things started to unravel.

Father returned to his original job, but not with the sense of triumph he had expected, and looking back now, I deduced that the Power Station Executive Group had come to realise that it was their mistake which sent him to an invaded Poland, but wanted to shift the blame to someone else.

Some bright spark suggested that the most prudent thing to do was to shift the fault to Father, by innuendo, whisper campaigns along with the usual corporate skulduggery of non promotional rewards, by moving executives sideways to eliminate any possibility of "bitching" by the recipient, and if such a person did raise some query as to what was going on, it opened the door to labelling them as "not being a team player".

End of story. Mission complete.

All the perpetrators go home and sleep soundly while the recipients are left bewildered, hurt, depressed and emotionally screwed.

Your friend Declan Sam, began to hide in the shadows of defeat as this iniquitous plan rolled out, never speaking of the Poland affair again and telling me to do the same.

My Mother did not help the situation, as she would regularly remind him that it was his entire fault, and by extraction mine as well.

The psychological pressure must have been enormous. Condemned without a trial.

My brothers were returned from boarding school, increasing the pressure on the household unit, and with more vindictiveness toward me.

They had learned some new tricks at boarding school.

Ear pulling and backside kicking became the norm and order of the day, and any *appellare* by me to Mother was generally rebuffed with "your weak like your father", or another, "you're a sissy".

This had such a profound effect on me that Treblinka did not seem so bad, but I did developed an uncontrollable temper.

Known in those days as a short fuse, I attempted to kill my teasing provocative sibling offender, as we grappled like two animals in a life an death struggle, I had him in a vice like hold that was making his face turn blue.

After being suitably restrained, and screamed at with 'stop it Martin you'll kill him' I was soundly thrashed by my Mother, with the branch of a willow tree, ideally trimmed to give maximum effect and pain to the recipient and fiendish pleasure to the perpetrator.

In the darkness of my place of solitude I did find comfort with "teddy" (yes, I still had him) who brushed away my tears and smoothed the welts on my arms and legs with his tiny smooth paws.

He was the only one I could turn to for comfort.

This environment drove me to become a loner, living in my own little world, dreaming, making up my own games, thinking of Rossie, and totally absorbed in reading, which she had told me 'this is the way you learn, and dream your dreams.'

An old lady who lived up on a hill not far from my home, had become fond of me, and had wondered at my introspective ways, gave me a book called "Tell Me Why?"

This was like an illustrated child's encyclopedia and was to become my doorway to knowledge and wonder.

This book provided an opportunity for a new friendship, namely Mrs Burt, my gift giver, who became my part time teacher and to some extent my confidant.

She had two children, an adult male, Allan who was married and lived close by, and a daughter, Schantel, who in my childish eyes was the most beautiful creature on earth. She had a gentleness and tenderness that melted me every time we met and her adoring eyes sent me into ecstasy, which made her laugh, in a slightly titillating way, and she would hold my face between her soft hands, and kiss my cheek, and I swear, I would almost wet myself.

On one occasion after an episode like this I overheard Mrs Burt say to Schantel, "I think he's in love with you," followed by female giggling.

I was mortified that my cover had been exposed.

However, Schantel never changed and without her knowing, or maybe she did, provided me with that little bit of love and tenderness that I yearned for.

Mrs Burt on the other hand, offered me milk and biscuits on every occasion of our meeting, encouraged me, teaching me, and before long I had a better handle on reading, writing, arithmetic and general knowledge than any other kid around.

My elders, outside of my family, would heap praise on me for my general knowledge of subjects far and wide, often saying, "you're a smart kid".

Mrs Burt took great pleasure in this but refused to take any credit for my development, but it was clear to all that she played a pivotal role in my progress.

It wasn't until some years later that I discovered she had been a school teacher in England before coming to Australia.

Rossie started this process you know Sam, from the first day we met.

Sam nodded knowingly.

At home my hiding place was behind a large shed that Father had built, and it was up close to the dividing fence of our neighbour, and there was just enough room for my then small frame to fit between the gap, which allowed an escape route for me when trouble was looming.

It was a spot where no one considered looking and they would call and whistle for hours in their search for me.

I took some satisfaction from this in that I had outsmarted my pursuers and was left in peace to devour every word of my "Tell Me Why? And dream.

Allan Burt would see me outside the front of the house dress in a hand me down cowboy suit that someone had passed on, which consisted of a leather vest and chapps, and he nick named me "cowboy" which stuck for quite a while even though my brothers, when they found out, would taunt me with jibes like, "you're no cowboy you can't even ride a rocking horse"

Allan on one occasion had heard this and in some way felt responsible, and said to me on the side, "would you like to ride my old horse Jill".

Jill was a 22 year old bay mare, and Allan warned she could be quite contrary and cantankerous at times, "so be careful."

Well Jill and I became instant friends, which had Allan tipping back his hat and saying he had never seen the like of it before in his life.

I walked gently up to Jill, and she lifted her head in a curious way, which meant her nostril, flaring slightly to take in my scent, was at the same height as my mouth, and I began speaking to her in whispered tones, the same way as I used to talk to Teddie, in a sort of secretive way.

I told her I was looking for a friend and if she was too, we could become great mates. As it happened, I had Teddie in my back pocket and introduced him to Jill, and she sniffed him thoroughly and eventually gave a bit of a snort and I took that to mean that Teddie was OK.

I had often wondered in my ponderings of the "How Do's" in 'Tell Me Why' as to how does a horse scratch it's ears and eyes as we do, and I had come up with the answer 'with some difficulty'. So I ventured a scratch around her ears and to my surprise she liked it and made those sounds that horses make like a pleasurable rumbling, and all the while I kept talking to her, saying how pretty she was, and that she had a beautiful coat and nice feet.

She was closing her eyes dreamily and as I slid my hand up to that area, she gave a bit of a flick of surprise but settled as I scratched gently around the periphery of the eye lids, removing some scale from the places where the flies had been irritating the base of her long lashes.

Rubbing her neck, I spoke even more quietly, because I did not want to upset her with my next statement.

"Allan said it was OK by him if I wanted to have a ride some day, but I thought I should ask you first".

I hesitated momentarily and then Jill's head turned and she nibbled and nuzzled me. I took that as a yes.

Allan was slapping his leg and laughing in amazement, and shaking his head saying that he had never see anything like it.

And from that day on Jill and I were the best of mates, and she knew all my secrets and to this day I still believe that horse understood and responded accordingly.

Some would say that I had an over enthusiastic imagination, but Allan was convinced that he had never seen the like of it "in all his born days"

His Mother was not phased by what was reported to her, saying to me with a caring smile, "you will be a great man Martin one of these days" and Mr Burt Senior, Mrs Burt's husband, who was a train driver, agreed.

I must have driven him mad over the years with my constant questioning of a subject dear to my child like heart, as you would know Sam, "trains".

But to his credit he never once tired of answering my never ending "Why's"

What a man he was, quiet, a deep thinker, and steadfast.

They will always remain in my memory as the foundation stones of my early beginnings. Never prying, never judgemental, always accommodating, always giving.

I loved them.

But in some ways I think I have let them down.

"Don't be too hard on yourself Martin.

Shakespeare said in 'Measure for Measure'

"They say, best men are moulded out of faults"

"Don't stop the flow. Continue my boy."

Jill enabled me to make friends that I could never imagine, who by and large were mostly adults.

Was I always trying to get acceptance from adults or was this just coincidental?

This has been a long held conundrum for me.

Anyway, while I was riding Jill around the back paddock near by, a man whom I had seen many times before, was bringing a mob of horses across and one split from the pack and no amount of shouting on his part had any effect on the horse.

I instinctively took off after the animal, and it seemed to me that Jill was enjoying the sprint, and soon we rounded him up back to the mob.

The man who was a known horse trader, after corralling the horses rode up to me saying "nice riding sunny Jim. What's your name?"

"Martin I replied"

"You can call me Reg" he said with his hand outstretched to shake man to man.

"Oh I can't do that Sir, I said, My Father would thrash me"

"Ah, one of the old school is he? Well how about Uncle Reg, would that do it?

"I think so Uncle Reg."

He laughed and shook my hand saying "I like the cut of your jib Martin" and I flushed with pride instinctively knowing this was a compliment without knowing what it meant, but I looked it up in my "Tell Me Why" and took extra satisfaction having read it's meaning.

Uncle Reg was to become another important mentor in my life, and even though he was not well educated in a scholastic sense, he had a wisdom that came from hard won experience, and an understanding of human nature.

His hands were worn and calloused from hard work, his nose broken from sport or standing up for the 'little man,' and yet his heart was full of the 'milk of human kindness'

He had a big impact on my life.

I fondly remember the day that I was up 'giving Uncle Reg a hand', when Father came striding aggressively across the paddock shouting my name in anger, "Martin you little bugger, I'm going to give you 'what for' when I get you home" and seeing this Reg wheel his horse around and rode across to meet Father, and getting off his horse, and with his usual outstretched hand and tipping back his hat, greeted Father with a "G'Day, I'm Reg Shoreman", and father, eye balling him, responded "Declan O'Leary".

"That's quite a boy you have here", and as they shook hands I could hear him say, I hope I've not been out of line letting him help me with the mob, but I have never seen a kid of his age ride a horse like he can, you must be real proud of him Declan, and he's smart too. Never in all my born days have I come across a kid like him, and he's always talking about you and what a great Dad you are. You must be real proud of him"

In no time uncle Reg had Father 'eating out of his hand' and Reg invited him to a brew of tea he had on the fire.

I can still see this flicker of change that the 'old Declan' had on his face that day as he enjoyed the company of a real man, exchanging yarns of past events, experiences and dreams, sitting around a camp fire.

Reg had bragged on me in such a way that when Father caught my eye I could see a glimmer of that which was there at Treblinka.

It is called love.

As we left for home old Reg gave me his customary wink and a nod saying "see you next time I'm through, and bring your Dad with you as I've got lots more to share with him. He's a great man Martin, and you have done him proud".

He patted Father on the back and as they shook hands I could see that the 'coast was clear' for me.

If ever there was a bush psychologist 'par excellence' that was Reg.

Father did join us on a couple of occasions but eventually he returned to his 'shell'

Reg in many ways was my mentor and educator, having a vast 'bush knowledge' on most things that a boy of my age was lacking in instruction, but dying to hear. Like making a camp, tying knots, sharpening your knife, fishing and how to find your way by following the stars.

I would pepper him with queries drawn from my "Tell Me Why" book, to which he would laugh "where in the bloody hell do you get these questions from Martin?'

The things he could not answer, I would rattle off my knowledge and Reg would shake his head in amazement and ruffle up my hair, with a "you're one smart kid" which would swell my chest with pride at having been acknowledged and appreciated.

On one occasion after we had completed the muster, I was sitting down with Reg on a stump, sipping my sweetened tea, just like an old cow hand, when I noticed a frisky young horse running back and forth along the holding yard.

I had tied Jill up to the fence and she looked a bit agitated, when all of a sudden this horse took a running jump and vaulted the fence.

"Uncle Reg the young one has gotten out!"

Reg looked up from writing in his log book, saying "bugger".

"Do you think he will get away. What's he doing?"

The young horse had come around to Jill, and to my mind he was trying to climb on her.

"No he wont get away Martin he's too busy trying to mount old Jill"

I was aghast at what I was seeing and as I watched him doing his thing with a "dick" so long and so big, I called out "he wont hurt her will he Uncle Reg"

Reg chuckled, "not a chance Martin if anything he might get a kick or two from old Jill."

Reg was quick to notice my distress and with a slightly serious tone, sat me back down on the stump.

"You don't know about these things Martin. Do you know anything about girls?"

I shook my head and looked at uncle Reg searching for an answer.

"Martin I don't know if it's my place to be talking to you about such things, but as you don't know what you've seen, and what's going on here then there is no reason for you to go away confused. So if your Dad gets mad at this, then I will just have to wear his abuse."

"I wont say anything Uncle Reg it will be just between you and me."

I can still see old Reg's weather beaten, hard worn face look at me saying, "Oh God what I wouldn't give to have had a lad like you."

Although I was not fully cognisant of the import of that statement I can still feel the warmth that it bought to my heart.

"Well Martin what you saw there is what we all do. That young stallion was having sex with Jill so that he can produce a young foal. But he's out of luck as Jill is 22 years old and she is more than likely unable to have a baby. She's just too old. But he doesn't know that.

That thing you called a "dick" fits right into a pocket like opening just under Jill's tail, and he releases some fluid that mixes with an egg like shape that Jill would normally have inside if she wasn't so old. After a while that egg becomes a baby.

We all come into this world the same way. At some time your father would have done the same thing with your mother, but in a more caring way for you to come into the world."

My eyes were wide open and I must have had a dumbfounded look on my face.

"No Martin you were not found under a cabbage plant, as we so often tell our kids, but you would have started off in your mothers tummy and when you were ready, you would have popped out and started crying.

Is this all too much for you Martin?"

I shook my head.

"One day when you are a man you will have children just like that. You think about it, and if you have any questions you just come and ask. Man to man. You know?. One thing I must tell you for the future is that if a woman ever invites you to her bed, don't go there smelling like a hog."

That advice has stuck with me to this day, even though the import of it at the time did not quite resonate. The bells did not ring until later.

This was a liberating moment for me as these things had been swirling about in my head without answers.

Now the dots were joining up.

Chapter 10

Little Things Mean A Lot

RELAX, JUST RELAX, Sam's voice intoned producing the hypnotic state for the beginning of another session.

"How did you feel after our last meeting Martin."

"It was like I had a long piece of rope with a lot of knots in it and I was gradually getting the hang of how to undo them and as each knot unravelled it was as though there was a new awakening and a new understanding and a sense of being able to view things from a different perspective.

Uncle Reg's portrayal of the meaning of life and how it came about was not only mind blowing, but a revelation to a young child in the midst of "tell me why." I was able to link up the gaps of my past childhood experiences with my mother, when at a tender moment in Poland she was trying to tell me about the mystery of my being, only to cut off after I made an innocent admission to her."

"What was that tender moment Martin?"

"You remember that bathroom in the house at Sporad? It was a monster in size and a favourite play area for me, the echoes of the walls was magic and when Father sang in there while he was shaving or what ever, it was as though you were listening to a record or a theatrical performance.

One day I was playing hide and seek with imaginary kids, and of course "Teddie".

There was a large laundry basket, made out of woven cane, which was used for soiled clothes that made a perfect hiding place, and as "Teddie" and I huddled in our secret spot, in comes Mother who stripped down to total nakedness, and began admiring her body by touching her curves and caressing her breasts and smiling at the reflection she saw in that full length mirror.

And as I peered through the gaps in the woven cane, in comes father, also naked, and they started frolicking and running around a rather large table in the centre of the bathroom, which was used for folding the clothes.

To my mind they were playing some sort of game, and for an instant I was tempted to get out of the basket and join them. But something with held that thought and I just continued to watch, and then to my childish surprise they stopped the game and fell into a passionate embrace, which ended with both of them on the table, which I understood much later on they were having sex.

When all of this was over and they had showered and retreated to the bedroom, *"Teddie"* and I sneaked out of our hiding place and the incident passed from my mind until, on another occasion Mother invited me to take a bath with her, which was an uncharacteristic showing of affection. This was a tender moment.

It was a time of almost bonding, as she allowed me to touch her breasts, prompting me to ask the "tell me why" type questions, which she answered quite frankly and in a matter of fact tone. This was when I learned that I started my existence in her belly. This bought questions of concern as to how did I get out, and she pointed to the vaginal area.

When we got out to dry down and we stood together on the bath mat, my nose was just about at the height of the pubic hair line.

"It looks too small for me to get out of there", I stated, and moved my hand toward this mystery, which received an abrupt slap. "You are not allowed to touch" she said with an angry tone.

Taken aback by this incident I said in my defence, "but Father touches you there", and looking somewhat hurt by the chastisement.

"Father is allowed to, but not you. Anyway, how do you know what Father touches'?

I related my previous story of *"Teddie"* and I hiding in the basket.

A torrent of abuse and screaming followed with a lot of smacking and her denouncing me as an "evil little devil, you go to room and just you wait until your father comes home. You are the naughtiest boy I have ever known. I wish I had never had you".

That day my heart was broken and I remained in fear and trepidation of the expectation of what my father was going to do to me. It seemed to be the longest day of my life and when the time finally came and I heard the front door close and my mother rushing to tell of the day's events, I crept out of my room and waited to take my punishment that I was sure my father was about to administer.

The anticipated physical pain was greatly diminished in my mind by the thought that I had betrayed my fathers love, that I knew he had for me, which hurt the most.

As I crouched on the staircase with Teddie in my arms, I heard the whole drama, which made me think *'maybe I am a devil'* for whatever that may be, as I did not know, but it sounded bad.

Then to my surprise after the tale had been told, and the 'what are you going to do about it' saga,

I started to hear Father laugh uproariously and saying "what are you going on about, this is part of his education, no harm has been done except your ego has been bruised. Where is the little chap?

He came up the stairs and took me in his arms, caressing me as I started to cry, "I'm sorry Father".

"There's nothing to be sorry about, you asked some very important questions. Now come along and have some dinner. Your Daddy's man. Mother will get over it" he whispered.

It felt so good Sam, but I don't think Mother ever recovered from that event.

"There are childhood memories, which in part, are worth while hanging onto Martin, because of your Father. But no matter what ever happened in the future, that seed buried deep in his heart, was a real and uncompromising love for you.

Your Mother on the other hand would seem to have been going through a crisis of her own. And like some people, unable to cope with change, and as a woman, the thought of loosing the very attributes that form part of her psyche such as diminishing beauty and career opportunities, together with small children responsibilities and the like, can tend to make them take out their frustrations in a manner that would not normally be part of their make up.

Coupled with this she was most likely approaching menopause which has it's own abnormalities that can be very disturbing if that person is in a distressing location, such as Poland was at the time, and the ever increasing realisation that this had been a bad move for her and she was more than likely out of her comfort zone.

No help for a little boy I know, but people often get release from these pent up frustrations by taking out their dilemma on the most vulnerable.

This was further evidenced by the way she took off for London at the first opportunity after arriving in Poland, to bolster her own personal shortcomings and inadequacies. It was a cry for help that no one recognised.

You were not at fault Martin, even though this may have translated to your own personal self esteem, and may account for your desire as a child to associate with other positively responsive adults outside your family.

A very normal reaction to such a situation, that followed you after your return to Australia.

This could be a marker for you even as an adult.

Now I want you to free your mind of all extraneous thoughts, take in some deep breaths, slowly exhale and say after me . . . "I was not at fault as a child" and repeat this five times . . . now I want you to say this five times slowly, "I reject any thought that says I was at fault".

This at first may seem inconsequential to you, however, you must understand that there is a long history of those negative thought processes, and even though we both understand, that there is no foundation for these thoughts to exist, it does take time and effort to erase them from the subconscious and therefore we must treat these statements as a mantra and regularly repeat them to ourselves to eradicate these negatives, and implant the positives.

Got it?"

Martin nodded in agreement and already some magic wand was doing it's job.

Martin continued on in this vein and was amazed that such a simple process was gradually easing the pressure and a sense of wellness was replacing the tired, worn out feelings that had previously dogged his latter years' of existence.

Sam had cautioned him not think that this was the end of the road for his *"come back"*, as there was more than likely a deeper process which had accumulated during his formative and adult years that needed to be faced.

Sam was also mindful that Martin needed the gentle touch, because of his learned conservative approach to change and the need to keep his cards close to his chest by not letting the left hand know what the right hand was doing.

Hence he set about instituting a family socialising regime whereby Martin regularly was invited to Sam's home for dinner, lunches and such things to enable Martin to build trust with those people who cared honestly about him.

For Martin this was difficult at first, but as time passed he became more and more integrated to the group and the old barriers slowly in part came down.

This gave Martin a breather from the sessions and a time to reflect, and to come to terms with his childhood experiences, and as Sam would say, *Forgiveness* is a powerful tool for healing both parties.

James Hilton said, "If you forgive people enough, you belong to them, and they to you, whether either person likes it or not . . . . *Squatter's rights of the heart.*"

"Lets say we start again in a couple of weeks. There's no hurry but it will be good to start peeling the onion again."

Chapter 11
The Gypsy Girl

And so they took up again with Sam feeling a flush of accomplishment and Martin looking and feeling better than he could ever remember.

Physically he was looking trimmer, not because he was working out, but simply because he was eating better, cutting back on the grog and dressing better.

All adding up to the creation of a new man.

The beginnings of each session followed the same pattern that Sam had established in the early part of their relationship, with the hypnotic "Relax" which put Martin into the *state* that was intended, and the mantras and the soft background music, got the scene set for the beginnings of another session, with Sam encouraging Martin with a few promptings to get him going and on this occasion said,

"Reg must have been a very important person in your life back then"?

"Yes, without him I just don't know what would have happened to me. He was never critical but always encouraging without carelessly giving out praise and was never too busy to say g'day'.

And always interested in how I was travelling. What a man. I always looked up to him and wanted to be like him. He had a heart as big as a Texas and was always willing to help others out too.

By the time I was twelve an interesting event took place. I'd probably only see him a couple of times a month and he would greet me as though I was his best friend and this made me feel strong and special. In between the times when Uncle Reg was away, I had struck up a friendship with a girl who live in a shack on a property nearby with about five acres attached where fifteen to twenty sick horses were agisted and she kept an eye on them.

At first I thought she was a boy as she was dressed in rags of men's clothing, and covered her face with a rough scarf and spoke with a foreign accent.

After a few meetings she told me her story, that she was a girl, who had come from Hungary, was a Gypsy, and had been in a circus until she sustained a near fatal injury and had been abandoned by the circus as she had to be hospitalised for an extended period of time at the Bay Hospital because of the seriousness of her injuries.

During her convalescence she was sunning herself in a deck chair on the hospital lawns that went down to the sea.

A perfect place to recover.

Up rides this man on a white horse who strikes up a conversation and introduces himself as Jim.

Because he appeared kind and caring at the time, she pours out her heart to him and tells him of her current predicament.

Jim of course sees an opportunity to exploit her, and says she can stay in the shack and care for the horses while he's away on his wood chopping events, which happen quiet often.

In the early stages it appeared to be going OK until Jim starts demanding his benefits with threats of violence, and to turn her over to the authorities as an alien.

Naturally she is scared and surrenders to his demands.

She eventually tells me the whole story, as she needed to confide in someone for help and hoping for some answers, even though I was just a kid and a good listener.

On one particular day I was hanging over the wire fence talking to the horses which had become friendly, and Jim comes up to the front gate, leading his white horse and says "what are you doing here and what do you want?"

"I'm a friend of Eddies, as that's what Jim had nick named her to make others believe she was a boy, and I'm just having a look at the horses." I tensed up with his aggressive tone and I could see her coming up the track and as she got closer I could see that one of her eyes was closed and there was blood on her face and scarf.

Unhesitatingly I said "what happened to you?" She was whimpering, and immediately Jim turned on me shouting "shut your fucking mouth or I'll kick your arse from here to kingdom come"

"You touch me, or hit her again and I'll tell my uncle Reg. You'll see then" I said valiantly.

Jim spat on the ground making more threats that if he ever saw me again he would break my neck, and then road off to leave two frightened, but not bowed, youngsters to 'shiver in their boots' although neither of us were wearing any boots.

Once Jim had ridden out of sight she said, "he's gone for a month on a wood chopping event, come and I'll make us some tea, but I sorry there's nothing to eat"

The bastard. He'd gone and left her without money or food.

I looked at her eye and cuts to her face and realised she needed some patching up so I raced back to Fathers caravan that he had in the backyard, and retrieved a first aid kit and a large packet of biscuits together with three ten shilling notes I had saved for a "rainy day". I tended her wounds and we feasted on the biscuits."

To persuade her to take the money took some effort, as to her thinking 'it was not the right thing to do.'

Martin did not tell Sam of the events that took place later that day, whether out of embracement or that he felt it was not relevant. It was a *'cross roads thing'.*

However he discovered her real name was Esmeralda, that she had been a Roma princess, and had joined the circus in Europe with her Father who had been originally a Roma King of the Gypsy's.

Her mother had died, during the persecution by the Germans and others, and the circus was their means of escape.

Esmeralda and her father were trapeze artists, but her father had to quit as he had injured his shoulder and she was joined on the trapeze by a Russian who was constantly asking for sex to which she refused, and he deliberately dropped her on a catch, and without a safety net she crashed to the ground hitting some metal framework on the way causing extensive internal injuries.

When the doctors finished operating, it was revealed that they were not able to repair her reproductive organs, and for a Gypsy this was a disaster.

Martin tendered to her needs, made a hot bath for her to have a soak and then medicated her wounds.

She was so overwhelmed by his kindness that she invited him to her bed, but before accepting, Martin remembered Uncle Reg's advice and washed himself off in the bath.

This was an episode that Martin never forgot and was truly one of the most exquisite times of his life.

But after the euphoria had settled, Esmeralda swore him to secrecy as she feared that if this got out she could be gaoled and deported as she was twenty two, and Martin who was twelve, would surely be sent to a reformatory school.

Martin swore on his life and vowed never to tell a soul. She in turn told Martin that he was the greatest of lovers and he marvelled at the beauty of her body, her face, and her breasts.

To him, although her stature was small, she was perfect in every way.

Esmeralda lamented to him that she had always wanted children but now that was impossible and no man would want her.

Maybe Martin was still keeping his vow, in not telling this story to Sam, but it was never told.

Martin waited for the return of Uncle Reg and on their first meeting related Esmeralda's story, and of her plight with the bastard known as Jim the 'wood chopper'.

Reg said he would see her on the next day and true to his word arrived with Danny his foreman.

Danny was a really nice bloke and had grown up under Reg's tutelage.

Danny had a baby daughter but his wife had died giving birth, and the baby was being looked after by Danny's mother, an old lady who had had a tough life herself, and to some degree was ailing with the added responsibility of caring for the child.

Next to Reg, Martin told to Sam, Danny was his next best friend. He was the kind of person that no matter what was going wrong he was able to put on a happy face. Tall and lean, as strong as a malley bull, he had a hansom face that could belie his toughness.

He was like Martins big brother.

Esmeralda was a bit apprehensive when the three of them turned up, but Reg soon put her at ease with his greeting, "G'Day love, I'm Reg, Martins uncle, and this is my foreman Danny. Martin told me of your situation and I want to help if I can."

"Martin has told me all about you uncle Reg and I'm so pleased to meet you because you are such a wonderful man", she said with the cutest of accents and a warm smile that won old Reg.

"I could see this was going well", Martin said, and over a cup of tea, Reg warmed to Esmeralda like a father to a daughter, and Danny was all attention.

When all the talking was done Reg stood up and gave Esmeralda a fatherly hug saying "don't you worry about a thing love, this Jim he wont ever be back I'll see to that, and Danny's going to get you some groceries and any thing else you need, and my missus will organise some ladies clothes for you, for we can't have you going about in men's clobber can we? Is that OK by you little princess?"

Esmeralda started to cry as such kindness had never been offered to her before. Danny slipped his arm around her shoulder in a comforting way saying "there, there my little girl, it's going to be alright."

After bidding Esmeralda a good bye and stepping outside Martin's heart was jumping for joy and I said "you are the greatest uncle Reg, thanks for helping her out as you can see how Jim has been belting her up."

"Well Martin my boy that is not going to happen ever again, and you my son more than likely have killed two birds with the one stone".

"What do you mean uncle Reg, have I done something wrong," Martin said full of concern.

"No Martin nothing wrong, what I meant is, did you notice how Danny was buzzing around like a bee in a milk bottle, or like a bloke on his first date. You Martin may have just fixed up two peoples lives in one fell swoop. There is no doubt about you my boy, you are a genius!"

Martin hung his head in embarrassment as Reg ruffled up his hair, at what seemed to be an undeserved accolade.

Marvels never ceased to amaze Martin as Reg swung into action, making Esmeralda a member of his family, and she was welcomed by Reg's wife and daughter as their own.

Esmeralda's life was on a roller coaster, and change was the order of the day.

Here she was dressed up as a fine young lady, looking more beautiful than anyone could ever imagined, with her coy smile and her gentle ways, that suddenly everyone wanted to know her.

Danny became quite smitten, and he said openly that he had fallen in love with her at first sight.

She on the other hand was reluctant to make too obvious a show of her feelings for him as her past had left her in such a damaged condition that a little time was needed for her to regain her self belief.

Danny was smart enough to know this and with Reg's counsel went about wooing her in a gentle manner, which he completely understood, because of his own experience, in loosing his wife. Feelings were still quite raw, and a kind word was the balm that was needed.

In the due course of time confidence was increasing on both sides and added to this was Danny's daughter who had stolen Esmeralda's heart as she bonded with her as if she was her own.

On one occasion Danny came into the nursery and found Esmeralda crying as she held the baby, and asked what was wrong, and Esmeralda said her tears were because she knew she would never have a baby of her own.

Danny looked at her earnestly saying "that's not a problem for me as I see this baby as being yours as well, and you can see she loves you as a mother.

I know this is not the same, but you'll see in time that you will feel the same way, and she'll need someone like you to love and care for her. So don't cry, be happy and enjoy this little one as your own".

Esmeralda thought about this deeply and not long after sought Reg's advice who responded, "you know Essy, as he had nicknamed her, I'm biased in all this as Danny is like the son I never had, and I've known him from when he was just knee height to a grass hopper and I can honestly say you will never find a finer, kinder, hard working loving man than Danny. He will do you proud and never let you down and will protect you no matter what.

Will he make a good husband and lover? The very best!

Don't let this moment get away from you. You deserve every thing he has to offer, I'm sure of that."

Esmeralda burst into tears and hugged old Reg until he was nearly blubbering himself.

Esmeralda went with the wings of a dove and a sense of freedom she had not experienced since a child.

When Danny returned from a muster a week or so later he rode up to Essy's place and she was waiting at the gate and as Danny got off his horse and cocked back his hat, smiling as usual said "G'day Essy how have you been?" Essy opened the gate and ran toward him and said "Danny do you love me"?

Well this fairly knock poor Danny for a loop and with a dumbfounded look on his face said "do I what! From the very first time I saw you I fell in love with you, you darlin' girl" and he swept her up in his arms and kissed her passionately, wondering no doubt, if he was dreaming.

Things moved fast from here and the wedding was arranged with all hands on deck with both Mum's, that's Danny's mum and Reg's wife, doing most of the organising, including the catering.

Reg called in a few favours from old mates and took care of the grog and soft drinks.

Reg was to give the bride away, his daughter was bride's maid and Martin was best man.

"This was going to be a shindig to remember" Reg said, and just about everyone who heard this statement agreed.

A marquee was set up in Reg's backyard, and Danny and Esmeralda were married under a big Moreton Bay Fig in the front yard.

Esmeralda certainly looked like the princess she said she had been, and Danny was resplendent in clothes he had never worn before in his life, but Reg said that it had to be done just right so that the memory would last forever.

Photos were taken of everyone including Martin, and Esmeralda and she said she would treasure this one as her very own.

Things moved on for Martin as he was now at High School and looking forward to a career that he had not as yet chosen.

When Martins parents decided to move to another suburb, many sad goodbyes were said with Reg, Danny and Esmeralda, with the usual promises of "we'll keep in touch," but dependent upon the circumstances, these things generally never happen.

Esmeralda as it happened was able to have a child of her own after Reg talked to a visiting American doctor, who agreed to rectify the problem.

"You know, Reg said to Danny, Martin found this Doctor while caddying for him at the golf course, and during one of his 'tell me why' questions, talked about Esmeralda's problem and asked if he would talk to me, Esmeralda's father, to see if anything could be done.

There's no bloody doubt about this kid, he said as he shook his head, he's the greatest bar none."

That's the story as Danny relayed it to Martin when he came to thank him for his contribution to his family.

Old Reg said to Martin at their parting, "you know Martin the good you do will always come back to you, and you've got heaps coming your way."

"Sounds to me, Sam said, Reg was one of the wisest men you have ever met in your life Martin. A true blue Aussie as they say, upright and honest, a man of his word, always there with a helping hand.

A man's ways you were able to emulate.

These are character building blocks, which I am sure you have taken into your life, and have held you in good stead.

All these things you must review as positive and extract the benefits to help clear out any negatives.

It's like a balance sheet Martin. You have a page with a line drawn down, top to bottom through the centre and on one side you write a heading, "Positive Events" and on the other "Negative Events."

In most peoples lives, regardless of the bad times they've been through, the end result is generally weighted in favour of the "Positives."

However, dependant on how our psychological disposition is working, we can sometimes believe that the "Negatives" have won the day and this can cast a long shadow over how we operate.

In your case I believe that the "Positives" far outperform the "Negatives" and therefore deserve our attention to put them in their rightful place of your conscious and subconscious mind.

Do you agree?"

Chapter 12
The Formative Years

"Now Martin my boy, we are going to explore your formative teen age years and into adulthood"

Martin had thought long and hard about this next step and was approaching the next expose` with some trepidation as it would not only go to digging up some matters that could be regarded as unsavoury but had the potential to downgrade his relationship with Sam, who when he heard of these concerns assured Martin that there was nothing that would shock him and there was nothing which would unseat his relationship with Martin. "I give you my word"

With this assurance in place Martin decided to go for it warts and all as this part of his life had held him hostage, and had formed a parameter of secrecy around his life, which as time went by was becoming at times unbearable with depression and nightmares being the order of the day, that would at times have him waking up screaming at the horrors of these suppressed memories that he had up until now never contemplated revealing to anyone. He was just living with it and not too successfully.

Martin began after surrendering his subconscious to "RELAX", by relaying to Sam that the last year of primary school had set the ground work for a some what dysfunctional life ahead.

The Headmaster, in the last year of primary, had thrashed him unmercifully with a cane, in front of the class, over a skylarking incident with another child.

The Headmaster had exceeded the customary six cuts to each hand, by adding six more, and then completely lost it, and had then torn the shirt from Martin's body and proceeded to thrash him about the torso and legs to such an extent that the class was traumatised, with the girls crying and everyone else in a complete state of shock and total stunned silence.

The Headmaster then locked him in the classroom and forbade him from going to lunch.

Martin escaped via a window and peddled his bike with all the urgency he could muster toward home.

Declan on seeing this atrocity wanted to go and deal with the Headmaster immediately, but Martin's mother won the day by saying she would see the Headmaster and sort the matter out.

This was the foundation stone of Martin's anger as he saw his mother acquiescing to the outrageous claims of this man, to the point where he looked at her and said "can't you see he's a liar" to which she had replied "behave yourself Martin" which lead to Martin screaming hysterically, "he's a liar, he's a liar, he's a liar", only to be dragged from the room with the Headmaster defiantly stating he was going to '*expel him*', with a menacing threat that '*no other school will take him, I'll see to that*'

The very next day Martin was coerced, under threat of further punishment, as well as being sent to a "boys home," to go and apologise to the Headmaster to avoid expulsion.

Martin right up until this day, had never forgiven his mother for this betrayal, nor had he respected his father in the same way he had previously.

However the experience had given Martin the determination to excel academically in his endeavour to gain a place at one of the better high schools, and had achieved second place in the class at the final exam, beaten by a girl he fancied, Janice James, a blond haired blue eyed Dux of the school, which would have automatically given him entrance to the best high school in the area.

However the Headmaster was not done yet, as he marked across the paper "performance inconsistent for the year."

Hence Martin was relegated to a non high school and his chances of academic achievement were thwarted.

Martin's parents, particularly his mother, failed to support him with this unjust action, and instead berated him as the trouble maker and insisted '*he had got his just deserts*'.

At least this was his mothers take on the matter and his father crept into the shadows which further infuriated him, and the first seeds of hatred and mistrust entered his heart.

Sam heard all this and was shocked, without disclosing his feelings.

And to call for forgiveness all seemed too hollow and he remained quiet on the commentary at this time.

Martin's demeanour was noticeably uneasy as he related this memory.

His face and mouth twitched with residual anger.

Finally Sam said," I can see and understand how hate would be a natural outcome to this miscarriage of justice, but I want to put it to you; who do you think is hurting the most from this outrageous misconduct.

Your parents have gone and no doubt the sick little man who perpetrated this crime has also passed on. Pausing momentarily he continued,

It's you my son. This hatred is buried deep and you are the only one hurting.

Now I know it's easy for me to say, but I know the only way you are going to get shot of this is to let it go.

Not for them, but for you Martin. You have faced bigger hurdles than this Martin, and you must let it go not for anyone else, but for you Martin.

You have paid a far too big a price for this, and you must set it free. Send it out into the ether where it belongs."

"I can see that Sam, he said, but no superficial statement will set me free at this time.

You see Sam this conflict just doesn't end there, there's more to this battle, even though I have had some very pleasant interludes along the way and I suppose I should include them so as you get the full picture."

"I agree Martin and don't forget my commitment to you."

"Well I went to this downgraded Technical School and persevered with it until I had completed the certificate course, but it was always in my mind to complete the high school certificate and go to university.

Interestingly, I was introduced to the Army Cadets in the last year of the Technical School, however they were always short of money and were unable to provide uniforms, and could only provided the training.

This sort of discipline caught my interest and imagination.

Father being Irish was anti anything 'English' which included the Armed Forces, and he blamed the 'Poms' in part for Treblinka.

'No son of mine will ever join the army or the police force' he would rant, so the absence of uniforms worked in my favour as I was able to take on the training without his knowledge.

I told my mother that I was going on to High School, to which she replied 'you'll never do any good there'.

A great vote of confidence.

However my perseverance paid off, and I was finally allowed to go.

I learnt later that mother was hoping to get my wages, via board and lodgings if I had taken a job, and *'start paying my way around here.'*

As I prepared to go on my first day to this new adventure, (*'you'll never do any god there'*) my send off was ironically, 'you will become a Doctor or a Priest or else', with a flourish of a wagging finger. Oh happy neurotic days.

As it happened I did have some very happy times at this school. I made new friends, and when it was discovered that I had been in cadets, I had a personal visit from a senior lieutenant telling me if I was to pursue my Cadet Army career with the school I would be most welcome.

I was flattered by the invitation and recklessly accepted without considering the ramifications at home.

I convinced myself that something would turn up to ward off this seemingly inevitable collision, all the time aware of a growing sickness in my stomach, which diminished to some degree at the kitting-up session where you get all your gear, and at this school there were no shortages.

I can still feel the excitement as I received my uniform, which fitted perfectly, and seeing my self in the mirror looking, as I thought, like a real warrior.

However that sick feeling started to return as I packed my gear into a kit bag and started to head for home, intensifying my thinking as to what am I going to say, and more embarrassingly, what am I going to say to the senior cadet leader when I return everything and possibly having to say 'my father wouldn't let me.'

Oh woe is me.

As I set off to catch my bus, another seemingly disastrous thing happened.

My bus was heading up over the hill and the next one was not for an hour and a half.

I dumped my kit on the ground in disgust, sat on it dejectedly and leant up against the front fence of a house and considered my misery and my options which were very thin, and at the same time racking my brain for a possible solution.

Then suddenly I hear these cries for help and turning around, I see this lady clinging to the edge of a gutter and the ladder she was on, was at a precarious slant and it looked as though at any moment she would crash to the ground.

Without hesitation I jumped the fence and went to her aid, grabbing the ladder and trying to right it, so as to prevent her from falling.

As she started to come down a gust of wind blew up and for a moment I thought I had lost my hold on the ladder.

Her dress went up like a parachute and the next thing I know is that it's over my head and my nose is right on her genitalia, and she is not wearing nickers.

Clearly upset by the falling ladder, I help her inside and sat her down on the lounge.

She starts thanking me profusely, and I in turn am saying 'think nothing of it' when it strikes me that I have left all my gear on the footpath, and it had to started to pelt down with rain.

With an *excuse me*, I rushed out to see if anyone had stolen the kit bag. Happily it was still there and I retrieved it to the front porch, and totally soaked I re-entered the lounge room.

While I'm apologising for my kit bag episode, she's thanking me for my help, and invites me to have an orange juice, and suggests I take my shirt off and hang it on the chair to dry.

I had inherited early chest hair from my grandfather, which was the envy of my school mates as it made me seem older to the girls.

We chatted and I tell her about joining the cadets, and missing my bus and so on".

Her name was Bella.

Bella was a young lady who entered Martin's life quite by accident.

She had not planned it, but life has a curious way of bringing two people together for mutual fulfilment, and this is Bella's story.

In Italian Bella means beautiful, and this was certainly the case with Bella. She was trim, naturally sensual and terrific.

Bella's family moved from Italy before the second world war when Bella was a small child.

Bella's father, Enrico Santasegori, established himself in a delicatessen business and was a respected member of the community.

Bella was fun loving, full of life and always had a gorgeous smile, and was the darling of her friends and family.

She had a natural talent for dancing and a very exciting singing voice. She was the kind of person who lights up a party or a gathering of friends and family.

In the spring of 1938 Bella attended a dance at the local hall with friends.

Her father objected vigorously right from the start, but she was having a fabulous time swinging away to the modern jazz of that time, in the arms of a very handsome young man who was in his mid twenty's.

To Bella he was her knight in shining armour, tall ruggedly good looking and resplendent in his army uniform, with his applets filled with his commission as a Major.

Bella was fourteen, looking eighteen, and her hormones were jumping like crazy and Major Tom O'Driscol could hardly contain himself in the aura of Bella.

As they stepped outside for a breather, Tom was gushing about what a great time he was having, and Bella enthusiastically agreed.

As they looked at each other Tom said with all earnestness, "Bella this has never happened to me before, but I'm in love with you, even though we have only just met I know you are the girl for me. Am I being silly?"

Bella reached up and took his head in her hands and kissed him passionately on the lips.

Tom took her by the hand and led her to his army staff car, which was a big Dodge Desoto, and on the back seat they made ardent love and surrendered to each other with abandonment.

Tom confided to Bella that he was shipping out tomorrow for France and when he came back would she marry him.

Bella without thinking of the ramifications of this proposed anticipated union, enthusiastically agreed.

Love is blind.

It didn't take too much time for Bella to become aware of her situation and discover that she was pregnant.

All hell was let loose in the Santasegori household with her father, screaming and shouting and pulling his hair out and all the while asking Bella "how could you do this to me"?

Bella's plaintiff reply was always "I love him Pappa"

His reply always, "you don't know what love is. How could you, you are only a child. Fourteen no less. "I will have him thrown out of the army."

And so the argument would go on with Mrs Santasegori 'the meat in the sandwich'

Tom's stint in France was short lived as he was soon back in Australia with a severe wound he had received from a mad assassin, who was attempting to take the life of the French President and an Australian Ambassador. Tom stepped up to the mark by shielding these men and then charging on the gunman killing him and his associate, but had taken three bullets himself and was now hanging on to life by a 'very fine thread'.

He was aware of Bella's pregnancy and some said this was the thing that pulled him through.

Bella took her father to visit Tom at the Army hospital and was shocked when her father completely lost it and started to abuse Tom and threatened his intention to go to the Army and have him 'thrown out'.

Tom even though he was seriously ill kept his composure and quietly replied to Enrico that he loved Bella and would marry her as soon as he was well enough.

Enrico was not placated by this and continued his rant, much to Bella's shame and distress.

Tom looked Enrico in the eye and said with an underlying threat, "you take this any further and I will see that you are deported, as you are an alien without papers.

Have you ever wondered why you are still here, and not in a detention camp.

Have you thought about that and why it is so?

It is because of my love for Bella that I have interposed on your behalf, personally guaranteeing your life, so that you can remain free in the community. I have risked my Army position and reputation for you, because I am going to make Bella my wife."

Tom had organised with his Commanding Officer for Bella to move into accommodation close by so as to assist with his recuperation and to enable him to watch his baby grow in Bella's womb.

Tom had become the recipient of the Army's highest honour and was awarded the Military Cross for his Valiant Bravery in the face of the enemy.

Despite the fact that Tom had engineered the respite for Bella's family, on the matter of detention and or deportation, her father remained unforgiving and eventually 'excommunicated' Bella from the family, and forced his wife to have 'nothing to do with her'.

Initially these were dark days for Bella but with the growing pregnancy and her marriage to Tom, which had some hiccups with her being fourteen, things started to straighten out after Tom had recovered sufficiently to leave hospital.

The French Government were so impressed with Tom's quick action and bravery that a sizable sum of money was made available in appreciation.

The Australian Government tried to prevent this happening with the logic that, 'he was only doing his duty' and any such funds should be directed to State Revenue.

The French on the other hand were quite adamant and insisted that the French Ambassador hand the money to Tom and warned the Australian Government that any interference would be considered a breach of their sovereign right.

Tom immediately bought a house and they waited for the arrival of their child and right on time Bella gave birth to a beautiful health boy.

Tom was over the moon and Bella was proud of the result.

Tom's health remained indifferent, and he was in and out of hospital on a regular basis. The war wounds seemed to have a mind of their own, and continued to niggle away, making Tom's life a living hell. But through all this he still managed to attend functions where he was treated as a dignitary and war hero to the delight of arm chair 'generals' and anyone else who wanted to perpetrate the myth that they had something to do with it, and it was a grand opportunity to use him up for their own ends.

1939 rolled around and Tom's health had improved sufficiently for him to be posted overseas to beat the drum, and be the poster boy to round up any Aussies for the stoush that was underway, and motivate the troops already there waiting to be deployed.

However on his first deployment and only three days into battle he was hit by shrapnel and took a bullet for good measure before dropping a hand grenade into the enemy bunker, and then collapsing from loss of blood.

Back home he went through the same hospital treatment and being hailed as a hero ad nauseam.

For all his heroics the only thing Tom had won was a life of continued ill health and the gradual theft of his still young life.

Bella with all her youthful inexperience, handled things extremely well and basically had the lone responsibility of raring young Tim, for that's what they named their son.

Tom wanted Tim for a name, as that was the name of his best mate whom he had to leave on the front line.

For reasons, which are not always understood, this gave Tom some sense of satisfaction as he looked at the little fellow, as he lay in his crib.

Bella went along with this decision as she thought the name sounded right . . . Tim O'Driscol. It had a nice ring to it.

Tom lasted another two years and then surrendered to his injuries.

The Army to it's credit before his death elevated him to Lieutenant Colonel and granted a TPI pension which allowed Bella and Tim to live comfortably for the rest of her life.

Still it was a bitter pill to swallow and she was isolated; no family, although her mother did turn up in fear and trepidation to have a look at Tim and to tell Bella she loved her, but she was not strong enough to do anything about the family separation.

Friends come and go, but eventually drop off if they get the idea that something might be expected of them, *'and when it was all said and done, Bella got herself into this scrape so she should get herself out of it'.*

And Bella did.

She absorbed herself in young Tim, and when the shock and depression lifted, set about re-educating herself in the arts, music and language which included her native tongue, Italian.

Time slips by so quickly and before you know it seventeen years have past and Tim wants to follow his father into the army.

Little did Bella realise that heart ache was just around the corner when the Korean War starts up and Tim is posted and lands in Kapyong.

In less than a week he takes a sniper shot and is killed instantly.

Some people just don't get a break. Bella is thrown into the black hole once again, and this time there is no life line-comfort from family, friends, neighbours or anyone else.

Suicide is a tempting consideration, as she wrestles at the bottom of the pit, but a still small voice within says, 'you're better than this Bella don't let the enemy win'.

Bella can't distinguish where the voice is coming from.

Is it from Tom or Tim, or is it from God.

She can't tell, but she decides to go with it, and dismisses the suicide jockey.

Like most wounds, time heals them, and she absorbed herself again in a re educating program with an emphasis on the classics and slow by slow the mending takes place and after about twelve months her spirits had risen and she was at peace with herself and the world.

Around about this time Martin happens to come along in a package, which was quite unexpected.

He was young, bright, full of enthusiasm and sensitive.

Who would have thought there would have been a connection.

There was and it fulfilled both their needs.

Martin continues with his story.

"After a while I notice that she is clutching her neck in some discomfort, probably from the wrenching on the ladder, and I volunteer a massage, which I tell her I'm good at.

99

She agrees, and says that there is some lotion on the bench, which might help.

So I wash my hands to ensure they are clean for this operation, and gently start the massage.

She is sitting on the lounge with her legs up on the cushions and her back against the arm of the lounge.

In my "Tell Me Why" book I had read about massage and the best ways of producing soothing results, and in no time Bella, was saying how wonderful it was. We had introduced our selves on a first name basis.

I must say I was getting pretty aroused by this time, and no amount of wrestling with the feeling was working.

Bella was a very attractive woman and had looked after herself, and as I massaged her neck the front of her blouse was open enough for me to see her breasts, and as she was not wearing a bra, I could see her nipples were upright and she was breathing in a way that made the breasts rise and fall voluptuously.

I was working the front of the neck muscles, when she looked up and said "you can rub down further if you like Martin".

I was beside myself and as I bent over I happily obliged.

I felt these magnificent mammaries, and at the same time our lips met.

The next thing we were on the floor and one of the greatest sexual encounters of my life followed.

This relationship went on for the rest of my schooling, with her attesting that she was not expecting any commitment and that some day I would fly the coupe and she would remember one of the most satisfying experiences of her life with joy.

She provided me with a solution to my dilemma in confronting my parents about the army cadets, by offering me the granny flat at the rear of her house, to store my gear.

This had been her son's hang out before he was killed in Korea.

He was born when she had just turned fifteen.

His father was an army man who had died of his war wounds two years after he was born, and the son followed his father into the army and was killed a few days after arriving at the front line.

Such tragedies must be overwhelming.

She would have got some TLC comfort from me, in the knowledge that there were no strings attached.

Martin mused, as his memory drifted to that time.

She felt secure that I would never brag to my school mates or anyone else for that matter, about our relationship and was happy if I ever had to introduce her to some of my pals as "Aunty."

I know this may appear weird Sam, but I learnt so much about life from her and how to deal with adversity, and get some balance in my life.

I grew up in that time, and the buffeting from my family was less important to me.

My schooling went on by leaps and bounds in this environment, which included my cadet training.

The whole army thing stimulated me.

I thrived on the discipline, the theory, the marching, and the military music infused me with a desire for leadership.

I soon reached my sergeants stipes and the Lieutenant made a big deal of it as he presented them to me. He probably thought this would inspire the others to become achievers.

Initially it had the opposite effect.

After we had finished training and taking a shower, one of the cadet's, who had a big opinion of himself and a chip on his shoulder, took an aggressive attitude toward me, saying "you don't want to slip over O'Leary when you're brown nosing the Lieutenant you might run right up his arse".

"I'm going to pretend I didn't hear that Jones".

"You can pretend all you like, you're both a pair of crawlers and he's a big shit".

My reaction was swift and direct as I whacked him with such force that he went down like a sack of spuds.

Blood oozed from his mouth and nose and in his semi conscious state started to whine, and I told him "you can say what you like about me, but don't ever say anything of that nature about the Lieutenant, *as he's a returned man*".

Still defiant he says "I'm going to tell on you".

I don't know what came over me, but I urinated on him, as I must have had such contempt for this individual.

"Any of you blokes want a bit of what Jones got?"

They all backed off and dressed in a mad rush to get out of the shower block.

Then it dawned on me that the Lieutenant generally posted himself up the back in an observation area to make sure there's no skylarking going on.

Dread entered my space as I thought this will be the shortest lived sergeant in the history of this place, but as I furtively looked around he was nowhere to be seen.

However I felt duty bound to go and report the incident to him and suffer the consequences.

As I entered his office the first thing he said was "Yes Sergeant?"

I was expecting an instant dismissal as he had already seen Jones and sent him to the Nurse.

"Sir I'm here to report an incident that happened in the showers and to turn in my sergeants stripes".

"Why would you want to do that O'Leary?"

"Well Sir, Jones and I had a bit of a set to and.".

"I know all about it as I was there and witnessed the whole thing.

You see O'Leary I was in my observation post bending down and doing up my boots when I heard the kafuffle start, and I heard the conversation that took place, and I saw you deck him.

I was not that impressed with you pissing on him, but he probably deserved it.

A small wry smile appeared, "that will be all Sergeant and don't forget to have those stipes stitched on."

I snapped to attention with a sharp salute, which the Lieutenant returned, and the matter was closed".

Chapter 13
The Lure Of French Perfume

"Martin you are a man of integrity and loyalty. That comes through to me quite clearly.

So far you have handled yourself in a way that most others would have been happy to just give up and not try.

But it does occur to me that you have a tendency to feel over responsible for your actions and the actions of other people and then find yourself to be in the role of a compensator.

Do you think I'm right in saying that?"

Martin paused for a time evaluating Sam's comment and finally said, "I think you may be right as it does seem to characterise many of my decisions and actions although it never occurred to me as to that was what I was doing.

It always seemed to be the right thing to do."

"It may well have been the right thing to do in most cases Martin, but it could well have been an over burdening of your responsibilities and thus putting added levels of pressure on your mix of activities.

Let's see what unfolds and hopefully this may act as a pressure relief valve."

Martin drew a thin smile and shook his head ever so slightly as these revelations started to change the pictured landscape of his life.

"Now just relax and relax . . . ."

"After I left school I decided to take a year off, get myself a job and some money in my pocket, as well as joining the CMF, the Citizens Military Force, an organisation sponsored by the regular army, that was attended on a part time basis, such as a couple of nights a week, an occasional week end bivouac away, together with a bi-annual camp at some remote army training base for a couple of weeks.

This suited me down to the ground. I loved it and I was able to hone some of my natural skills and those that Uncle Reg had passed on, along with those of the army.

It was also a time of upheaval as I moved out of home, with the condemnation mantra of my mother, "so that's all the thanks I get for all the sacrifices. You'll be back with your tail between your legs, trying to put your feet under the table.

I don't think so."

Father continued to be in the shadows and all he could muster was a pat on my shoulder as I passed through the front door, but it said more than a thousand words to me as I surveyed what I was leaving behind."

"What an incredibly sad outcome for such a gallant gentleman. Post traumatic syndrome I suspect." Sam interposed to which Martin could only nod in lamented agreement.

"I moved in with Bella and the following twelve months were simply bliss.

Having got some money in my pocket, and a move up in the ranks to Captain, my life to me was turning out OK.

Bella kept pushing me to start university and get some "education" which seemed like a good idea, and now that I was receiving a small army stipend, a casual job on the side and a few bits and pieces here and there I was on my way.

Time flies and the next thing I knew the final year of my degree was staring me in the face.

Walking up to the library on a spring afternoon it seemed to me that the world was my oyster. As I walked through the doors I became aware of someone following close behind and as a courtesy, held the door open.

Right before my eyes was a vision of beauty supreme, wearing a black cape, a black French beret beneath which was beautiful long shiny black hair and the milkiest of skin with bright red lips and a smile, which captivated me instantly. All this and wrapped in a French Perfume.

I was smitten.

"Well hello, I'm Martin" I found myself saying without any compunction, and trying to look as cavalier as possible.

The sweet gentle voice that followed knocked me off my feet like never before. Her hand came out as she said "I'm Jacqueline, but my friends call me Jackie, do you come here often"?

"I've almost lived here for the past three years" I braggingly replied.

"Would you help me find my way around, as I've only just started?"

Could I what, I thought and like a puppy dog followed and showed her around.

Like all women she knew from the out start that she held the upper hand, with all the aces, and used that advantage over this bedazzled creature too stupid for his own good.

Well this bedazzlement led to a full blown romance of the "over the moon" type, a proportion of which I had never experienced before, which obsessively concluded in me believing that this must be love.

Bella was extremely understanding about the whole thing, reminding me that she had predicted this would happen, and was happy for my happiness, and even offered me the granny flat as a way out of any embarrassing conclusions that some may jump to.

I finally decided that it would be best if I found something else.

One thing leads to another and before you know it we were talking marriage and this is where things can get a bit whacky, with nervousness on my part, helped along with objections from my family, who did not seem to be able to find anything good in what I might do, whether romantically or academically.

Women have a way of helping this scenario along by insisting on taking charge of every detail of wedding proceedings, in the manner of how many to invite, cutting right across from the original idea of having a quiet nuptials, and then turning the event into a side show with hundreds of invited free loaders, to the flowers, rings, presents for the bridesmaids and flower girls which eventually adds up to a three ringed circus, with attending angry, argumentative scenes aided and abetted by the future mother-in-law, and my participation being not up to scratch.

There's no father-in-law, as he had passed over years before, so I'm driven to the only sane counsel I know, and that's Uncle Reg.

This was to be another eventful time and as per usual I'm greeted with some much needed warmth, TLC, understanding and compassion.

This is a real family celebration and all the old faces are there with one exception. Danny had bought his older bachelor brother along, whom he had never mentioned to me before, and here I am looking at this man in disbelief, who has the demeanour of a wealthy businessman, and as it turns out, he's a high profile Bond's Broker, and has been away from home, mostly overseas, since he was sixteen.

Danny and Ben when they stood side by side were like chalk and cheese.

Danny the horse breaker come cattleman, and Ben "the Investment Banker".

It was hard to believe, but blood's thicker than water as they say, and it was obvious as they both eyed each other off with mutual admiration.

"Ben . . . that's Benjamin?" I enquired. "No just Ben. When Mum named me, she did so after the famed Labor Politian Ben Chifley and hence I have the moniker Ben Chifley Du Maurier and that provides some after dinner entertainment.

Danny was named after the Irish song Danny Boy, which was playing in the hospital at the time of his birth. Hence he is Danny Boy Du Maurier".

Everyone had a good chuckle, and the mother of these two great men, Jess, sheepishly had a tear in her eye as she held her boy's.

"If you don't mind me asking, where's Dad?"

Danny spoke up, "Donny's gone a drovin' and we don't know where he are, but no, we think he's gone with Clancy, Clancy of the overflow".(A paraphrase of AB Banjo Paterson's Clancy of the Overflow).

I gave a head shake of disgust at having asked a stupid question but Danny gave me the *old pat on the back* with "It's okey-doke my little brother, no harms done".

My business end was tied up with Reg agreeing to give the bride away, and Danny to be my best man.

During the night Ben announces that he has two tickets to the Opera for La Bohe`me and he's looking for a partner.

This was not an Opera crowd and there are no takers.

Then suddenly I have a brain wave, and think of Bella, who was always saying how she would love to go to an Opera with some one who understood these performances.

With everyone's agreement and to Ben's bemusement I give Bella a ring and tell her of the situation and would she be prepared to go on a blind date with Ben.

Ben takes over the phone, and an expected couple of minutes conversation turns into twenty minutes and Ben is clearly impressed.

"How do you do these things, and how do you know such beautiful people?"

Danny answered for me saying, "this man's a genius and there's nothing he can't do if he puts his mind to it".

Naturally I give Ben a doctored thumbnail sketch of my knowing Bella, and what a terrific person she is, intelligent, funny, a great conversationalist and well read, widowed and lost a son in Korea.

"But she's not flat, I assure him, she's a fun lady".

Of course there is no hint of breaching my confidentiality agreement with Bella, which was never in doubt, and Ben was over the moon with the anticipated date, and was soon asking questions of what food Bella liked, her music preference, and flowers.

"A small orchid corsage should fit the bill" I advised Ben, knowing full well that Bella adored orchids.

This was going to be a black tie event and I knew Bella liked the dress up part of an evening out.

This was shaping up to being a seminal event, which Bella certainly deserved after all she had been through, and Ben with his sleek Mercedes Benz was going to cap it off.

This could be the beginning of something good, and the others thought so too.

Ben was a man of style and booked a table for two at a classy restaurant, noted for it's superb food and fine wines.

As it happened Ben and Bella were made for each other and the night at the Opera was the beginning of a wonderful relationship and I got more than my fair share of credit for supposedly making things happen.

The pity is, Martin remarked in a down cast mood, that I don't seem to be able to make it happen for myself".

Sam looked at Martin realising that this was a hurtful recollection and as Martin slowly came out of the hypnotic trance, he reassuringly said, "this can happen to any of us Martin. When we are dealing with third parties we have the benefit of viewing the subject matter without complicating it with emotions and distracting outside influences, and therefore are able to make judgements, which are objective. So don't go laying any unnecessary blame at your own feet by comparing what you were able to do for other people and seemingly not able to do for yourself.

The most important thing here is that you are able to face the situation as you see it now, recognising it for what it is worth, and to examine the ways that things can be done much better in the future".

Chapter 14

A New Direction

At the next meeting, Martin swung into the therapy session as though it had just finished from the previous occasion.

"Our wedding went off without a hitch. Everyone played their part and most importantly everyone declared it a *'Great Shindig'*.

Jackie's freeloading friends all got shit-faced on the free grog and at one time I had to ask Danny to settle them down before the venue management asked us to leave.

Danny was good at that sort of thing for when he fixed that eye ball to eye ball stare on you, only a fool would ignore his request at his own peril."

Martin paused reflectively and before earnestly asking "Why is it Sam that after the marriage certificate is issued things seem to change? The ink is hardly dry, and all that *lovey dovey* business gradually goes out the door and is replaced with a Boa Constrictor wrestling match which puts the vow of *'until death do us part'* in a new light."

"Well Martin I guess it depends on how two young vibrant people go into the marriage contract.

For instance, are there any hidden agenda's on the part of either person? The one who holds the greater passion for control, will make a move early in the relationship.

I have here my own collection of quotations, which I call "*my book of wisdom's,*" gathered over the years, and may throw some light on this conundrum.

George Bernard Shaw said it so succinctly, *"When two people are under the influence of the most violent, most insane, most delusive, and most transient of passions, they are required to swear that they will remain in that excited, abnormal, and exhausting condition continuously until death do them part".*

"Jackie may have been one of those people who when the passion drops off rather quickly after the event, she replaces it with control, and she gets off on the power play and if you don't recognise it for what it is, then in no time she's calling the shots.

If you are still in the passion mode you are reluctant to recognise this situation, because you are still on 'cloud nine' and your natural desires for love in all forms is blinding to what's going on, and before long you have a predicament that you don't want to face".

"That was just it Sam and I felt hoodwinked and resentful. Every time I'd raise the matter I was shut down with comments such as, 'you're exaggerating, that's your ego talking, you have become paranoid, or you're a man who can't stand a woman to have opinions'.

And that's the way it went Sam and I started to engross myself in my work and studies and little by little we started to grow apart and would basically adopt a position of normality in front of friends and hiding the true situation.

A child came along, a little girl, after a night of lustful passion, and the arrival of a new born did seemingly patch up the disconnected relationship temporarily, but in the due course of time the old wounds would surface again, which would bring the attending stress and a sense of loathing.

I was eventually pushed out of having a relationship with my daughter as Jackie smothered her with obsessive possession.

Then out of the blue a series of circumstances bought about a dramatic change in my life which initially took the pressure out of our *'cooker'* relationship.'"

"What was that?" Sam enquired.

"Let me step back a bit here Sam so I can fill in the whole picture.

In my frustration at the stress that had built up in me I was looking for a way out, and initially I did not know what I was looking for. Was it a job, or an idea that might set me free, I don't know, but in my pursuit I came across a magazine called Popular Mechanics which listed pages and pages of 'new ideas' as well as a random assortment of adds from people who were selling their ideas.

In here I found an ad from a man in Hong Kong who was advertising the concept of 'teach your self' Kung Fu.

His description of the course with it's attending disciplines and Asian philosophies, twigged my mind into thinking that this could be a way for me to get my stress levels down and get my mind straight.

After a lot of haggling by correspondence on price we finally settled on a figure and in the passage of time the Instruction Course came and to my surprise it came in a direct typing format with the demonstration figures personally drawn by the author, and appropriate extra comments written in the margins to give extra instruction to the reader. It was very detailed, well written in English with a politeness and words of encouragement that one does not expect, but immediately it was evident that this was a man of character and integrity, signing himself off 'To Martin, from your friend Bruce'.

This made me chuckle a little as it was quaint, direct and sincere.

It wasn't until I went to the cover page of the manual, which was plain brown paper, where I read, written in modest type setting,

TEACH YOURSELF KUNG FU
By Bruce Lee.

At that time I had not the faintest idea who Bruce Lee was, but in due course, after asking around, I became aware that this man was regarded as the worlds greatest exponent of this art.

I could not believe it, and the many letters that followed regarding certain techniques that needed clarification I did not let on that I knew of his fame, but after a time I felt it was necessary to offer my apologies for this ignorance and my seemingly disrespectful comments said during our negotiations.

As ever Bruce came back with a most humble reply and in no sense was there ever a rebuke, but always continuing encouragement in my endeavours.

What a man.

I had done a small amount of boxing in my youth and as I got older I had a look of "pretty boy or baby face" setting me up as an easy mark, that would attract certain characters who wanted a fight to boost their own ego's or status with the girls or their mates.

I generally was able to handle myself and most times win the day, but more often than not I would come off with a black eye, a busted lip or a nose swollen from a short right cross.

The Kung Fu seemed to answer my needs in this regard as Bruce taught a strategy in that a series of punches delivered in a precise order could do all the damage I needed to bring any confrontation to a quick and decisive end and boost my standing to any audience that may be looking on.

Hence I got the reputation of a *"bloke you don't need to take on"*.

This training had the added bonus that I was seeking to get the stress out of my life and bring calm and tranquillity just as Bruce said it would be. He had a breathing component and meditation mix, which I am sure got me out of many a psychological jamb."

Martin looked at Sam who had an expression of 'I wounder where this is going'. Sensing this Martin said, "I'm leading up to the next stage in my life, which in times past, I could never have contimplated.

I used to meet up with some mates on the way home from work for a few beers, at a pub that had a bit of a reputation for it's dodgy clientele, but for all that it was our 'watering hole'.

One such night it came my turn to buy the next round, and as there were five of us I needed a tray to carry the drinks and on my return, right in my pathway was an individual who was known by some, but not by me, as a 'stand over man' and a vicious thug.

'Excuse me' I said hoping that he would stand aside, but with one swift movement he up-ends the tray, the contents of which soaked me through and through, followed by a whole heap of gooforing laughter.

Without hesitation I let fly with my new found skills, much to the shock of everyone looking on with the thoughts of, who'd have the balls to take on 'Grunt', the nick name this character.

This manoeuvre that Bruce had taught me, I named the six pack, as it consisted of six short shock punches suitably aimed at the soft part of the face down to the heart area, and was delivered with extraordinary force which was a method that Bruce had perfected and had made his style of Kung Fu unique. I had studied and practiced this technique unceasingly until I got it absolutely right, which some might say, with fanaticism.

However Bruce thought that I had got onto the dedication that was required to make his program work.

The result was devastating. Blood poured out of every orifice of Grunt's face. He was out cold, and but for a slight twitch now and again he remained motionless, and his hangers-on backed off in fear that I was about to attack them as well.

The Publican came over to survey the mess and immediately pointed to the hangers-on "your banned now get out of here". They left without a murmur or looking back.

"It's OK son, he said to me, I saw everything, this bastard had it coming to him.

I've never been able to get rid of him. You've done me a favour. Let me call an ambulance and get rid of this shit, and I'll replace the beers and get you a towel to dry down".

Sam looked at Martin in half shock and wonderment.

"That incident set me on a path that changed the course of my life. As weird as it may seem for a bloke like me Sam, who never ever contemplated taking violence to another human being, out side one of my family, is suddenly transformed with a confidence I had never known, but at the same time it seemed that I was still an unaggressive character but an unintimidated one.

Bruce had taught me a philosophy of peace and mastery of my own emotions not unlike that of St Francis of Assisi. It stood me in great stead until Vietnam and that era, when I started to unravel. I just could not make sense of anything about my life. I started to feel like I had been used up and that nothing I did was good enough".

"You were in Vietnam?"

"Yes, but not as an enlisted man, even though I wore a uniform.

Not that long before the 'pub scenario', I was working for one of the largest industrial corporate groups in Australia, and my appointment had been confirmed by the Deputy Manager in the absence of the holidaying General Manager, who had the worst sociopathic paranoid condition I'd ever seen, and on his return I was summoned along with the Deputy General Manager to his office where he proceeded to ask intimidating questions as to who was responsible for my appointment in his absence along with a string of insulting interrogating questions designed to humiliate his Deputy and to undermine my presence.

In my defence I showed him my Science Degree, to which he snapped out, 'what was your major, physics or chemistry?'

Industrial Psychology, I replied and his response was to say, as he threw the document to the floor, disparagingly, 'not worth the paper it's written on. This is not a degree but a sham'.

He abruptly left the room leaving the Deputy in total humiliation and me thinking, what a piece of shit.

Oh boy I thought, as I sat in my newly acquired office, this looks like this is going to be one hell of a ride.

I was not wrong as this psychiatric blow fly was determined to make my journey as uncomfortable as possible.

I wont go to all the inns and outs of what went on as I don't think that detail would be profitable to our discussion, but things came to a head when this maniac got a factory employee to intimidate me with some aggressive behaviour with the intent of causing a fight and thereby rendering an excuse to sack me.

Part of my duties was to inspect, from time to time, all safety areas, which included toilet facilities.

Instead of using a clip board to record these inspections I had hit upon the idea of carrying a voice activated tape recorder, which at the time was a state of the art management apparatus.

As I walked into one of the toilet blocks I was confronted by this employee, a cleaner with a wet mop in hand, who had a reputation I was told as being a 'knuckle man', who brazenly said with a scowl "what do you want"?

"I'm here to check your work performance".

With that he sloshed the mop across my shoes giving them a good soaking and at the same time said "fuck off ponce or I'll knock your block off".

"why you son of a bitch" I belched, as I felt the stinking water seep through my shoes, and with that he launches out in an attempt to king hit me.

This was not going to be his lucky day as the first of my six pack, crunched the soft flesh about his eye, cheek bone area and his nose, followed up by the second of the pack, right on his jaw bone below the ear. It cracked like a dried twig. I then swung him around and forced his head into the toilet bowl, which he was yet to clean.

Instinctively I yelled at him, "who put you up to this you miserable piece of crap. Give it up or your head stays permanently in the bogg hole.

It did not take long before he was asking for mercy and blow me down if he doesn't say, "the old man wanted you to fight me so as he could sack you. He put me up to it with the promise of the gate keepers job".

"I confided in the Factory Doctor of the real events, but asked him to corroborate the story that 'it looks like the cleaner had slipped and fell striking his head on the toilet bowl and thus causing his injuries as the most likely result of events.

However the 'Old Man' was not wearing it and attempted to lay the blame at my feet, and to enforce his position called for an Executive Director from head office to come to the fray of my expulsion.

We all gathered in the Board room and the General Manager was fairly frothing at the mouth with anticipation of an execution.

The Executive Director had counselled me before the meeting, urging a voluntary resignation and thereby eliminating any nastiness or controversy.

As we sat around the table the incumbent psychopath was giving forth on how I had never fitted in right from the start, and now I had brought the management staff into disrepute, blah blah blah.

The Executive Director cut right to the chase and said to me, "what's your take on all this"

I described the events of our first meeting and his abominable behaviour to his Deputy and his degrading and disparaging remarks about my university degree. I handed the document over for inspection to which he said, "this is a thoroughly legitimate accomplishment and I congratulate you on achieving an honours award".

"This is all so much poppy cock, the GM burst out, no one is going to believe his drivel".

I turned to the Executive Director "I'm not finished yet Sir, this man set about to destroy my reputation, even though I have not ever given him the slightest provocation for his behaviour. I have here a record of events that happened just recently, whereby I was set upon by a factory employee at the behest of the General Manager".

"Lies, lies, lies" was the out of control scream of the GM.

I produced my small tape recorder with an explanation that I had been using this device to record my factory inspections as against writing the information.

The GM went from accusing, to whimpering excuses for his behaviour.

A private conference followed between myself and the Executive Director whereby he explained the Company position on this unsavoury matter in that the dismissal of the General Manager was probably remote as he had given the Company more that thirty years of unblemished service, and that he was on retirement schedule.

As for me, I could stay on, but his advice was that even though I was in the clear, some of the mud would stick and it was probably in my best interests to start afresh.

So with a negotiated severance package which included my company car, I packed my history of this sordid incident into a card board box and left.

Too embarrassed to go home and tell my wife of these happenings and to avoid her carping criticism of my perceived failure,

I would continue to leave each morning, as though going to work, to search for new opportunities and to avoid alarm bells of a domestic nature.

This had rocked my world.

On this one occasion of despair after it had become clear to me that the mud that sticks was becoming a reality, as I was getting knock backs on jobs that were beneath my competence, I resorted to the pub to calm my growing anxiety as to how long I could keep up this sham.

I was studying the froth on my first beer, when my contemplations were interrupted by a young man I had not seen for some time, and at best had only a passing acquaintance with him previously.

"Why so glum chum" he said cheerily with a pat on my back.

"Oh I didn't notice I was that glum. Just quietly having an ale, not thinking too much."

"Well from where I was standing you looked like you were carrying the world on your shoulders".

Now he was really starting to piss me off, and he was able to see the irritation in my face.

"Sorry old mate, I don't mean to be too flippant, but you did seem to be a bit tired, probably not down. The truth is I have been looking for you, and knowing this is generally your watering hole, I've been hanging out here in the hope of catching up with you".

"Catching up with me?" I said in a surprised tone, "why would that be. We haven't seen each other in years"

"I was telling my boss about you, he said, and how you demolished the local thug that everyone in the whole of Sydney was afraid of.

I was just standing over there in the corner and watched the whole thing. Wow"

"I'm generally not in the business of beating people up, but that was a case of extenuating circumstances and I had no idea what reputation he had".

"Well Martin you probably don't remember what I do for a living'.

"I never knew what you did", I cut across.

"Well you might say I'm a recruiter for the Government, and once I told my boss of that incident and your Industrial Psychology background he jumped at the opportunity of wanting to meet you".

"Wait a minute, the last time we met I don't even think I had started my Degree".

"Martin I'm a recruiter, I make it my business to know peoples' background, and even back in those old days you impressed me, and with not wanting to flatter you too much, I used to say to myself that's the kind of bloke I want to be".

"Get out of here. Now I know you're bull shitting. But I'll say this, you have brightened up my day. Let me buy you a beer".

"Sam that was the beginning of a most extraordinary set of events, followed by a life style that I would have been hard pressed to imagine.

John, that was his name, wasted no time in setting up an interview with his boss, and remarkably they knew of all the events that had taken place at my previous employer, including my severance details. It freaks you out what they know.

Things started to move fast after this and the next thing I'm meeting Johns boss, who knew as much about me as I thought I knew about myself.

I cautioned him not to make contact with my wife Jackie about this discussion as she was not good at handling change".

"No worries there Martin my boy, the big boss said, by the way call me David, if you agree to our terms of arrangements, (which included a much improved salary, a car, a very well appointed office, a secretary and other benefits that had not been part of any previous package) you can tell her yourself that you have moved up in the world, working for the Department of External Affairs as an Executive Adviser to the Minister.

Do we have a deal?"

Sealed by way of an extended hand shake,

I must say I left that meeting feeling as high as a kite, bemused, bewildered and down right star struck. It was hard to believe.

Jackie received the news with a measure of satisfaction, but I was left with the impression that in some way she was jealous that I was receiving such acclaim.

I spent the next two months on an induction program of what this appointment was all about, and like anything else that seems too rosy and hard to believe, there's always some sting in the tail that can make one feel a little uneasy.

The sting was that the Government had some mining interests that were vital to the country, and they could not afford to have any disruption to productivity or potential sabotage to their operations, because of international events, and as I was supposedly an industrial conflict resolution expert, then I was the man for the job.

However these mines and other interests were invariably way out in the sticks in the middle of nowhere, which meant that I would be away from home for weeks at a time and even longer.

As this scenario unfolded, I thought to myself this is not going to go down too well with Jackie, but my "pal" John had a plan that he thought would work perfectly. Not only was he a recruiter, he was a spin doctor as well.

The plan was to sell Jackie on the idea that I was serving my country on vital strategies, and that while I was away my salary would be deposited directly into her bank account and she would be issued with a fuel card for the car.

To my absolute amazement she bought the plan without a whimper, and assured me she could manage without a problem.

Our small child by this time was a cute and cuddly a little girl we named Louise. She was picture perfect and right from the start she was as smart as a whip and at a very young age was talking like a chatter box to everyone's amusement, and would entertain anyone who was present with her extraordinary recall, such as 'where did I leave my keys' and she would take off and bring them back triumphantly.

Of course Jackie took all the credit for these attributes and smothered her with attention, and it seemed to me at the time that she did this to spite me.

I never understood why.

An extension of the deal, which Jackie never got to know about, was that in the other hand, I would receive a subsidy plus expenses over and above my salary entitlement for my living away allowances, which would be deposited into another account to which only I had access.

Things were starting to heat up and my assignments were laid out, subject to change at any moment, as that was the nature of the business.

Generally these were so called *'industrial dispute matters'* that needed sorting out, and I was asked what I thought would be the best approach.

In view of the fact that these sites were way out in the land of the never-never, trying to take the "manager" approach would probably not work. But if I dealt with the problem from a worker perspective, say as a 'leading hand,' I could resolve the matter without disruption to production, and with the men's consent, fill the expected vacancy with one of their own.

This would minimising any friction that may develop, and should restore moral and get the site back into optimum production and at the same time get another of their team appointed to my job after I left, as a leading hand, and thus restoring harmony.

David was overjoyed with the plan and with much hand pumping and back slapping looked me in the eye and said "Martin you're the man".

They even set up a system of post cards that I would fill out in advance to Jackie saying that I was well and how much I missed her and so on, which would appear that they were sent from supposedly where ever I was, or meant to be, but were actually posted by them for me, so as to *"keep the home fires burning", and 'nosey parkers out of the loop'*, as well David would say. *"Must keep the little lady happy"*.

They had thought the whole scenario through and were not going to leave any stone unturned, and to a large extent it worked right throughout my time of working with them until the sting in the tail.

Chapter 15
Covert Sting In The Tail

S am looked at Martin saying, "what an incredible journey. After what you had been through I don't know how you pulled this off."

"Well that's the beginning of a journey where I pass through hell.

In the beginning I was doing small incidental jobs designed to draw me in, and to see how well I was able to cope with the rough lifestyle and the 'being away from home script', which I did not feel too bad about.

But next cab off the rank was a job way up in the Gulf Country near Weipa.

Oh my God, what a place, humidity and heat like I'd never seen before and the only way in was by boat or plane.

I opted for the latter and when the plane door opened I just wanted to go back inside. The heat was overwhelming.

As I made my way over to the terminal I was scratching my head at these extraordinary circumstances when I heard someone calling out my name "Hey Martin" I stopped and looked around to see this tall lean Aboriginal man with a mile wide smile on his face, casually leaning up against a post that held up the awning of the "terminal" which was just a wrought iron shed.

Bugger me I thought, that's bloody old Turtle. Never in my wildest dreams would I ever expect to see my old school mate here even though I knew the Gulf Country was his birth home.

I dropped my bags and wandered over with an ever increasing grin on my face and greeted him like my long lost brother with a great big bear hug. "Go easy on my rib cage Bro", he said and we stood there looking at one another with me being the more incredulous of the two.

"How in the hell did you know I was on that plane?"

"Well you know we've always had a spiritual connection, so I just tuned in and there it came up on my radar"

I stood back at arms length and said "you what".

I had held this belief myself but had rarely put it to the test.

"And I checked the flight—in manifest". This was followed by a gufforing laugh.

"But I have been thinking of you lately and trying to make contact" he said with a sheepish grin.

"Well you are a sight for sore eyes. Is there any place around here where we can grab a beer?"

"This is the bush mate, but we never go dry. Dump your swag and lets go'.

There was so much to talk about that words just tumbled out as we reminisced about the days when we were kids together, from the school yard to the boxing ring at the Royal Easter show.

Finally Turtle asked me 'what in the hell are you doing here', so I told him of my new job with the Government and what I was doing.

He frowned and looked concerned as he said "bloody Governments mate, they are not to be trusted. Are you sure they're not making a patsy out of you?

"I don't think so, but what do you mean?"

"Those bastards have habit of finding blokes like you, talented, easy going, can think on their feet able to take care of them selves in a fight, setting them a task no other prick can do and then screwing them over big time. I'm not trying to put the mockers on this Martin but you be very careful, that's my sense of what's going on and now that I know, I'll be watching your back every chance I get".

"That's a sobering prediction Turtle and I really appreciate your insight".

As we parted he slapped me on the back and said "you keep in touch with me. You know how".

With more hand shakes and good wishes we parted and as I watched him go, it seemed to me as though he had just disappeared into the shadows of the evening sky, and I stood there some what bewildered.

Sam I can't begin tell you what a good man he is, and how he has watched my back in more than one sense.

From here on Sam the telling of my life becomes somewhat dark and I feel hesitant to reveal it to you as there are some passages that to this day make me cringe at the recalling of them and I'm afraid that this may create a chasm between us, but now that we have gone this far and to hold back would make my relationship with you and your family a lie".

Sam reached out his hand and took hold of Martin saying "there is nothing in this world that you could say or tell me that would persuade me to think any differently of you than I do now. I am but a clearing house for you Martin and I want you to be free to tell me anything that is troubling you and I will do my best to set your conscience at ease for as *Robert Burton once said 'A good conscience is a continual feast'*".

Every line and wrinkle in Sam's face poured out compassion for Martin as he watched the struggle that he was facing in this recall situation.

Martin took a deep breath and ventured into the Weipa assignment explaining to Sam that it was one of the larges bauxite mines in Australia and it was in continual disruption via disputes, strikes and the like which had become a desperation stage for the Government with production being used as bargaining chip that was getting out of hand.

"My job was to sort it out no matter what".

*"Too many things at risk here Martin, heads might roll further up the line".
They said.*

"I did some research on the main cause of the trouble, and it was the union delegate.

I discovered he was basically an illegal immigrant having overstayed his visa and was not a paid up member of the union, and it would seem, had not passed on the other union members dues.

This all looked too easy but I knew I would have to tread warily as this would be a gross embarrassment to the Government if the whole thing went pear shaped.

I joined the team as a leading hand and soon got to know the men and some of their grievances, which seemed fairly minimal.

The foreman was a nice bloke but needed retraining in supervision skills.

One day in the lunch hut I started to question the men about how they felt about all this down time and almost to a man said they were sick of it and were disappointed in management.

I said to them "I don't know about you blokes but I came to this hell hole for one thing and that was to make money".

They nodded in agreement, as I said I was not going to work with all this crap and I aim to do something about it.

The union delegate worked the afternoon shift, but soon got to hear of what I had said and when he came on line, jumped into his front-end loader and aggressively drove his vehicle straight at me, pulling up just inches from where I was standing, and leapt out shouting abuse, with his face all red and quivering in his rage demanding "who in the hell do you think you are, I make the decisions around here regarding union matters".

He was a short fat fellow in bib and brace overalls with a north England accent, and if the occasion was not so serious it was a big laugh, and as the men stood around to see my response as I said "you don't make the decisions of what I earn here so bugger off".

I turned to walk away when a couple of men gave a shout *'watch out'*. This character had taken a large wrench from the tray of his vehicle and was about to clobber me only I jumped in time to miss his swing and I immediately put a choke hold on him. A technique I had learnt from Bruce Lee.

"You miserable piece of shit I'd kill a man for less than that".

He had almost passed out before I released him and he lay on the ground coughing and spluttering before screaming what he was going to do to me. "I'm going to the police and I'll see the boss, you can't do this to me"

"You can do what ever you like but I don't think it will get you anywhere when I tell them you are an illegal immigrant, paid no tax since you've been in the country, and listen to this boys, I addressed the men standing around, he hasn't paid your union dues in for twelve months. He's been squandering your hard earned cash on his own luxuries at the Gold Coast. Wine, women and song. Can you believe this scum bag?"

"I'll pay it back, I'll pay it back . . . promise".

By this time the men were about to give him a kicking but I said "hold it fellers this piece of dog shit is not good enough for your boots I've got a better solution that I will tell you about later"

I got this miserable piece of humanity and frog marched him over to the foreman's hut, and as the Foreman had been previously advised as to what actions I was taking, I got him to formally sack him and to tell him any monies he thought were due to him would be with held and distributed among the men to compensate for the money he had stolen from them.

I then informed him that there was a boat leaving that night for England and he was to be on it and all authorities will be notified of departure and arrival times.

These shock tactics had such a profound effect, that this bloke was speechless, and was ultimately loaded onto the boat blubbering, with the Captain being informed not to let him off until London where security would do the rest.

Within a couple of weeks this whole saga was stitched up, and the men were happy to see the last of that fat character and a new shop steward appointed from within their ranks.

The Management were able to see their way clear to subsidise any short fall with union dues and attended to other small matters which the men has been grumbling over.

Production was back in full swing and in due course another one of the boys was appointed as a leading hand.

My report to all the "old boys" back at freak show central, meant they were generously patting each other on the back at having achieved a desired result, even though in some quarters the method was seen as a little unorthodox.

But then again, a win's a win and they were happy to take it".

Political creatures are like hogs, they'll eat anything".

Sam looked at Martin in a studious manner for some time before saying, "You are a most intriguing character Martin. You think outside the square with an audaciousness I don't think I have ever encountered before.

Are you being reckless or just fearless?"

"I think I see a technique in problem solving quickly, and I'm prepared to back myself that I can pull it off. I always remember my old mentor Uncle Reg saying, 'if you can see the solution don't hesitate, act immediately or the opportunity will pass".

When I was a kid, a small time circus used to come around regularly, and they had a bucking donkey contest.

The audience was invited to try and master the donkey and the prize was a block of chocolate, but no one ever got to win the chocolate.

Uncle Reg had said to me "Martin, knowledge is everything. The next time you go to ride that beast, screw up his ear before you jump on and the prize will be yours".

And it worked. So much so that the circus owner would never let me ride again after I had taken about three blocks of chocolate from him".

Sam marvelled at that story commenting "Reg must have been a great teacher and you an ample student".

"Well what he taught me I've hung onto and it has got me out of a few scrapes".

"Martin my boy, mountains appear more lofty the nearer they are approached, but great men know that they are not impassable. You are a great man".

Martin stumbled over this comment.

"Really Sam, I don't see myself in that light and by the time you finish your counsel with me you may have to retract that opinion".

Unhesitatingly Sam retorted "Shakespeare said, 'but be not afraid of greatness: some are born great, some achieve greatness and some have greatness thrust upon them'.

"Take hold of it in your hands Martin, embrace it. This is the doorway to your freedom.

Start forgiving yourself for whatever you think you have done that you see as *your fault*.

Move forward through that doorway Martin and you will discover a new world".

Chapter 16

The Big Red

"You know Sam, that light at the end of the tunnel is starting to look a bit brighter and it's all thanks to you. My mind was like the inside of a golf ball with all those thin strands of elastic tying down my brain. The pressure was wearing me out, but little by little I think it's easing up. I think there's hope".

"There's more than hope Martin, there's victory" was Sam's flourish.

"Well let's see what today brings. Relax . . . relax . . . just relax."

Martin lay back in the chair and almost immediately his mind locked on to the next assignment the Minister had given him, and he spoke with Sam as though he was reading from a book.

"The memories are as clear as if it was yesterday, of the time in Kalgoorlie.

There was a general background briefing by the Chief of Staff at the Ministry, regarding the gold mine called JYMBindi at Kalgoorlie, that had an all too familiar work place disruption scenario, which had spiralled got out of control and was now an embarrassment to all and sundry at a Government level.

The master protagonist was again a union delegate with a British coal mining background and although he had a bad reputation for being a trouble-maker, an investigation cleared him of any criminal activity and as well, his Australian citizenship was in order.

However his repeated behaviour for causing unwanted and unnecessary disruption which had severe ramifications down the line, caused the Government to take some action to bring this activity to a holt, asap.

Time was of the essence in this matter and I was tasked with job of *fixing it.*

I lobbed into Kal, as that was how Kalgoorlie was known by the locals, with the initial instructions to pick up the 1 ton 4wd Flat back ute, from a holding yard, then head around to the local Police Station, make myself known to them, as they had been pre-informed by the Department, have a couple of beers, just to let the locals see the new face in town, make an intro' to the publican and then to get on my way to meet up with the JYMBindi Manager at the Camp of one the biggest open cut gold mines in the West.

Found the 4wd OK and had a yarn with a mechanic by the name of Jake, who informed me he'd gone over the vehicle and everything was in order including the electric winch on the front bar.

He also filled me in with a bit of gossip relating to the history of the events leading up to the ute being in the yard.

Apparently the previous leading hand had got a rough deal from the union rep, who had made his life miserable with verbal threats and intimidation, based on cultural animosities, along with this bloke seeing himself as a bit of a knuckle man, and as the leading hand was a smaller man, a Scot by birth, this treatment went unabated, behind the scenes. He finally quit as he could not handle the pressure and ridicule and ribbing from his workmates.

"He even left those two bags of lime in the back, he was that anxious to get out, my informant said. Just thought I'd give you a heads up".

"Thanks. Where can I get some provisions around here and which pub do you recommend?"

"Ma Kelly's just around the corner and she's got every thing you'll ever need and she has all the gossip.

There's a couple of pubs here, but my pick is Shannons just down here on the left side. He gestured with a wave.

They know how to chill the beer and they have the best brothel in town.

The bloke who owns it is a tranny, and he likes to be called Mavis. But don't be fooled, he can still go the knuckle if pushed.

Most of the "miners" drink there and you'll get the drift of what's going on.

If your luck holds out, you'll be able to get a fuck or a fight any night of the week"

He gave me a grin and a knowing wink".

Ma Kelly was my next port of call and just as Jake the mechanic had said, Ma Kelly had everything no matter what.

I detected a slight Irish accent, so I put on a bit of the 'brogue' and that started a feisty conversation of 'where are you from, and what's your name, and what's your fathers first name, and to my amazement Declan had gone to school with her father.

We were like blood cousins, and there wasn't a thing that Ma wouldn't do for me.

It's a small world even out here in this vast expanse.

The cops were pretty laid back and wished me the best of luck.

The pub was as usual patronised by local regulars, and "bar flies".

There was a knowing grin and chuckle when they found out I was the new Leading Hand at "Bindi".

The Bar Manager was typical of the blokes who run an establishment like this in the bush.

In a word, laconic.

I got to meet Mavis and she turned out to be tops.

I'd parked outside the pub and when I swung into the drivers' seat I was confronted by a 'snarling teeth baring' blue heeler cattle dog, who snapped at me in a vicious manner and I promptly grabbed him by the scruff of the neck and threw him out the window.

With that I drove off and two or three kilometres out of town I checked the rear vision mirror and to my amazement here's the dog back in the distance chasing the vehicle and as I slowed down I could see his tongue hanging out to the side, as he ran full pelt in the hope of catching up.

I stopped and waited for him to catch up and to my astonishment he made straight for the passenger window and tried to jump in.

I gave him the same treatment as before and stared him down, and pointing directly at him saying 'I'm the boss around here and you don't ride up front. If you want, you can get in the back. He hesitated so I grabbed him again by the scruff of the neck and helped him on his way to the rear of the ute.

I think he soon got the message, and even though he eyed me off with some distain he settled down and we were off again.

The Camp Manager filled me in on the dog, as he was with the previous leading hand and he always rode up front.

With me? Not until he's learnt some manners and realised I was the *alpha male* in this partnership.

The manager took me on a guided tour of the mine and we finally ended up high on a man made ridge that overlooked the operation.

It was bloody red dirt as far as the eye could see.

Looking around I notice a large iron dome with a handle on it capping off a concrete block. When I asked about it, he explained that the mine originally was under ground and that the cap was on to a disused air ventilating shaft which went down about three hundred feet to an under ground cutting which had run out about five years ago.

Back to business again, I gave him a thumb nail sketch of what I was proposing to do to resolve the problem with the union delegate. He just nodded saying "you're the expert".

"Start up was is 7am, he said, and I'll meet you at the Foreman's shed and we will deal with formalities and you can meet the men".

My accommodation was a one bed room, lounge/living room arrangement with air conditioning, TV and all the facilities to live comfortably.

It was situated up on a ridge about fifteen steps above the road way. The front door faced North and had a dust-come weather shield at the top of the steps.

You've never seen dust until you come to a place like Bindi. No matter where you looked the place was all red dust, and the slightest breeze would send it whirling all over the place.

I had bought some provision in town and as I picked them out of the truck, the blue heeler dog looked at me with some apprehension.

He stood up, and for the first time, I noticed that his tail had been cut off, making his rear end look a bit like that of a bob cat.

As I started up the stairs I looked back to see the dog still standing there. Looking and waiting for orders.

"Are you coming up" and immediately he jumped down wagging his backside and at the same time tried to get ahead of me.

"Where do you think you're going I barked. Heel!

Don't ever get ahead of me again Blue".

Low and behold he understood. And so master and dog relationship had been established. He was smart. And while not a young dog he picked things up quickly.

I've never liked dogs inside where I'm living, even though someone had built a '*doggy door*' into the front door, Blue got to understand that his billet was outside.

I put a mat out near the weather shield and he was happy with that arrangement.

We eventually got on like a house on fire so much so that after a week or so of him jumping up onto the back tray when we left for work, I just looked at him and thought, if I'm ever going to have a friend in this god forsaken red dust hole, it will be Blue.

I opened up the passenger door and said "come on boy you've earned your stripes, get in".

I have never in my life seen a dog express more gratitude both in looks, rear end tail wagging, if he'd had one, and wanting to lick my hand until I told him "there's no need for that", and then we were back to business as partners.

I had a real respect for that canine, and he became my mate.

The more I started to blend in on the job I felt my work mates had an increasing respect for me as I tried to make their work load more acceptable, adjusting the rosters, organising regular equipment maintenance, which meant less break-downs and overall a better work place, which included occupational health and safety.

All done with the agreement of the site manager and the foreman plus one guy I had sorted out for grooming and training, without his knowledge of any outcome that would eventually come his way.

He was liked by his mates and had the necessary initiative I was looking for.

A week or so went by with the men sensing a positive change in the air, expressed their approval.

The union delegate didn't take long to try his standover tactics, endeavouring to dominate the pace and putting on a threatening face and the boys were watching to see how I was going to handle this arse hole.

When he started to whinge, I let him know I was the leading hand, and he was the union delegate, by saying "stay off my patch, do your job and we will get along".

"I don't think you know who you're talking to sunny Jim, don't try to order me around, I've been here five years and you just blow in and think you can take over. I'll kick your arse and send you running out of town like that other coward before you".

He had a nasty east-ender accent which pissed me off.

Well these were fighting words Sam and they could not be passed up in front of the men, or all respect would go out the door, and they all stood around in anticipation of what was the next move.

This guy had a nasty ugly face, which he used to intimidate his victims and he thought he could try it on me.

135

"You take a hike before you do something you might regret. You're ugly, and you don't have any brains otherwise you would be able to see what a fool you are".

With that he makes a charge at me swinging his fist as he moved in.

However I was determined to make this short and sweet and I let go with the 'six pack'.

He went down like a sack of spuds, squirming around on the ground and all the while the onlookers stood there in shock as one of them said later they had never see a demolition so fast, except when the dynamite went off.

Even though he was in shock, and the claret was running freely he got up and tried to continue, I shouted "enough!"

It didn't stop him, so I was left with no alternative but finish him off.

That was ugly and I got no pleasure from doing it.

Management stepped into the breach and fired him and he was told to "go get your kit and get off the site".

It was a Friday night and as I was rostered off for the weekend, I decided to go and have a feed at the pub, have a few beers and chill out after all the excitement of the day.

As I sauntered up to the bar to order a well-earned beer a young lady, very attractive and blond was sitting there as pretty as a picture looking very much out of place in this bar. She looked at me with a hello smile and said "care to join me?"

"What's a beautiful flower like you doing in a place liker this" I asked, with a beer in hand I accepted her invitation to join her as I could do with a feminine chat.

Without so much as a flicker, she replied, "I work in the brothel"

I nearly fell off my bar stool, but she was as composed as if she had said "I'm a scientist".

"How old are you"? I said.

"I'm twenty, how old are you?"

"I'm nearly old enough to be your father, do you mind if I ask just out of curiosity, why are you working here?"

"I'm a university student studying psychology. My parents don't have a lot of money and my uni fees never stop increasing, with tuition, books, study excursions and the like, and rather than fall into the debt trap I decided to give this work experience ago.

If anyone knew of this back home they would be aghast and my parents shamed. So I've taken on another name, dyed my hair, and before I go back to uni I should have made enough to pay my dues for the next twelve months.

So there you have it. Are you shocked?" she asked.

"No, I admire your courage for being such a young lady, and making such a decision, and no doubt you will be able to write a thesis on this in due course."

"You're so sweet she said. The way I look at it, other girls are giving their sexual favours away free of charge and receive less respect than I get. I'm achieving my goals and I wont have anyone chasing me for money".

"I like your logic"

"That's the nicest thing you could have ever said to me".

We chatted about this and that and I gave her a story about what I was doing in Kal without revealing any of the truth.

In the middle of this conversation she suddenly said with a touch of fear "Oh my God, here's a man who is hunting me down as a customer, and I have refused him several times because he has a cock as big as a donkey and I don't fancy being torn up by him, as I wont be able to work for a month.

He has a bad reputation. He's an animal and it looks like I'm cornered".

I turned to see the bloke pushing his way through the drinkers, and everyone was standing back.

The man was built like a brick shit house and ugly to boot.

Big head and a body better than twenty stone, and once he spotted the girl, was making a beeline in her direction and yelling out some nonsense as he came.

She just froze in fear and I touch her arm and said "hold on this is going to be OK".

This buffoon started saying "I want you Cindy and I mean now".

I stood up to assess the situation and the words of Bruce Lee came into my head, "If you are going to fight a bull don't try and hit the bony part of the skull, go for the fleshy parts and make every punch count as though your life depended on it".

I could hear the crowd yelling "get out of here Bull" and then Mavis appeared on the scene and started to remonstrate with him, and Bull's response was to shove her out of the way like he was swatting flies.

I looked at him, eye ball to eye ball, and said "she's my girl Bull so bugger off".

When he looked at me I saw a fleshy face, big nose, big mouth with lips like a horse and I saw my target, together with a gut swollen from excessive beer drinking and being on the 'bludge'.

Now that I had distracted him, he came at me like a wild animal, dangerous, aggressive and out of control.

The crowd were holding their collective breaths with anticipation that I was about to be smashed.

My stance was good and my breathing regular as I faced him, and then I let fly with the first six pack all directed to the soft parts of his face and he opened up like melon, with bones crushing and teeth flying onto the barroom floor.

He stood there like a dismantled statue, stunned, but still aggressive. His body heaving with the pain and disorientation.

This was followed up with the second six pack to his abdomen and I felt his sternum surrender under the impact.

Down he went like a giant human rhinoceros, and he was still.

Totally unconscious lying in his blood.

Not a pretty sight, but there was no other way to do it.

His size alone was awesome, and I understood why this slip of a girl was terrified at the prospect of him penetrating her.

The crowd stood back in awe of the spectacle and looked at me as though I had come from outer space.

Mavis came over and said "man I have never seen the like of this and I have seen some brawls in my time but nothing matches this. You are the only man who has ever been game to take Bull on and beat the crap out of him. Even the coppers were afraid of him, and it took more than six of them to handle him.

Speak of the devil here they are as per usual after the event.

Don't worry son I can take care of them".

It took four men to drag Bull outside so that the ambulance men could treat him and take him to hospital.

The sergeant finally made his way over and asked what happened.

I gave him a brief run down on the events, and with a casual nod, he said "this is OK I'll write up the report just to cover all bases but you'll be in the clear.

This might encourage this bastard to leave town. He's been a thorn in our side for ages".

It took some time for the girl to come to her senses, and recover her composure, which was followed by her gushing appreciation for having been saved.

Her real name was Rebecca and she was from Adelaide and lived in a respectable working class suburb.

What would they think if they could see her now.

She coyly said to me that her digs were just up at the end of the veranda, and if I liked we could have some fun together 'no charge'.

I declined politely saying it's not that I wouldn't like to, as you're a very pretty intelligent girl, but it would be like having sex with my sister, or daughter, if I had one."

"You are quite a man Martin O'Leary and I would be privileged to be counted as one of your friends".

"You are a friend Rebecca and I will not forget you in a hurry"

I confided in her that my work here had almost come to an end and that I had another job offer waiting for me to accept. But "keep it under your hat".

With a hug and a kiss on the cheek we parted and I told her I would drop in before I left.

I went around to Ma Kelly's place for a few items, which included one of those long baguette French sticks, which I planned to stuff with some cheese, tomatoes, some lettuce and cold meat.

I'd fancied something like this to remind me of home, and with a long black coffee it should do the trick.

It had been a big day and Blue and I just ambled along the dusty road that didn't look too bad at night and the air cooled down so that it was almost habitable.

We parked at the bottom of the stairs to our accommodation, and I grabbed the paper bag of groceries, put my yellow hard hat on and proceeded to climb.

Half way up, Blue stopped and made a low growl and when I had a look at him his hair was standing up so I knew something was amiss, and as I look up toward the wind break at the top of the stairs I thought I saw a bit of a movement that had set Blue off. By this time he was in a crouching pose which indicated he was ready to pounce on what ever was up there.

I took off my hard hat and put it on the end of the French stick and proceeded with caution until I was about to step onto the landing and then I pushed the French stick forward with my hat at the end and as I did so, swish came a star fence post which sent the hat flying and if my head had been in it, sure death would have followed.

I sprang into action, as the person swinging the star stake did so with such force that he came out onto the landing.

I grabbed him and at the same time delivered some pretty severe blows. The last one hit him on the jaw just below the ear and I felt and heard the bone snap just before he went cascading down the stairs and ended up just before the bottom with his head wedged between an upright and the lower rail.

Blue stood guard over him, hair bristling and teeth bared, combined with a guttural growl to show he meant business, just in case he bolted before I could get a torch to see who it was.

Damn me if it wasn't the ex-union delegate trying to kill me before he left.

One eye opened as I stood over him and I said you had better be gone by morning or I will kill you myself.

Blue and I had a late supper, he had dog biscuits and water and a couple of pieces of the cold meat, and I had a coffee and a couple of beers and what was left of the French stick. Then we turned in.

At about three am Blue started to make some noises outside the door and I thought bugger, who is it this time.

I pulled on my trousers and boots and a fleecy jacket, as the nights can get cold in this part of the world, and poked my head out only to see Blue looking down the stairs and growling. I got the torch and had a look and there was the bloody union guy where I had left him.

On closer inspection he was dead.

Oh boy, I thought this is going to cause heaps of trouble, for me, the mine and the government.

I started to wrack my brain for a possible solution and then it hit me.

"Martin, old Reg would say when he was giving me his pearls of wisdom, there is not a problem if your faced with it that can't be solved, and if it ever happens to you, just take stock of the situation, weigh up your options, select the best one and do it immediately because if you dilly dally, you'll screw it up".

What were the options?

Call the police and explain the situation. Call the site manager and do the same?

This would be too messy for me, for JYMBindi and the site manager and External Affairs. Too much explaining to do, too much paper work and bureaucratic crap.

And how do you give a reasonable explanation with no witnesses?

I followed Reg's advice and then it came to me like a bolt out of the blue, the abandoned air ventilating shaft.

I lumped his body onto the back of the ute, threw a cover over, and headed for the shaft.

I undid the electric winch on the front bar, hooked it onto the handle of the lid, put the ute into low range and into reverse gear and worked the vehicle and the winch together and up came the lid.

Quickly I searched the body to remove any ID and then dragged the body to the shaft and let it go. It took longer than I thought for it to hit the bottom, which made me think it was deeper than first thought.

The two bags of lime that I had been carting around on the back of my vehicle since I arrived went down the shaft, which in the due course of time would dispose of the remains.

Closing the lid went without incident.

Blue and I went home to complete our rest.

What a day. I was absolutely snookered.

I made an exception with Blue that night, as in reality he saved the day, and let him come inside and sleep on his mat. I'm sure that little bugger knew that this was a variation to the rule, but was happy for the consideration.

The next day I fed the mine furnace with the rest of the gear and ID information this guy had been carrying, which appeared to confirm that he had no living relatives either here or the UK.

Time is always of the essence, and I quickly got to a meeting with the site manager and the foreman to sort out a replacement for my role as leading hand and as well put up a suitable man for the post of union delegate

This was not too hard as both parties were happy to allow me to organise this process.

With an appropriate lapse of time this was duly organised to the satisfaction of all concerned.

I told the men whom I had been working with that I had accepted another position out of state and it was an opportunity not to be passed up.

On my way out and back to Kal, I called on Rebecca and even though Bull had moved on out of town I felt she needed an extra bit of protection if a similar incident should happen to raise it's ugly head, and so I convinced her that Blue was the man for the job.

I know this sounds silly, but I had talked this over with Blue before hand and I'm sure he understood that Rebecca would be his new 'Master'. Mistress is out of context here.

"Blue's easy to get along with if you maintain all the protocols necessary to make this happen. Don't ever let him mount your leg, and make him sleep out side except under exceptional circumstances, like if some bastard is acting up the wrong way.

If someone gets completely out of hand, tell Blue "attack' and he will go for the blokes balls. He's good at that.

Feed him once a day, give him plenty of water and he's yours forever. And when you go back to Adelaide, he'll fit in, as he knows his job is to look after you".

Sam looked flummox.

"Martin I'm finding it hard to believe this is you. What a remarkable journey you have been on. This surely must have taken you out of your comfort zone and raised your inner anxieties to one incredible level". Sam observed.

"I'm only half way there yet Sam.

My usual personality traits are changing, my response to violence is going up, and my mind set has become more accommodating to this physical confrontation method as a problem solving, come resolution practice.

In between times, I had received a phone call from my cohort back at External affairs, and along with congratulations on bringing about a speedy conclusion to the tasks that were allotted me, I was also warned that things were deteriorating on the domestic home front.

My wife was petitioning for a divorce and at the same time demanding a continuation of the financial status.

Chapter 17

Hell Hath No Fury

This was bringing some fire into the department, and there were some unhappy campers in the mix.

It would seem Jackie had hooked up with some smart arsed lawyer who was pushing this agenda, and by way of an indirect blackmail, was seeking to involve the Department in his sleazy scheme, in an endeavour to embarrass the Government.

When I arrived back at Head Office the *nervous nellies* were almost running out of control, as one old operative said to me, like a '*bunch of old molls at a poofters picnic*'.

This was partly due to me, and as well the Government was up a dry creek and without a paddle in it's ensuing demise.

The blame game was in full swing and everyone was running for cover.

Sam you have never seen so many gutless wonders in one place at the same time.

Again I applied old Reg's theory, "there's no problem that can't be solved" so my first thing was to hot foot it out to see Jackie and try to talk some reason into the situation, but it quickly became clear that she had been planning this manoeuvre for some time and no amount of persuasion or cajoling would bring her to her senses.

The daughter gave it away when she said to me "Michaels going to take us to his house and he's going to be my new daddy".

I was gob smacked and at the same time furious that I had been taken so cheaply.

I set about seeing who this Michael was, and as you would expect, he was a bloody muck sucking lawyer.

But anyone who'd try and pull this sort of stunt must have some history.

I set my ASIO contacts on to him and up he popped on their radar as a person of interest on insider trading, dubious share issues, and dealings with some undesirable characters, and questionable safe haven off shore banking, and trust fund issues.

ASIO were going quietly on him to see what developments might take place.

I got one of the office girls to make an appointment with him for me under an assumed name, as a stockbroker.

When I got into his office I came right to the point of what he was doing to my family.

I ripped him up against the wall and made it clear I was fully aware of his so called business dealings and insider trading and that if he made one move to derail my position with the Government and make any attempt to implicate my office in any way, I would have ASIO pick him up and see to it that he was goaled for a lengthy time.

I could also let the Mafia in on his tricks, I threatened.

No telling what they might do if they thought he was sand bagging them.

My final threat to him was that he had better write a letter of retraction on all the demands that he attempted to bring against the Department and me, and it had better be on the Ministers desk no later than tomorrow at noon or I will come after him myself and it wont be nice was my promise.

What Jackie does with you I don't care, but if you cause my daughter to come into harms way, you're a dead man.

Now do it! As I don't want to come back here again. Get the picture."

While I wasn't a good husband Sam, I don't know what Jackie saw in that creep".

"Well what was the out come Martin"? Sam said,

"Right on noon next day a special delivery letter came with a full retraction of all demands had landed on the Ministers desk".

"Martin, he said, you are a bloody genius"

"I'm not really, I just work harder than most"

"Well son I just hope your family situation works out. If I can help, don't hesitate".

Nice sentiments, but there was no way in the world I was about to let these socially inept characters get on my case.

With all these pressures coming at me Sam I could feel some internal rumblings going on, which were robbing me of my sense of balance and giving me an edginess which was foreign to my make up.

A man's got to have balance.

No amount of cajoling was going to change Jackie and she was hell bent on pursuing her course of action, but an 'interim adjustment' was made to our financial arrangements until the lawyers got things sorted out.

The interim judgement was that she would receive an amount to cover rent, food and welfare for the child and utilities.

About one third of what she had been previously receiving.

Chapter 18

Into The Firing Line

Just when I thought I was desk bound, my new assignment was put on the table, which was to pack me off to Vietnam, and as this subject was a political *'hot potato'*, and a serious matter of urgency, in that some skulduggery was going on at the base in Nui Dat and it was assumed some Australian soldiers were involved in *"flogging off"* some weaponry, ammunition, and assorted armaments to the North Vietnamese.

External Affairs was in full blown panic mode, with no desire for this to get out into the public arena, and to set up a military enquiry would certainly attract the journalists, hungry for a bit of Government scandal, which would offer an excuse to get up off their lazy arses.

Straight away I took the view that this was a 'put up job', as I could not believe any Aussie would be involved in such a traitorous operation.

Call me naïve, but it was totally against all my instincts.

Several things needed to be sorted out from the get-go.

One being a total background report, on the commanding officer of that base, which was to include any dodgy dealings to which he may have been accused, as well as embracing a psychological profile, along with a check by my mate in New York on Pentagon chatter.

This raised some eyebrows, but persistence and logic won the day.

Another condition was, there would be no way in hell that I was going to carry out an investigation at an army base in a war zone as a civilian.

Considering my army background, I demanded a full battle uniform kit as a sergeant, with a minimum AK47 weapon and a standard issue side arm.

"No arguments please. My way or no way", was my stance on the subject and as my track record so far put me in a "he knows what he's doing" league, hardly a murmur was made.

My role as a sergeant would allow me to get close to the men and at the same time not appear as a threat to the other Officers.

I hooked up with an American aircraft out of the RAAF base at Richmond direct to Saigon.

That was an interesting flight as the American boys were inquisitive as why a 'one out' Aussie soldier was going to Vietnam, and what was he proposing to do there, and what unit was he attached to and they were super surprised to learn that I was attached Lieutenant Colonel Frank Drake.

I asked them what kind of a soldier was he, and to a man, said he was of the 'old school' a real hard guy, you're in for a rough ride with him.

Naturally I did not disclose the purpose of my mission and they seemed to swallow the made up story I gave them.

Upon arrival I was to report to a Captain Sartorsky.

Sounded Polish to me.

When I fronted up to the reception desk at the Australian Army Communication Centre in the heart of the city, I was surprised to discover that the Captain was a female and a pretty one at that.

"Don't be surprised Sergeant that I'm in-charge here, we all have a job to do in making this thing work."

As I saluted her I stumbled out something stupid like, "I just didn't expect to find an Officer this pretty running this show"

She flushed a little saying "flattery will get you nowhere Sergeant so in future mind your mouth".

Now it was my turn to flush for having made a tasteless and disrespectful comment, and I apologised immediately.

Documentation and procedure concluded I was directed to the Hotel Continental and informed that I would be staying over night and Lt. Colonel Drake will arrange my pick-up the following day.

The room was comfortable but the hotel had seen better days. In '*her time*' she would have been a grand old lady with a definite French influence and charm.

It was getting late in the day so I showered and got cleaned up.

Fortunately I was able to sleep in the old US cargo carrier, despite the noise of the engines and the rough ride from the buffeting winds, and so I arrive relatively refreshed.

1930 hours the dinning room opened and I casually strolled in to size up the situation, and was happy to see that they were still offering table service.

Finding a table looked to be a bit of a challenge as everyone else seemed to have cottoned onto the first in first served idea.

In the midst of my observation a voice called out "Sergeant" and low and behold the Captain was motioning me to come over and join her.

I could have swallowed my tongue.

I stood at the table and gave a sharp military salute.

She responded with a casual flick of the wrist and said, "you can dispose of the formalities for the moment, sit down and join me if you wish".

Naturally this was an unexpected pleasure and I gracefully accepted.

"By the way my name is Martin".

"I know I read all the paperwork, and I'm Glenda, but most of my friends call me Glen".

We clicked almost immediately, recalling bits and pieces of our past and as you would expect she was interested to hear my story of Poland and the 'Great Escape'. Her parents were Polish and went through the terrible times we were exposed to in the war.

The food was just great and the hotel had some great French wines, after a little financial encouragement.

She asked after my marital status and I frankly confessed my situation, saying that I had been gutted by the whole episode, and she told me of her 'engaged' relationship to a Navy Commander which was on the rocks due to their continued separation in different parts of the world, so there was a considerable amount of mutual commiserations going on between us, aided and abetted by the wine.

We had a few laughs over the brighter things of life, and she laughed easily at my jokes.

It was a great night.

We made our way to the stairs with a controlled stagger trying to be as dignified as possible so that no one would noticed, although that should not have mattered as this seemed to be a 'get drunk' night for all who were attending the restaurant.

Arriving at our respective doors it dawned on me that we had adjoining rooms.

My mind, I must admit flashed the possibilities of the situation, but I rebuked myself with *"cut it out!"*

I had no sooner stripped down to my boxers when, there was a gentle tap on the internal connecting door, which had been locked,

And a question was posed from the other side, "would you care for a night cap"?

I heard the safety latch click as I turned the knob and there was Glen standing there in a negligee saying" I've only got whiskey".

"My favourite", I returned, and as they say in the classics, the rest is history.

Two lonely people crying out for some affection.

My scheduled departure time was 0900 and I hitched a ride to the helipad and right on time was a Bell 47 with skids and carry platforms on either side.

The pilot waved me to put my gear on the platform secure it and climb into the cock-pit.

He was wearing a full helmet which didn't allow me to get a good look at his face, and it wasn't until we fitted up the intercom ear phones that we were able to communicate.

He confirmed my identity, shook hands and took off.

I called him Sergeant and he called me Sir. He decided to give me a quick reconnaissance of the area before heading onto Nui Dat Base.

There was something going on here, as this man kept staring at me, which made me feel uncomfortable, but I brushed it off as 'he's just trying to size me up'.

When we landed he removed his helmet and the first look nearly bowled me over as it was just as though I was looking into a mirror.

We just stood there looking at each other in disbelief, grinning foolishly like two teenaged kids.

I broke the mesmerising situation by saying "I'm Martin"

He replied "I'm Chuck"

"Are you kidding me" I said in a non offensive way, "back where I come from, chuck is what you do if you're about to vomit or you're about to pick up a house brick and throw it at someone. No offence old mate you just caught me off guard."

"No offence taken, my Christian name is Charles or Charlie if you like".

"Would you mind if I called you Charlie, as that would make me feel more comfortable".

"No problems at all Bud", as he slapped me on the back.

"There's just one question I have to ask you, did your father ever go to Australia, because when I look at you I see almost a mirror image of myself even though I'm about ten years older.

This is uncanny and it's only that you are a great guy that I'm not spooked out.

We're going to get along just great I know it."

So help me Sam this man Charlie was so like me that I felt bonded to him like a brother.

When I entered the Colonel's office he did not look up straight away as he seemed engrossed in some documents and gave me a greeting like "OK you're here O'Leary take a seat while I check this stuff".

Colonel Drake was an obvious New Yorker by his gruff accent, chomping on a cigar and had the features of a tough military campaigner. But when he finally looked up and was about to stand up to formally greet me, he let out with a "What the fucking hell is going on here" as he dropped back into his chair looking at me as though he had seen an apparition.

"My God you and Chuck must be related".

I snapped out a salute saying "I thought so too Colonel".

"Take it easy O'Leary, just call me Frank"

"I appreciate the privilege Colonel, but if it's OK by you Sir I'd like to maintain the formality on my side. I know I can operate better with that discipline in place".

The Colonel looked at me as though I was a nutter. "I don't make that concession to everyone son, but from the get go you sure are different".

"I appreciate that Sir and I mean no offence by my request".

"Have it your way".

Later on in our journey together he raised the question of 'what's behind that position' and as we partook of one of his favourite tipples, that is rum, I told him the story of my father not allowing me, as a child, to call an adult or a person in a superior role by their first name. This was so imbedded in my psyche that it had carried over into my adulthood.

"Some time down the track you'll have to have someone look at that" he said with a wink and a nod.

The Colonel was himself a complex character as he opened up to me on many occasions after the day was done, and as hinted to me, he felt in his long journey of life that he had found someone he could trust.

During my passage in Vietnam we became good friends and it used to make him chuckle that I still called him Colonel, no matter how much our mutual respect grew.

"Don't you like my name? call me Francis if you like". He would chide me.

Charlie and I were really like brothers in an almost eerie way. At times our thinking processes were so similar, and our likes and dislikes in music, literature, politics, religion, women and humour, were so compatible that we could spend hours talking just off the cuff or in deeper matters, of things like what makes you tick, what are your ambitions, what are your great loves in life, women, children, parents and God. These were great times that will not be forgotten easily.

Charlie an I bunked together, and as I started to formulate a plan and examine the area of concern, which was the armaments dump, which was a large converted machinery come maintenance igloo type building, which had originally been built as an aircraft hanger.

It became increasingly clear to me that neither the American or Australian soldiers could be involved in this heist, of the disappearing armaments, simply because of the logistics needed to carry out the operation. It was just too exposed.

I executed a complete reconnaissance of this storage facility and the surrounds, and came to the conclusion that this was indeed the work of a very tricky operation carried out by some trusted person or persons, at a time when surveillance was at it's lowest.

I had taken up the role, for all intention purposes, for those looking on or watching my movements as an audit, come bean counter operative, and was therefore regarded as a person of low interest, just wandering around doing a clerical job.

I had noted that on certain days when the armament shipments went out to various locations that the dirt floor looked like it had been swept as there were no foot prints or tyre tracks visible.

This sparked my interest with a Professor Julius Sumner Miller TV question, *"Why is it so"*.

I was drawn to an old inspection pit in the floor, which had been installed when the shed was used for vehicle mechanical repairs, but was now closed over with a retractable cover, which was on metal tracks.

This had a large pad lock on it to prevent it being opened and I had almost ruled the pit out of the equation until I noticed the brass casing on the lock was showing signs of handling. It had some bright rub spots on it, which led me to think, *"this should not be so"*.

I conferred with Colonel Drake and put my suspicions on the table that these signs seemed to appear the night before the armaments were destined for a particular engagement in the field which to my mind, there was someone with inside information involved here, as this knowledge was only available *on a need to know basis.*

"So who have you got in mind O'Leary as it seems you have this investigation pretty well taped"

"That Vietnamese Major who is on secondment to you. I've got a gut feeling about this guy and there is something wrong there, but I just can't put my finger on it as yet. He's a slimy looking bastard. Can't look you in the eye. But when he thinks you're not looking he's watching every move.

I've seen him hiding behind the door when I'm having a conversation with someone else, covertly listening and then scuttling away when he thinks you are about to go to the door.

But I also feel that there has to be some outside help, transmitting information here because the timing is to good to be coincidental.

Sorry Colonel but that's the way I see it at present".

"So what's your plan. 'cause I can see by the way your mind works you have one".

"Well for starters I would like to secrete myself in the "dump" the next night we have intelligence on the armaments requirements and the destination, as I'm sure this will reveal how our suspects are getting the gear out from right under our nose.

Then I want to do the same thing here in your office on the nights your Vietnamese cleaning lady comes in".

"What, you don't think Mrs Ng is in on this do you".

"Well, high level information is getting out and I don't want to leave any stone unturned and I've noted myself Colonel, that certain areas are vulnerable here".

"God dam it O'Leary, is there anything you don't see around here".

"I'd also, with your permission Sir, like to wander down to the local watering hole, which I've noticed is a meeting place for some combat soldiers coming back from a mission or are prepping themselves before going out on one, and just have a listen to what they talk about and see if I can pick up something from that area".

"You got it Sergeant, and I don't have to remind you to be careful. Just keep me in the picture on a daily basis as the *Brass* expect me to have a hands on approach with this activity".

My first thought was to try and get to know the guy who was running this lean-to liquor bar.

I had observed him at a distance previously, and my impression was that of a sleazy little fat guy dressed in a somewhat soiled white suite, forever with a cheesy smile on his face and had all the earmarks of a hustler.

When I first approached him, he was apprehensively nervous and went over board to ingratiate himself.

I was as usual dressed in my full battle fatigues, wearing my slouch hat, and carrying my weapon and side arm.

I was of the view that I was not about to be caught out in this hostile place without being able to look after myself.

He put out a fat hand saying "me Yimmy". Which of course was Jimmy.

The boys had named him Yimmy Wot, because every time you asked for anything, he would blurt out "wot", dropping the "t" at the end, as this was his pronunciation of what.

"You need beer Sergeant? It's on me"

"No thank you Jimmy but you might be able to help me with this question" and I could see him freezing up a little and his eyes were starting to flick backwards and forwards, right to left, as a defensive mechanism for his brain.

"yeth, yeth, what can I tell you?"

"How does a guy talk to a lady here, you know to just say hello. How does he say it in Vietnamese".

Immediately the colour came back into his face as he realised his unfounded concern was unnecessary as he chortled out amidst his unusual snorting, "me tell you for pretty lady".

He paused for a moment trying to make it look as though he was giving some consideration to this request and then studiously saying slowly, so as I could write it down phonetically, and learn this script.

"Ban muon quan he tinh duc".

"you see, velly easy Sergeant, you see".

There was a certain amount of glee in his voice which I was to learn why much later.

However at the time I took it on board and this encounter allowed me to hang around 'Yimmy's place without suspicion on his part.

A couple of young US soldiers came in for a booze up, and immediately spotting me, wanted to get a conversation going, with all the routine questions of what's your name Sarge, and where are you from, have a beer etc, and me reciprocating in the same way and shouting a couple of beers and at the same time explaining I was on the water, with that hand flicking quiver move that indicates your in recovery mode.

We were having heaps of laughs and 'Yimmy' was trying to get in on the act by saying, "I tell Sergeant how to talk girl" Ho Ho Ho. To which they replied "fuck off Yimmy Wot' and get us some more free beers you fat little prick".

To which he laughed "You velly funny, velly funny".

"You wont think I'm velly funny when I stick my boot up your fat ass".

This made Jimmy think he was the life of the party.

"He's a sneaky little mother fucker, always asking questions. If he ever gives up looking after us I'm going to smash the prick".

My mind twigged to this comment, 'looking after us' which made me look at the boys more closely.

My God they were just kids, Johnny and Jethro, both eighteen from the same country town in the US, out to see the world as they had thought, and now here they are out here fighting a war that they had not the faintest idea of what it was all about. Mind you they were not on their own.

"What the fucking hell are we doing here Martin? They would ask in bewilderment.

They were definitely not on their own.

I was adopted as their 'big brother' and as they were going out on a mission tomorrow they almost begged of me to agree to meet up with them in a couple of days 'if we make it back' in a somewhat bravado tone.

"You bet no problem, just don't keep me waiting".

I had a meeting with the Colonel and told him of my suspicions regarding 'Yimmy Wot' and that he could be a link in what was going on as he was always pumping the boys and any other army personnel he could get into their ear with, "Yimmy bly you flee dlink'.

The Colonel thought I may be drawing a long bow on this one but conceded that I should track it down if I felt so strongly about it.

"Come on Martin have a drink with me as you're the only son of a bitch I can talk to now days".

So the Colonel and I settled in for a session and just reminisced about our lives, the ups the downs, work, marriages, children, hopes and dreams and what the hell after this mess.

We discovered we were both children of migrants, him being Greek and me being Irish.

I was able to tell him of my mentor Reg and what he meant to me, and after I had finished he just looked at me and said "One hell of a man".

And he was so right.

Colonel Frank had grown up in New York and had learned all the smarts of that city, and his father decided it was time for him to get some discipline into his life, and had him signed up for the Rangers in the Army.

"Made a man of me" he said wistfully

"Well Martin, I don't often say this, but I have full confidence in you and I believe you will do your country proud along with the rest of us".

This vote of assurance really meant so much to me at the time, and I was about to say my thank you's when the Colonel cut in, "Go on get out of here" and with a pat on my shoulder sent me on my way.

I had so much to share with my new found brother Charlie that we talked into the wee hours of the morning. He was a great sounding board. So much wisdom.

"I've told Dad about you and how we look so much alike that it's all too uncanny, and asked him as a joke as to whether he had been to Australia. Sent him a photograph as well".

"Poor old bastard he'll have hell to pay if your mother gets a hold of that letter and photo".

Charlie thought this was an uproarious joke, "Nah, they'll see the fun in this. You'll love 'em".

So this was it. My world was expanding without me trying.

The very next day an order for armaments had come in for despatch the following day.

A truck was positioned and a store operative was organising the loading, and I noted, so was the Vietnamese Major.

When I quizzed him as to what was his role here, he promptly replied that there were Vietnamese soldiers involved and he wanted to be sure their requirements were met.

The truck was secured for the night ready for early despatch next morning.

I secreted myself inside the building and in a position which allowed me good visual access to the loading area as I wanted to confirm my suspicions that someone was getting into this facility illegally.

It was a long wait, and just when I thought that I had got it all wrong, there was movement at the front door, which was a large ill fitting sliding contraption, that I knew was chained and padlocked at the closure. There was a bit of a gap at the end, but I concluded no one could fit through there. Too small, I was wrong.

As I focused on this, the door rattled a little. There was a cautious movement and as I watched, a small child squeezed through the opening and went directly to a key, which was hanging on the wall, and as quick as a flash went to the inspection pit and unlocked the padlock on the cover.

Slowly and quietly the cover was pushed back from inside and out popped at least a half dozen men, who seemingly were adept at knowing where everything was on the shelves, and started to take what they needed from the racks and straight down into the pit.

I had never seen so few men move so much gear in the short space of about twenty minutes.

Once gone the cover was rolled back in place and the small child quickly replaced the padlock, took out a broom, almost twice his size, and brushed out the foot prints of his comrades. Replaced the key and slid out of the front door into the night.

A child soldier!

When I relayed this to the Colonel, he was absolutely dumfounded, and a further inspection discovered a tunnel in the pit, which had obviously been used many times for this operation.

One thing I was able to reveal, was that no US or Aussie soldiers were responsible at this end, as the tunnel was too small.

The tunnel was too close to the armaments racks, so detonating the tunnel was out of the question. We decided to pumped a vast quantity of gas down the hole and anyone down there who had the idea that they were in the clear would not have had the chance to think again.

"There's a link up here Colonel, and I bet they will be trying to get a hold on what you are going to do next, and as it's the cleaning lady's night, I want to secrete myself in your office and we'll lay some dummy papers about to look like top secret, and let's see what happens.

Then I want to chase down this bloody Yimmy as I've got a gut feeling he's in on this in some way. He's too inquisitive for my liking. He doesn't look smart, but he's as cunning as a rat with a gold tooth."

Sure enough, as I lay in wait for the cleaner, she quickly started to search the Colonel's desk and the 'in' and 'out' trays. She spots the dummy papers, and brings them over under the desk lamp and starts to photograph them with a cute little camera she had in her apron.

That done she goes about her cleaning activities as though nothing had happened.

I felt vindicated with my hunch, but this needed to be kept under wraps.

This, the Colonel must never let get out, or there would be hell to pay as a certain enemy of his would just love to get this information out to further discredit him.

As far as I was concerned he was too damn good of a soldier and a hell of a man for this to happen, and I would counsel him that way at our next meeting, and the following next day I revealed the events of the previous night and advised that he keep it secret, permanently.

"Why", he asked I've got no reason to hide this".

"I didn't want to tell you this, but I'm a 'blood' trained investigator, it's in my blood, and before I left Australia I pulled a few strings and dug up your files and saw all of your achievements, your rise to one of the highest levels in the military, adviser to the Presidents War Cabinet, on first name terms with him, seen as one of the only guys he can trust, and then whammo you end up in this shit hole doing a job that any junior officer could handle, and I wanted to know why.

I'm sorry, but it just did not seem right to me, and as I did not know you, my inquisitiveness went deeper.

As I said it's in my blood, and if I think there is an injustice having been done I want to know why, and I wont rest until I find out.

Do you know why Sir?"

"Oh for Christ's sake stop calling me Sir, and no I don't have an accurate take on that, only suspicions. Don't tell me you know".

"Well Colonel," and before I could say anything more he said "if you keep this up we're going to have a falling out"

"OK, OK I'm sorry, but on one condition I call you Frank in private, because publically I believe you are entitled to that courtesy and respect by me calling you Colonel. Is that a deal?"

"You're a stickler for protocol God damn it".

Well here it is Frank, while I was rooting about, I ran into a dead end, which did not add up, so I contacted a mate of mine in Washington and ask him to find out what he could about the President going sour on you.

I suppose you're wondering how someone like me has a contact in Washington.

My life Frank has had a series of 'come by chances'.

One night I was working late when I was with a company before I joined the Government, and knowing that I would probably not have a feed waiting for me when I got home, I decided to stop off at an Italian café that I knew about and have a bolenase and a couple of glasses of red.

This place was situated near a music hall famous for it's jazz concents.

I'd parked my car nearby and as I walked to the cafe I spotted a couple of town thugs bailing this guy up and demanding his wallet. He was well dressed and did not look as though he was up for this scenario and was a bit slow in producing his wallet and without warning one the street mugs whacks him and down he goes.

So I step in and said "hey what's going on here this man is a friend of mine".

One of the assailants says who the hell do you think you are?"

And I quip back, "I'm Ray Charles and if you hang about I'll sing you a tune".

He responds, you ain't black mate but you must be blind and if you don't fuck off out of here we'll give you a good kicking as well".

Well that was enough and I whacked both of them, and two coppers who were watching from across the road came in to join the fracas, and belatedly took control.

My new found friend turned out to be a jazz nut, by the name of Harold Schwatz and was employed by the US Government in a high level security post, and over a couple of beers we exchanged a lot of information about ourselves and ended up great mates with him saying to me that if he could ever help me in some way that I was never to hesitate to make contact. We exchanged business cards and I drove him back to his city hotel.

I made contact with him about you, as I wanted to be sure who I was hooking up with.

I was able to get the low-down on your back ground, which included your army achievements and your rise through the ranks to Presidential adviser, and then to be moved side ways.

I hope this is not going to piss you off, but a certain Lieutenant General Anton Biggs got into the Presidents ear and spread malicious rumours about a drunken party you were at, and it was said you bad mouthed the President about his inability to make decisions as the only brain he had was between his legs.

Some how this Biggs character was able to con someone into corroborating this bull-shit and the President bought it, and Biggs moves up a notch or two in the Presidential hierarchy and you get busted to a war zone".

"By this time Sam, the Colonel was getting agitated and showing signs that he was about to explode and I thought my new found friendship was about to end in disaster".

"You're a brave man Martin, he said, not many would take these risks of honour. You've got courage and you've got conviction and integraty".

I had to move swiftly to try and placate this situation, and his growing anger.

"Hold on Frank, I said, I knew there had to be more to this scenario, so I dug deeper and finally discovered that Biggs had found out about his wife's infidelity with you and it was his way of pay back".

"How could he have found out. No one knew, there were no witnesses and it was a one off occasion".

"Your right, no one knew, but Biggs and his wife were having a blow-up one night and things got out of hand as they do when husband and wife set to at each other, and in the heat of the moment she tells him he was not half the man that you are, and then it all tumbled out about you being a great lover and so on".

"Martin you are an absolutely incredible bastard. How do you find this stuff".

"If you want honey Frank, you have to find the bees hive. That's the thing I do".

"You know Martin this has eased a burden for me. It has been eating my guts out over and over, and now the truth has thankfully set me free.

I was at this very formal White House party and it was as boring as dog shit, and so I took a wander down one of the many hall ways just to get away from all the crap these bastards go on with, and there was a room with big oak doors that looked enticing, and I tested the door handle and the door opened. Inside it was wall to wall paintings, by some of the masters and as I have a passing interest in these things I decided to go in, closing the door behind me.

I was looking over some of the works, then suddenly there was a cough behind me, and to my surprise there was Biggs wife Nancy, who started by saying 'I did not know you had an interest in the arts Frank'.

She was also escaping the mind numbing party.

One thing lead to another with the aid of a fine brandy that was there for the taking, I made delicious love to the finest woman, I've ever known, whom Biggs did not deserve.

It was great with a capital G, and I pledged not to reveal our tryst".

Franks eyes rolled up as he remembered the ecstasy.

"Well there you have it Frank, I don't believe it's worth the risk of reporting this office escapade, as it could be argued, by someone with an axe to grind, that you had been careless in your personal security and therefore cop some unwanted scrutiny of your leadership. You know the bull shit I mean".

"A very sound point Martin and I thank you for your good advice".

"Sam this man's mind is compartmentalised and no sooner had we gone through the exercise just mentioned, and without a beat he says to me, "Martin this is something I want you to have, and he opens his locker and pulls out an M16, saying I want to swap you this for your old AK47.

It was certainly a fine looking weapon with timber inserts and looked as though it had just come out of the box.

"Frank I said, that's very nice but I've have had this old AK tricked up. I've improved the action and the recoil and above all the accuracy. It's a great weapon".

"I appreciate what you are saying but this one is better and I've had this one tricked up as well, and it will out perform that AK47 any day of the week I guarantee it.

It's lighter, has a longer barrel and it is good for 500 metres right on the button. If it does not live up to the performance I say it's capable of, I will give you back your AK with a case of whiskey. Oh and it comes with a case of 30 round clips, and they are lighter as well.

What do you say?"

"Frank I say thank you very much but I'd hate to think I'm depriving you of such a fine weapon".

"Already you are turning my life around and as a way of appreciation I want you to have it and it would hurt me if you turned it down."

I could have hugged the guy, but I knew that would be out of order, and so I graciously accepted the M16.

Three days had passed and I heard the boys, Johnny and Jethro had made it back from their mission.

As I made my way down to the boozer I could hear them laughing fairly uproariously, followed by silly giggles.

A sheet of corrugated iron stood vertically beside the boozer shed, to give the patrons a little protection from the wind, dust and the rays of the setting sun and this was the favourite spot for the boys as they sat on rickety bar stools that Yimmy must have got from the tip.

I sidled up to beside the corrugated iron sheet, which had a slit in it, probably from someone giving it a whack with a machete.

It allowed me to see them magging away with Yimmy who was trying to get in on the act asking questions like "where you go, how many kill that shit, and where you go next.

You tell Yimmy".

"We're going to tell you nuttin' until you get us our shit you little fucker".

"Yes yes yes, but this is velly good shit, don't you tell no body".

Then Yimmy ducks down below the counter and comes up with a hand full of small plastic bags with white powder in them.

"Where's the rest they demand".

"More next time you come in. Before you go on next fwight to kill bloody Gook".

He flashed that wicked smile with all those gold teeth.

The boys looked at one another, as they stored their stash, with a silly grin on their faces and Johnny said to Yimmy,

"You seen Martin? He was going to come here today"

"No, but him come, you see"

So this was the game, Yimmy was feeding them with drugs for exchange of information on troop movement.

Here's the link I thought. This little prick was relaying this information to the tunnel mob and before every deployment, ammunition and the like, would be loaded up the night before and they would come in under this cover to steal what ever they wanted from the store and when the short fall was discovered the blame was being put on the soldiers who were loading up the truck.

Now we're cooking I thought.

I strolled around the corner and made it look like I had just arrived.

"We didn't think you were going to show Bro" as they got up to give me the Ghetto hand shake.

"How you Guys doing anyway, you look like shit. Have you got any protein bars or something like that to refuel after stomping through the jungle in this humidity?"

"Yeah man we got some medicine back at the camp. It's a real pick-me-up". Followed by silly boisterous laughter.

"What's funny about that" I said.

"It's nuttin man, we just can't believe you're interested in us, that's all".

I gave Johnny a slap on the back and said, "we're mates right? Mates look out for one another. You two are like my brothers. Not this gangland bull shit brothers, but real brothers, you know blood brothers".

As I looked at these two kids, and they were staring back at me they both started to tear up, just a little.

"Than means a lot to me and Jethro Martin, a real lot.

You know I wrote to my Mum the other day and told her about you and I sent her our photo. She'll love you".

Yimmy was noticeable by his absence, but he came back looking a bit agitated, and it crossed my mind as to what had this slimy little prick been up to.

The boys were beefed up with our little conversation and Johnny with the help of all the lubricant he'd been drinking said, "Martin, as we are blood brothers would you swap your hat for my cap as mementoes of this time"?.

I had a feeling he had been eyeing it off for some time and dropping little hints that it would look better on him than me. But I had pointed out to him that my *slouch hat* was a symbol of my commitment to the army and my country.

It identified who I was.

It only increased his desire to have it and when he asked this time around, I pondered the request for a moment and genuinely recognised why he wanted it and so I said "sure, wear it with pride when you get home".

We made the exchange and he immediately put the hat on, stood to attention, saluted me and I returned the compliment.

He then linked arms with Jethro and then marched out on to the street a little unsteadily.

Suddenly there was a flurry from behind by Yimmy who started to yell out frantically "Yohnny come back, Yohnny come back".

"I see he's wearing your hat.

He's one of mine, and just a kid.

I'm Captain Harrison Young".

We were about to shake hands and as we watched these two lurch across the road, the sun was setting and the long shadows bought a picturesque atmosphere to the place and we stood there watching and as Yimmy was making his last frantic call, Johnny looked back and gave us a casual wave and at the same instant a cricket ball size object came out of the thick foliage of the tree that hung toward the centre of the road, and a god almighty explosion went off hitting the boys.

The Captain yelled cover me, and clear that tree.

I swung into action automatically and unloaded the thirty rounds I had in my clip and was in the process of reloading another when these seemingly bundles of rags started to fall from the tree I had almost shredded.

The Captain yelled he had it covered, and was busily giving orders for a medivac team.

I walked over to these bundles and turned one over with my foot and to my horror it was a small child and the other bundles were the same.

Oh my God, the shock horror of such a sight almost split my brain in two at the sight of this ghastly scene.

I freaked out, and as I snap on my new clip I turned on the crowd who had gather and screamed, "what kind of fucking people are you that you send your children to war". I spotted one man who was crying hysterically, and said in a very unkind manner, "Shut up. I should shoot you for sending your child up the tree to carry out this attack".

"Not me(between sobs) Yimmy give the children one American dollar each to go up the tree and throw the bomb at man with funny hat"

The Medivac guys pronounced all the children dead and at the same time I saw that miserable little prick Yimmy madly stuffing all the American dollar bills, of the day's takings, into his coat pockets, and when he spotted me heading his way he took off like a jack rabbit and me after him.

Down this narrow passageway, running at full pelt, he thought he had reached safety, but the back gate had been locked and I had him cornered.

I stood over him threateningly with my side arm drawn and said "you miserable little fucking cockroach. So that's your game. Screwing information out of soldiers with your low grade drugs and then killing them, using children to take the blame".

By this time Yimmy new the game was up and got very cocky with his attitude.

"You Americans are all shit. We beat you in war and your CIA helps us with the drugs. Not shit drugs but best grade.

That hand grenade was for you not Yohnny. That's why I call him back. Silly boy".

Sam I have never felt the fury that I felt at that time, and I was out of control with blind rage, because not only did this bastard cause the death of Johnny and Jethro and the children but right up to the end he had this self satisfied smirk on his ugly face and those teeth. The whole scene just blew me away, and I shot him at point blank range.

As I stood over him, not thinking anything in particular, except contempt, there was a slight movement from behind and I wheeled around with my M16 ready to open fire, only to see this old man standing in the door-way of what must have been his house and he raised his hands in a pose of surrender.

He was dressed in a monks' type habit, and a small hat on his head.

"Who are you I demanded".

"I'm the town elder and priest", he said in understandable English.

"Put your hands down, but don't make a move or it may be your last.

Do you know this creature", I gestured to Yimmys body.

"Yes he is a velly velly bad man, and we know he is velly bad working for the Vietcong, but we can not tell anyone other wise Yimmy has us killed".

"OK now I've got to figure out what to do with his body".

"Don't you worry Sergeant we look after. We get rid of Yimmy".

"What ever you do, I do not want him found or popping up somewhere. This could be big trouble".

"I understand, my sons will help, and Yimmy will never be found again. You no worry please".

I went through Yimmys pockets and took out all the US $ bills he had stashed. There was about $500 in total and I said to the Town Elder, "you divide this up equally for the parents who's children have been killed. No cheating now, because if I hear of that, I will come back looking for you. Understand".

"Me no cheat Sergeant. These are my people. I am Elder and Priest. My sons also follow our tradition".

The old man looked at me with sorrow in his eyes and a look upon his face that said he knew tragedy and heart ache. He was looking into my soul Sam. He placed his hands on my head and said, "be at peace Martin, not your fault"

He just blew me away Sam. He used my name and without knowing it saved my sanity.

I don't know why, but I felt I could trust him.

"Can you find someone to run this bar as I would like to keep it going for the soldiers".

He agreed he could, so as we re-entered the bar, I pointed to a brass plate in the dirt floor and said, "that's where Yimmy kept all his cash and I'm trusting you to do with it what is required. No drugs, OK?"

"We no like drugs. Velly bad"

I gather up all the drug pouches that Yimmy had under the counter, and had one quick look at where Yimmy was, and to my surprise he was already gone.

I looked at the old guy and he said "You no worry Martin. Every thing OK".

I walked out to the front and everything was just about all cleared up and the Captain came over and said "I'm sorry I got you involved in that, but thanks for watching my back. How many kids involved."

"Oh Christ there were six. They were just babies"!

"I'll do all the paperwork on the boys, and do you mind if I send your hat back with him to the states".

"Not at all I'm honoured.

It breaks my heart with those two young guys".

"Well you made a big impression on them.

By the way I'm Harrison Young from California".

"Martin O'Leary, Australia".

"I'll report to your Colonel Martin".

With a salute we parted company.

As I turned to head back to HQ the old Elder/Priest was still standing there and I said to him, "I don't know what to say to these people, my heart aches for them"

"You no worry Martin I will take care of them and I will tell them what a good man you are and that this was a terrible accident, caused by velly bad man Yimmy. They will understand. Not your fault Martin".

How in the hell do you understand a thing like that.

I had a new respect for these people and the total tragedy of their lives. They just pick up from where they left off, and keep moving forward.

They were an inspiration to me, but could I follow on? I don't know.

When I got back to base the Colonel just looked at me and said this is a sorry state of affairs, but let's put this together so that we don't leave any gaps that can come back to bite us on the ass.

I pointed out to him how this Jimmy almost bragged about the CIA being their drug line with the idea of feeding the allied troops.

Unbelievable, but some of the papers I had dug out of Jimmy's pocket did seem to verify his claim.

The Colonel thought about this for sometime and finally said "I think we should keep this under our hats Martin as I believe it would go against us to bring this up, even as shocking as this might be, proving such an allegation would be difficult and those bastards would find some way of weaselling them selves into the clear and then sticking the blame on us.

Leave it for the moment and we will see which way the cards will fall".

Captain Harrison Young turned up and briefed the Colonel of the incident, and confirmed he had given me the order to watch his back and to clear the tree from where the grenade had come.

The Colonel turned to me and said, "take some time out son, you weren't to know that the tree would be lousy with kids. I understand how you must be feeling about those kids. It was an accident. We don't go around killing kids.

Those two young guys were close to you, but this is war and shit does happen.

Now Captain will you join us in a drink, just to ease the pain?"

"Well thank you Sir, I would be much obliged as my nerves have been rattled by today's events, and I want to say to you Martin, 'you done good today'. The outcome is not what you wanted, but 'you done good'. You got rid of that little shit Jimmy, God only knows how many of our brave soldiers have fallen because of him".

"These were comforting words Sam, but that incident with the children buried deep into my gut even to this day. I still have nightmares. Oh God I am so sorry".

"I can understand your despair Martin, I really can, because I have been there and I know that we feel there is no hope, but I have taken comfort from a small piece George Elliot wrote "But what we call our despair is often only the painful eagerness of unfed hope".

There is hope Martin and you can achieve it. We have to work toward letting go. And we will conquer this letting go with *"nothings impossible"*.

Martin returned to the events of Nui Dat and continued with his narrative. The Captain left, and for reasons I do not understand, the Colonel and I went straight back into planning. Must have been the military way.

We determined, because of the events of the day, that this group of armament invaders would strike again soon, because they would realise that their number was up and with the tunnel blocked and Jimmy out of the way they would more than likely strike again soon.

We were mulling over the possibilities, when the Colonel happened to mention that a truck was parked inside the hanger with 3000 anti-personnel mines on board, that had been dug up by the US Army under an agreement to stop using these devices in the field, and were destined for detonation at an area away from the base and current operations.

"That's it Frank, these bastards will try and break out the vehicle in the middle of the night.

My suggestion is that we let them do it, because to try and prevent them moving the truck might cause the whole thing to go up in the ammunition dump.

Let them take the vehicle out, and as they will move north, which will be advantageous for us, as it gets the cargo out of harms way.

Charlie and I in the chopper, can track them to a point where we can take them out as well as the cargo".

Frank rubbed his chin as he was examining all the alternative possibilities as well as the risks.

"OK, lets do it. I'll leave the details with you to swing this thing into action, and to get Charlie on board for all the flying co-ordinates".

I outlined the plan to Charlie of how I thought we should approach the mission and he made some important submissions, which tied it up nicely.

We then laid in wait for the next moves, and sure enough we didn't have to wait too long as two operatives, with the help of the small child soon had the sliding door opened, and as well secured the truck keys and were soon rolling out past the sentry, as all the documentation for despatch had been signed the night before, the guard innocently let them through, and as the Vietnamese Major was driving it all seemed to be in order.

Charlie and I soon had the chopper airborne, and our emergency pack, which weighed about 80 lbs was behind my seat.

We sighted the truck and waited for a suitable spot before lining it up for a clear shot, and when it arrived Charlie banked, and with the door opened on my side I had a clear shot.

The Bell 47's are noisy little buggers and as we banked, the roof turret of the truck flew open and the passenger popped out with his AK47 blazing.

I got him first shot and pumped a couple into the wind-screen for good measure and killed the Major.

"We've got trouble here Martin, that little bastard must have hit one of the hydraulic lines and we are loosing pressure fast.

I'm going to try and land this thing, so when we get to about 10 feet off the ground, you jump and roll away as far as you can and when I hit dirt I'll do the same".

I gave Charlie a look of hesitation, but he barked out the order, do as I say, just do it.

As I hit the ground the 10 feet seemed further than I thought, and I fell badly but continued to roll with our emergency kit, and my M16 in tow.

I looked back over my shoulder to see Charlie leap from the chopper and as I watch I momentarily in that split second said to myself, old Charlie made it too, and then there was this God almighty explosion.

The chopper had gone up with an enormous blast, which had propelled Charlie when he jumped, onto a land mine.

One they had missed in the clean-up.

Charlie had gone arse down.

"Shit, shit, shit. Fucking hell, Charlie had copped it".

Without hesitation I gathered the pack, ignoring the fact that I had injured my back in the jump and had collected some shrapnel in my legs also, and raced back to Charlie.

"Christ Almighty Charlie, what a fucking mess, but don't worry mate I'm going to get you out of here".

One leg was blown off at the thigh, and a nasty piece of shrapnel had torn his balls off and his penis hung on by a thread.

I madly tied a tourniquet, but the blood was gushing out in such a way that it was difficult to get a grip.

"Charlie I'm fucking sorry mate I got you into this shit, I'm so sorry".

I was coming apart Sam.

I was loosing it.

I was helpless and hopeless in this situation. I had killed my best mate.

In the midst of all this he said, "It's not your fault buddy, these things happen.

You are the only brother I ever had and I'm satisfied with that. I want you to give this letter, pointing to his shirt pocket, to my father when he comes and tell him I love him".

This mans life was ebbing away right before my eyes, and he has the decency to put me at ease.

The tears were rolling down my face and when I looked again he was gone.

He had the letter to his father in his hand.

When I had gathered myself together from my emotional grief, I took out a ground sheet and gathered all of Charlies body parts that I could find and tried to assemble them in their correct order.

I removed his dog tags and put them around my neck, as a symbol of our closeness and took his fathers letter and some other personal effects and put them into a medivac envelope.

His side arm I put in my gear.

The land mine had made quite a ditch, and after I had wrapped Charlie's remains in the ground sheet, and lacing it up securely, I dragged him into the blast ditch and covered his body with dirt and stones to deter any wild animal from digging it up.

The hardest thing I've ever had to do in my whole life.

What a terrible place this was. Hot as hell, and dry and sticky with sweat all the time, with every insect known to man kind, swarms of mosquitoes at night, and a quagmire when it's wet.

My thoughts and attention was bought back into focus when I heard some gun-fire and a lot of screaming.

I moved into a secure position and looked in the direction of the noise and there, not more than 150 metres away, was three Vietcong soldiers screaming at three women and by the looks of it there was a man and a small child lying on the ground, and they looked as if they were the recipients of the gun fire, as blood was quite evident on the ground.

As I was contemplating my next move regarding this incident, there was a movement in the bushes near me and as I looked, M16 at the ready, the face of a buffalo appeared. He looked and then casually sauntered off in the direction of the melee.

I picked up a stone and hit him right in the 'aristotle', which made him buck up and charge out through the brush giving me the decoy that I needed.

Three easy shots and down went the Viet Cong who were threatening the three women.

They were kneeling and blind folded.

"This bloody M16 was better than I thought. Frank was right".

What a weird thought that was, under the prevailing circumstances of the day.

I cautiously made my way toward the women, ever mindful that other Vietcong could be in hiding waiting, but that was not the case and as I looked at the bodies it was evident that the man was the father, and the child, probably his only son.

God what a terrible place this is.

I took the blind folds off and they all looked hysterically at me, thinking the worst was about to happen to them, one of the girls was able to see my Aussie shoulder flashes and relayed the information to the others, and when I demonstrated in gesture fashion that I had shot the Vietcong soldiers, some form of assurance was restored.

They inturn were beside themselves at the sight of their two loved ones lying motionless.

I picked up the child and placed him on a table that was on the veranda of their small house, and did the same with the father.

Their grieving and wailing was heart wrenching to say the least, and I knew how they felt, and really wanted to join them in my own distress over Charlie, but it was not to happen.

To give them space, I notice the old buffalo just standing there, and it might have been that he knew something was wrong and wanted to help in his own way, and did not hesitate when I harnessed him up with a couple of ropes which I then tied to the bodies of the enemy and dragged them to the site of the truck which had stopped between a cutting offering ample protection for what I was about to do.

I gave the buffalo an order to go home and remarkably he turned and ambled away in that direction.

I checked and searched all the Vietcong for official documentation, identification, maps and their written instructions, which were relatively few and packaged them accordingly.

I did the same with the Major and his companion in the cabin up front and it was clear that the Major was a Viet Cong plant with documents to prove it. He also carried a two-way radio, which I confiscated.

I strategically placed their bodies and then proceeded to soak the whole show with fuel, from the jerry cans that were part of the trucks equipment, up to and including the land mine stash.

I was about to make sure these things never got into the enemies hands.

From behind the tallest culvert I let fly with a couple of hand grenades, and the mother of all explosions went up and when the dust and shit settled I took a peek and sure enough, the job was done to perfection.

I made my way back to the farm house and the girls had wrapt the two bodies in straw woven mats with flowers attached and had started to dig what was supposedly to be the grave.

I took the shovel from them and signalled that I would do the rest and made short work of it as the soil was a sandy composition, and easy to dig.

When it came time to bury the two I lifted them into the grave and all the women threw some flowers and dirt.

When I had filled in the grave I stood there not knowing what to do next, and then it came to me that a few prayers were in order to send the deceased on their way, and to help those who were left behind.

For the life of me I don't know why I did this as I had left Catholicism a long time ago, and God was not foremost in my belief system, and I had not done this for Charlie, my best mate.

Just weird.

I'd had a Catholic up bringing, and had been an alter boys during the Latin Mass times and knew the Requiem Mass routine.

I stood at the end of the grave and made the sign of the cross and proceeded to pray in Latin.

The women fell to their knees, made the sign of the cross and followed me in prayer. I felt like a charlatan.

Their recovery and resilience was remarkable, and as it was close to lunch time, they produced some delectable food stuffs and by gesture and movement sat me down for a mini feast.

Not an understandable word was spoken between us and as the afternoon progressed I unpacked my kit and surveyed the layout to put my tent up, as it soon became obvious to me that help was not just around the corner, as my wireless system had not stood up to my crash landing and the bits of shrapnel that had pierced the haversack and the radio and not to mention my bum and legs that had been peppered when Charlie met his demise.

I selected a patch not far from the house that was flat and had a bit of bush cover.

The ladies offered the veranda, but I figured that if there was to be another attack they would strike the house first, and with a lot of bowing and head shaking I proceeded to erect my camp.

There's no doubt about the Yanks I thought, they know how to make a good tent that's easily put up and with a blow-up floor for comfort.

The family had a Nanny Goat for milk and it also had a kid.

So I tied the Nanny to a tree close by, with a bell around her neck as an alarm system in case there was an invasion during the night. Any foreign movement and she would sense it first.

In sign language I asked if there was a bath, as I was filthy with blood and dirt from head to foot.

I was shown a kind of tub that you could sit down in if you scrunched up your legs and it was filled via a gravity-fed pipe and as well, an over head bucket with holes in it to rinse off when you are finished.

It was primitive, but to me it was luxury, as the cool waters ministered to my aching needs and gave me the opportunity to survey the damage to my body.

The pieces of shrapnel in my bum were small and I guessed they would work their own way out, providing they went in the right direction, but the one's in my left leg were deeply embedded and looked nasty.

I had some items left over in my first aid kit and poured some Benodine into the wound in the hope it would kill any of the bugs lurking there.

One of the girls came down with a mug of some delectable drink and I thought as a matter of courtesy I would try my little piece of Vietnamese I had learnt from Jimmy.

As she gave me the mug I said, Ban muon quan he tinh duc.

She looked horrified and quickly turned away, and it was obvious that it didn't go down too well.

I must have pronounced it incorrectly I thought to myself, and it doesn't look as though I'll get any supper either.

The survival food in the kit turned out to be not too bad, and with the aid of my spirit stove was able to satisfy hunger.

I settled into writing up my report and journal and as the evening sun goes down quite quickly in this part of the world, set my small light, and with the tent zipped up and a mosquito wick burning I was snug as a bug in a rug.

My trusty M16 lay close at hand and my side arm was never out of reach. With the light out I lay back and started to relive the days events, and as I went through them my emotions became a bit raw as it all felt like a bad nightmare, and the blame and shame thing had taken hold of my mind.

In the midst of this mental trauma and chaos I was jolted by the tent door being unzipped, and I thought, so much for that bloody goat idea, and I snapped the safety off on the M16 and raised it to a point, that I thought who ever comes through that flap is about to loose his head. All sorts of things run through your mind as the adrenaline starts pumping.

Then this pretty little head pokes through saying Su-Lin . . . Su-Lin.

"My God, I could have shot you". Tragedy was stalking me this day; is there no respite for this wicked man?

Now I was sounding like I'm crazy.

I figured Su-Lin was her first name so I gestured her to come in, wondering all the while what she wanted. For a moment or two she just sat there as did I, just looking and then she touches my wounded leg and I made a bit of a jump, as she noticed the bandages she put her hands together in a prayer like way and then nervously takes my head in her hands, drawing it to herself and as this happens I see that her breasts are bare, smallish but plump and her nipples are out.

Then it dawns on me what the game is and I hold her ever so gently, not wishing to crush such a beautiful flower.

She smelt wonderful and Reg's instruction came home.

"Don't ever rush a lady.

Just go gently, caressing her sweetly with slow hand movements until you feel that she is relaxed and comfortable with the moment".

And it works!

I don't know what's going on here, but what ever it is I'm going to take it.

That day had been one of, if not the hardest days of my life. I didn't sign up for this. I dreaded the ramifications of this day's events and I was scrambled.

This little lady had saved my life and when it was all over there was no fuss, she just disappeared into the night and I was left rejuvenated.

So many things go through your mind when you are in this state, caught between the elements of fear, exhilaration, doubt, sadness and despair.

I lay there looking at the stars that I could see through the fine weave of the tent fabric, and I guess it must have been about an hour or so when the fly of the tent started to unzip, and as I steadied my rifle again, in pops this same head that says Ky-Lin. This is the other twin, and Su-Lin must have told her about my wounded leg as she carefully manoeuvred herself around to avoid hurting it.

I knew this had to be the other twin for even though it was almost impossible to distinguish them apart, as they were a mirror image of one another there was something that made me recognise the difference. The Ky-Lin's name helped.

She was slightly more bustier, and smiled more readily.

Oh what gorgeous bodies these girls had and I thought I must have died and gone to heaven.

Her beautiful nakedness lay close to me and I applied all of Uncle Reg's advice as I gently suckled her breasts and tenderly touch her, I was able to rise to the occasion and she moaned ever so sweetly to the orgasmic experience.

Ky-Lin and I had a chemistry which transcended all things, and I was so enamoured of her and in that moment after we had finished, I started to sing a Nat King Cole classic 'Darling Je Vous Aime Beaucope, Je ne sais pas what to do, you know you've completely Stolen my heart.

After few more French lines she sat up and looked me straight in the face and said with all earnestness, "Parlez-vous-francais?"

"Oui, school boy francais" I said and from then on it was question and answer time for both of us as we stumbled through memory lane trying to make sense of a language I had almost forgotten and surprising myself of how much you can remember with the right company.

Ky-Lin told me that they weren't Vietnamese but hMung people from Cambodia, and she and her sister had gone to a school run by French nuns and they all spoke French during school hours. However her people were persecuted by the Cambodians, and they were forced to move to this place which was owned by their fathers brother, but he died within a year of them arriving and so their father took over, but they were not able to go to school.

Then came the cruncher when she said to me why did you ask my sister and I in Vietnamese did we want sex?

I was mortified as I recalled to her how I came about that question via a Vietnamese man who was obviously trying to insult me. I thought it said hello, how are you.

Ky-lin put her arms around me in a passionate embrace and said "I forgive you. My sister and I thought it strange, because you were such a nice man".

She left before dawn and in the few short days that were left, I was in the good books with both girls.

They had felt that my statement in Vietnamese was like I was exacting some repayment for my help.

Two more days past, which were the most pleasurable I can remember, under the circumstances, and finally I was able to fix my radio, by cannibalizing the radio I had taken from the Viet Cong Major.

The signal was weak but the receiver '*rogered*' it, and the co-ordinates understood, we were to be picked up by a returning mission.

Two choppers came in and it was decided that the three women travel together in one, so I told Ky-Lin to wear Charlies dog tags at all times and show it to the Americans back at the base as it was possible I may be required some place else.

I put Charlies dog tags around her neck and we said our good byes.

They took off and I assisted the crew of my chopper to locate and collect Charlies remains.

Chapter 19

Gong And Gutser

When the Medics saw the extent of my wound and the swelling and infection that had taken place they started to freak out.

The Colonel listened to my account of events, and read my report and journal of the five Viet Cong operatives, Charlie's death and my demolition of the truck and rescuing the three women, Colonel Drake looked at me and said "you are one hell of a tiger. I could do with a platoon of your kind and this mess would be over in no time".

I had stood there fully expecting a roasting, but instead was receiving a commendation for the actions and courage I displayed.

"Your one of the few men who can make me tear up Colonel and I'll never forget this moment".

"Now get the hell out of here as I'm sending you to Hong Kong with that leg, because I would hate to see some silly bastard cut it off".

I had packaged every thing up with my log and report of the incident concerning the chopper going down and the nature of Charlies death, but I forgot to tell him about Charlies dog tags and that Ky-Lin was wearing them.

It didn't take long for this over-sight to surface and a day or two later the Colonel himself came to my base hospital bed, where I was waiting to be transferred to Hong Kong, saying we have a problem here, both these girls were examined and found to be pregnant and when asked, they showed Charlie's dog tags. You have to shed some light on this son, as it would be impossible for Charlie to father this pregnancy unless there is some difference in the time line.

"I'm sorry Colonel I'm blaming the morphine for that lapse. I wasn't trying to hide it, I just had a mental lapse".

I told him the story of Jimmy giving me a bum steer, and all the events leading up to my having sex with the girls and stressed there was no duress and this would be confirmed by them if questioned by a hMung interpreter, or French speaker.

She thought the tags were mine and I put them around her neck, with instructions that were to help her identity, and at the time of getting onto the helicopter there was not an opportunity to give her a realistic explanation.

Sorry Colonel, I messed up".

"No, no your OK. Get better son and don't let them take your leg off".

With that he was gone.

As I lay in the Surgical Unit of a Hong Kong hospital, having had every man and his dog poke at my leg, and then shake their head and walk away, I over heard one pair who stood outside the curtain talking about my condition and in the end they concluded by saying "we will have to take it off because there is a possibility of gangrene setting in.

"We will make arrangements now".

I lay in my bed frozen by this information and felt trapped.

Sam you cannot believe the level of fear that set in.

The sweat started to pour out of me, and in the middle of my dilemma in the next bed area, which had a curtain around it, came a familiar voice that I recognised, and I called out "Is that you Tom"? The next thing this head pops in with the usual grin on his face, that I had seen so many times when he was my hometown GP and says "who wants to know" and immediately recognises me and says, "Martin what the bloody hell are you doing here?".

"It's a long story Tom but these bastards want to cut my leg off".

That immediately caught Tom's attention and he's onto it straight away. Hospital protocols were not his long suite in medicine.

He's an action stations man, and after an examination of the said leg, with a bit of probing and a running questionnaire like "can you feel that, does that hurt, and if I bend your leg what happens, and so forth, Tom finally looks at me and raises his index finger and says, "one moment and we will get this thing right. Only a minute".

I could hear him further down the hallway calling on the surgical nurses, "darling I'm going to need this, and to another, "darling could you help me with that? Good girl your tops".

It was Tom's signature way of dealing with the nurses and they loved him.

I thanked my luck stars that I recognised his voice from the other side of the curtain for as sure as God made little green apples these white coated scalpel jockeys, with all the best intentions in the world, would have had my leg off and they would have notched up another win.

Tom set the scene, and with a flourish pulled the sheet back, set the girls about their duty, gloved up and turned to me and said, "this may hurt a little Martin, but I know your up for pain".

"You're the boss Tom and if there is anyone I would like to give me pain it's you".

"Good man", and with a style for drama, he lifted this very large syringe for all to see and plunged it into my leg without a skerrick of pain.

"What have you been doing to your self Martin?".

"I had an accident Tom".

"An accident indeed Martin my boy, but I'm here to the rescue, and I'm sure you will make a quick recovery".

Tom set to work and with the aid of surgical scissors and a scalpel made a couple of incisions, all the while encouraging the nurses with "look at this girls as his fingers went deep into the leg scooping out the clotted blood, which he deposited into a dish and as he did so, noted a couple of metallic sounds, and he fished out some pieces of shrapnel and announced to his girl's, "here is the cause of this man's discontent".

And they all gathered around to examine his discovery.

He showed them to me saying, "you didn't get these swimming Martin".

"I'll be here until tomorrow Martin, and I will call in and have another look. Don't worry I'll give them all the instructions they need, as well as telling them you're a special friend of mine. He gave a wink, turned and then left.

What a man I thought. I love you Tom Boland. No wonder the women just adored him.

I was given further sedation and a notice was pinned to my curtain "DO NOT DISTURB!".

However this did not prevent a visit from the Australian Embassy, who were not about to deliver any good news and in my drugged up state told me that I would be escorted back to Australia forth with and would be charged with unseemly conduct and that all privileges would be suspended forth with.

The next day I phoned Colonel Drake, after persuading one of the nurses to organise a phone for me, and told him of the situation, and his only response before hanging up abruptly was, "Fucking idiots".

Tom came back and his response was, "no body moves you until I say so".

The upshot of this sorry saga was that the Colonel got onto the American Embassy, informing them that I was up for a Presidential citation for the actions that I had taken on behalf of the Coalition, and that the President would not be pleased if such an action by the Australian Government took place.

Well did the shit hit the fan. My friend Glenda told me later that there was a frenzy of activity as all concerned were trying to shift the blame from one to another.

Two days later I have a visit from two American Embassy officials, who solemnly presented the "Bronze Star Medal" to me, with a written commendation from the President himself.

"I do hope you understand that I am not an enlisted soldier from Australia", I said.

"We understand that perfectly, and your confidentiality in this matter is fully respected".

Into the fray enters the two morons from the Australian side of things, offering their apologies and blurting out a whole lot of bull shit, and their congratulations on my award and offering their hands, which I refused by saying "piss off".

The Yanks saw the humour of it all, but the dear old Aussies looked miffed.

"Tell Mr President I'm honoured by this award, and thank him for his even handedness in this matter".

A couple of days later I was on my way home, not in a military aircraft but in a big Boeing 737 with business class accommodation and adorable hostesses. I was able to stretch out and enjoy the ride.

I can tell you Sam that by the time I left Vietnam via Hong Kong I was starting to unravel. My nerves were frayed, I was highly fatigued, and now I understand that I was suffering from post traumatic stress, which at the time no one recognised or just plainly did not want to recognise.

This combined with the interrogation I had to endure from those arm chair Generals who had never worn a uniform or seen a battle field was getting all too much.

They were happy to take all the credit but none of the blame and in one interview I had with a whole group of them poking, probing, asking inane questions which all related to my integrity, and after about an hour of this I just exploded and stood up and told them what a bunch of inept fuck wits they were, drawing to my conclusion by pulling out the Bronze Star Medal that been awarded to me by the President of the United states in recognition of my work, having single-handedly tried to save the life of my American comrade, stopping and dismantling an army vehicle loaded with at least 3000 land mines, capable of killing many thousands more in enemy hands, rescuing three women from assassination, and all you can do is to try and incriminate me with all your bull shit notions.

You're all scum and from this moment on I'm out of here. Fuck you!

I left that meeting as mad as hell, and went back to my desk and threw what ever was personal into a box and was marching out in high dungeon when the Ministers toe rag David, along with John, the guy who had got me into this shit, came running after me saying, "what are you doing".

"I told you and your flea bag mates I'm out of here and I mean it, and by the way I want that M16 as it was a personal gift from Colonel Drake to me.

And here's a message from me. If ever you two see me in the street, do not approach me as I will see that as an act of aggression and I will kill you. Stay out of my way and don't try to speak to me or the consequences will be serious. By serious I mean dire. You have been warned.

Communicate with me from now on through my lawyer, as I will be placing any connection to this matter in his hands".

"You can't do this Martin, and I wont let you".

I was burning as I looked him in the eye and said, "Don't mess with me David". I think he got the message.

They turned deadly pale and scuttled off like rats to a hole.

Well I got a lawyer Sam, and he was a bit of a shonk, unreliable and a liar and in one of his manipulative session, I just could not stand it any longer and I said to him, "If you fuck me over in this I will not be happy and there's no telling what I might do".

He tried to squirm, and in the end suggested I see another lawyer. I told him that was not an option, as I had revealed classified information, and I was not about to do the same again, so get your sorry arse into gear or there will be a falling out of huge proportions. He got the message.

My mind was in such a spin that I was having bouts of vertigo and a sense of paranoia would haunt me at night.

As luck would have it, Glenda Sartorsky got a transfer back to Australia on compassionate grounds as her Navy Commander had been severely injured and died.

She returned to Canberra and made discreet enquiries about me, from behind the hand, if you know what I mean, and found out where I was living, and at the first opportunity made her way to my door.

I sensed that she was trying to open up our short-lived relationship, but I quickly put that one to bed by telling her that I was not good for her and that she should set her sights higher. She was kind enough to let that one go to the keeper, and over a couple of shots of a single malt whiskey I told her of the trouble I was having with my lawyer, that I suspected he was a bum, and how I was now caught between a rock and a hard place.

Some of the many attributes of this girl, was that she was smart and quick to fossick out a solution.

She had heard that there was a crackerjack American Army Lawyer, Major Eric Ricardo who had settled in Sydney, and thought that he was worth a shot.

She took it upon herself to go and see him to test the waters and in so doing happened to mention my work with the Americans in Vietnam and my association with Colonel Drake, and my Presidential commendation.

As it happened he and Colonel Drake had been at Fort Benning together training soldiers to join the 75th Ranger Regiment, and he had formed a high opinion of him.

She told him of the shabby treatment I had received from the Australian Government, "who were openly trying to wipe their hands of him", she said.

Major Eric Ricardo sensed the challenge, and forthrightly told Glenda that he would call Colonel Drake to verify some aspects of the situation, not that he did not believe her, he said, but information from the "horses mouth" was a valuable start.

"If everything checks out, I think your friend Martin will have an advocate on his side and we will drive these bastards into some honesty".

Major Ricardo eventually negotiated a deal with the Government which primarily stated that any pending charges would be dropped and that I was to be exonerated from any perceived notions that I was in any way responsible for events that happened during my tour of Vietnam, and that my record would clearly state that all Governmental requirements of me were carried out to the entire satisfaction of the Government, and that there would be no requirement of me to sign a confidentiality/

secrecy clause regarding my appointment and activities carried out on behalf of the Government.

The Governments only rider to these conditions was that I was required to agree to a psychological examination by a Doctor Harry Dailey.

Major Ricardo thought this to be a fairly innocuous requirement and agreed to this inclusion.

I agreed to go along with this, as the whole matter was dragging along interminably and I just wanted to get shot of the whole incident.

That night I went home and called up Glenda and told her of the outcome and said I had a niggling concern that I just couldn't put my finger on, and it concerned this Dr Harry Dailey.

She confirmed as well that this situation also had a worrying aspect to it that she could not identify.

That night Sam, I went to sleep with this cloud hanging over me and just before I dropped off I found myself subconsciously calling out to Turtle, which had an echoing character to it, and from time to time I would intermit this with 'Kenny' having the same echoing sound.

This was cloaked in an overall sensation of knowing that Turtle had my back.

There was an eerie aspect to all this as it felt as though I was in a mountainous setting with mist all around and I could see my voice being carried out on this vaporous cloud.

The words looked as if they were extended like a ribbon, "T u r t l e. K e n n y"

When I awoke next morning confidence filled my being that Turtle had heard me. This was intermixed with another voice that said I was going mad.

The Government was moving swiftly on this and an appointment had been made for me to see the Doctor, which had the overtones of undue haste.

It was quite evident that they were extremely worried that this incident would spill over into the coming elections and would not go down too well if the media got hold of it and the whole grubby mess would hit the fan.

I arrived at the Doctors office in the late afternoon and went through the formalities of signing in and completing endless pieces of paper work.

I was ushered into a large room which in it's self was a small ward and was asked to remove all my clothing and put on this gown which had an open back.

When I questioned the nurse, asking was this really necessary, as I thought I was here for a consultation not a medical procedure. She assured me that this was Doctors way, in that he gave each patient a medical examination before proceeding.

It all seemed a bit strange, but after being offered a warm beverage, I seemed less reluctant to object.

With everything that had happened to me Sam it seemed as though all my resilience was seeping out of me and my preparedness to surrender rather than fight became quite disturbing as I did not have the where with-all to resist.

I sat on the bed that had been allocated to me which seemed to be higher than most as my legs dangled over the edge in a way that allowed me to swing them back and forward just like when I was a kid.

Dr Harry Dailey came in, and his own presence was disturbing, as he was a tall man with incredibly bushy eye brows hiding behind these enormous horn rimmed spectacles, with lenses that made his eyes enormous and a face that had a disturbing appearance, with a deeply frowned forehead, a large bulbous nose with fine red veins running through, and a mouth that turned down.

Dressed in a white coat with the ubiquitous stethoscope draped around the neck and a pocket stuffed with pens, an examination torch and a few other bits and pieces that as a whole looked like a character from a Marx Brothers sketch.

He did some routine stuff with a few grunts and an air of discovery, followed by a question to the nurse, "did Mr O'Leary have his warm drink?"

And that was that, with the assuring words from the nurse, "Doctor will be back in about fifteen minutes. Do you want to lie down?"

I shook my head in the negative.

While he was examining me he tossed a manila folder on the bedside table, which I recognised as a Government security file and at the top in bold letters was my name and then in the top right hand corner, three separate heavy stamped letters,

UDPOI DP T.

I had seen these acronyms in my early research when I first started in the Department.

UDPOI = undesirable person of interest DP= deprogram T= terminate.

He proceeded to write his initial examination findings on the enclosed papers.

My position of advantage gave me the opportunity to view what was going on in this *'ward'* and as far as I could see there were eight beds and all were occupied.

A dimmed light was illuminating the room, and on a closer look, the occupants of the beds were in such a formation that I had to stare intently.

In my semi drugged state, and to my surprise it seemed as though they were all laid out and the way the sheets were covering them, I thought, "Oh my God, I'm in the morgue".

Sam, a sense of fear gripped me momentarily as I thought I must have died and this was the morgue and now I had woken up.

I looked up to the office, which was no more than a glassed in cubicle and there was Dr Dailey staring down in a most peculiar manner it seemed to me, and what ever they had given me to drink rendered me unable to make a sound. I was mute.

As confusion enveloped me, and what seemed to be the next thing I know, but in point of fact could have been twenty minutes or more, in marches Turtle closely followed, by Glenda, and he gives me a knowing look saying "It's OK mate, we're going to get you out of here right now.

Stand up while I put your clothes on you".

And as I got up, the gown fell off and there I was starkers.

Turtle says to Glenda, "I'm sorry love, are you OK with this?"

"It's no problem I've seen him naked before".

"Oh I see", Turtle says with a bit of a grin.

Dr Dailey tried to intervene, but Turtle just said "Out of my way old man", and I was whisked away in a car and then onto a motel that Turtle had previously arranged. "Old mate of mine" he said.

After a couple of hours I had regained my senses and said to Turtle, "thank God you turned up Turtle how in the hell did you find me?"

"You called me?

"I did?" I said incredulously.

"Of course you did you silly bugger and I heard you loud and clear . . . Turtle . . . . Kenny . . . and I knew you would only call if you were in trouble, so I got onto Glenda and the rest is history".

Turtle put on his six-day smile and gave Glenda a wink.

"We found out what the Government was doing.

This Doctor is a proponent of the deep sleep therapy, designed to erase memories, which could have had devastating results for you. Those people you saw in the other beds had been there for two weeks and regularly they are injected with a chemical that eventually cleans out all your memory. Spooky stuff", Turtle said.

"More than that, I got onto some mates of mine who work on the inside of Government bureaucracy, and they found your file and it had been marked UD/ POI/DP/T. In laymen's terms this means Undesirable/ Person of Interest/Deprogram and terminate if necessary.

How did you find out all this Turtle?

These bastards have been trying to get rid of my mob since Cook arrived. You gotta have someone on the inside Mate, or else we would never know what's going on. Self protection Mate.

Old Harry Dailey is going to be in a pickle for letting you go. You know they had an ASIO car outside keeping an eye on you to make sure you didn't escape, but my mates had the fellers outside called away long enough so as we could make the snatch".

This was followed by one of Turtles trademark belly laughs, and Glenda and I saw the funny side of it as well.

"Where do we go from here" I asked, and Turtle promptly replied, "You're coming with me up to my Old Man's place, and you're welcome too Glenda, but this bloke needs some good old Blackfella TLC".

"Glenda will let old Ricardo know what's going on.

There's going to be some wild shit hitting the fan on this one".

"Sam I have been blessed with a few really good friends in my life, and on this day two of them came to my rescue.

I lay back on the bed and heard Glenda say to Turtle that she would be unable to take him up on the offer, and old Turtle replied that's OK love maybe another time.

My eyes started to rim as I thought of this man Turtle.

I started out by saying to him, "have you got a house there?"

"No, he said, You'll be staying with my old Mum as I have to leave for America in a couple of days as the band has a few gigs on the go"

"But your mob's not going to look after me Turtle, I'm white, they'll more than likely want to kick my arse"

"No way Bro you're family".

"How do you make that out?"

"Do you remember when we were kids we made a blood pact, and we cut ourselves and mixed the blood. Do you still have the scar?"

I pulled back my shirt sleeve and Turtle did the same, and there on our wrists were the scars made when we were just children.

And like kids we showed Glenda and we all had a chuckle.

"With my mob mate, that means we are blood brothers and that makes you family!"

Sure enough Turtles family was all that he said they were, and his Mum was a big fat old girl with a heart of gold and tireless energy.

She took me under her wing and it was so good to feel the real love of a parent.

When I first arrived there I asked her what I should call her and she said "you can call me Jean, but then again as you are truly Turtles brother I think you should call me Mum".

And so Mum it was, and I loved that old lady from that day on.

Turtle was ready to get on his way and just before his departure I got a letter from Major Ricardo telling me that Colonel Drake had been seriously wounded and after a lengthy stay in hospital, had been repatriated back to New York. He was living in a villa and now had 24/7 nursing care, as he was totally blind.

I found this information devastating and asked Turtle if he would visit him and render any comfort he could on my behalf.

"Pity they don't have any gum trees in the States as I would be able to do one of our healing ceremonies and smoke the gum leaves. Of course I would have to get Elder permission but I don't think that will be a problem when I tell them of his great deeds as a warrior".

"They have Blue Gums in California, I said, I could have some sent to you in New York".

"You just give me the details little brother I'll handle the rest".

That was typical of Turtle.

"By the way, while you're there you should look up Harold Schwartz and tell him you are my brother. He could be a good contact for you in the future".

We both exchanged a wink and a nod and our usual silly grin.

Chapter 20
The Good You Do . . . .

The Vietcong had been desperate to get the upper hand in the continuing conflict and were prepared to throw anything they could at their enemy, and in the ensuing months after I left, there was one engagement where it looked as though they might well overcome the US Forces. General Biggs was venting the last of his bile on Frank by putting him in as Field Commander, and as he was a '*hand's on Colonel*', he was there in the thick of it directing the traffic, and inspiring his men on to victory.

However, close to his vantage point was a fox hole under heavy siege, and one of the key soldiers in the hole took a severe hit and their calls for a medic were not able to be answered due to heavy operations else where.

Frank grabbed his Medic kit and raced to the fox hole himself, jumping straight in and tended to the wounded soldier, who was encouraged that his Colonel would come to his rescue.

To Frank's surprise there were three Bazooka's there. He immediately loaded them all and without hesitation took aim at the masses of 'Army Crab' like formations, maybe two or three brigades that were headed their way, and let fly.

The injured soldier took heart from this and called out "I'll keep reloading for you Colonel".

Frank must have killed hundreds that day and as he hit the two-way radio with "where in the fucking hell is my air cover, these bastards will not stop.

"Roger that."

No sooner had he got the call away when there was a thud in the fox hole and one of the soldiers yelled, "Behind you Colonel!"

In one reflex, uninterrupted move, Frank grabs a sand bag, which would have weighed up to 200kg and drops right onto the grenade, his body and all, and there is a simultaneous explosion and Frank gets sand blasted from his gut up and looks as though he is dead.

He saved the lives of the other four men in the fox hole.

The air cover followed soon after.

When he's finally removed, he has been skinned all the way up and the Doctors believe there is no chance of survival. But Frank's a fighter and survives except he has lost his eye-sight.

A small price to pay for the lives of his men he's heard to say later.

The overwhelming consensus for his bravery is that he should receive the highest award the country has to offer.

The Medal of Honor is normally presented by the President, but on this occasion he was unable to perform this duty due to extenuating circumstances.

It was an election year.

General Biggs was nominated to deputise on this occasion but when he approached, Frank refused to acknowledge him and told him to stick the medal up his fat ass.

The medal was returned to the President, and he no doubt was mortified by the outcome, he placed it in the top drawer of his desk in the Oval Office.

Turtle and his mates are a smash hit in New York and after a month decide to take a breather for a few weeks before heading off to Los Vagas.

Turtle rocks up to Frank's villa and is greeted by the nurse and he asks to see the Colonel.

Frank, who has the hearing of a fox, hears the request and yells out "No he's not home, and in any case we're not buying anything".

"I'm not selling anything Colonel", Turtle calls back.

"Well what do want you dumb ass".

"Don't want anything, just got a message from a friend of yours Colonel".

"That's just bullshit I don't have any friends".

"Well this one says you do and his name is Martin O'Leary and I can tell you he will be really pissed off if I tell him you refused to see me".

"Well get in here you block head, why didn't you say so in the first place?

"I wanted to be sure you were the right Colonel Drake".

The Colonel gave a bit of a chuckle and said "smart ass eh".

"Let me shake your hand, any friend of Martin is a friend of mine. As they shook hands Frank said, musician I see".

"Very perceptive for a man who can't see".

"I like your forthrightness, what's your name".

"Turtle".

"Turtle, what kind of name is that".

"As a kid I went by the name of Kenny but my folks called me Turtle because I would always stop and examine everything on the way, hence slow as a turtle".

"Well your folks are wrong as I sense that you are as sharp as a tack and nothing gets by you, and I can understand how you're a friend of Martins' because he's the same way.

It's good of you to come and see me Turtle, tell Martin I'm OK and he'd better get his sorry ass over here to see me as I could do with some of his mental 'home cooking'.

"Well that's just the thing Colonel, Martin felt that you'd be all stressed out and in need of a good therapeutic massage, and this is one of my specialities".

"That little fucker knows too much about me. That bastard could read my mind and knew what I was thinking before I did.

I don't know".

"Well what do you say Colonel, will you give it a shot. No cost and nothing to loose".

"You drive a hard bargain Turtle when do you want to do it?".

"No time like the present. I'll just need a little time to set this up".

There was a courtyard just beyond the lounge room and Turtle found a small dish brazier which was perfect for the blue gum leaves he had bought with him and in a short time had them smoking perfectly.

The first whiff made Frank call out "Christ almighty Turtle you're not going to set me on fire are you?"

"Take it easy Colonel this is all part of the process for the massage, it just adds ambience".

"OK I'll go along with it but you are just like Martin calling me Colonel all the time. This is not a parade ground you know. Just call me Frank. I'm more comfortable with that".

"Sure thing Frank I'm comfortable with that too"

As the fragrance of the gum leaves took hold, Frank commented how they seemed to relax him.

Turtle went quiet and surrendered Franks condition to the spirit of his ancestors and gently began his massage and after a short time Frank was under the influence of this treatment letting out some gentle moans as the inner tensions of his life escaped into the aether.

When Turtle asked Frank if he could lie on his stomach, without difficulty Frank readily accepted and it was at this time that Turtle was able to see the extent of his injury.

This poor bastard has been skinned alive, belly up, and even though the skin was growing back it still looked angry, which encouraged Turtle to be extra gentle with him and to understand that he was dealing with a very brave man who deserved respect above the norm.

"What's that you are rubbing on me Turtle" Frank asked.

"Emu oil Frank, I brought it here from Australia".

"Feels good", he said.

Some how Turtle sensed that a marvellous event was in the process of happening and sucked in the smoking frankincense of the leaves.

As he ran his nimble fingers up the spinal cord, his hands stopped just below the neck line where the skull joins in and there was a special place of significance to his fingers and as he gently manoeuvred that spot his arms suddenly stiffened in a straight out format and both thumbs and index fingers set upon this small bone formation, and 'click' something happened that made this area to feel just right.

Frank felt it too and dreamily said "what in the hell was that?"

"That's your life Frank all back together. You have been set free and now you will see everything in a different light".

Frank eased himself over and sat up a little bewildered but feeling like he had never felt before.

"OK Frank let's try a little experiment. I want to take the bandages off your eyes. Are you up for this?"

"Why not, I have never been like this before".

Turtle started the unwinding of the bandages ever so carefully, and finally said to Frank "Open your eyes Frank and have a look at me".

Frank tentatively opened his eyes, moved his eye balls from side to side and then exclaimed "you're black!"

"Do you have a problem with that?"

"I'm sorry Turtle I mean no offence, I just don't know what I was expecting".

"None taken old mate".

Frank began to weep, right from the depths of his inner being, and spluttered out "they said I'd never see again. Thanks to you Turtle you have saved my life, because I was convinced I'd have no life. How can I ever repay you for this".

Frank shook his head in bewilderment. The wide eyed nurse stood there gobsmacked.

"A simple thank you will do Frank that's all".

Frank got to his feet a little unsteadily and gave Turtle a hug and many thank you's.

"I think you should wear some shades as your eyes have been covered for at least six months.

And as well you'll be able to distinguish between friends and enemies, if they think you are still blind. Frank liked that suggestion.

Frank if it's OK by you, I'd like to stay a couple of days just to keep an eye on things. You know what I mean?"

"It'll be my pleasure Turtle. I have a spare room and I'll get the nurse to make up the bed".

"No need for that Frank, a mat on the floor will do. Any place that's convenient".

Turtle continued with his massage therapy during his stay with Frank and the conversations got deep and engrossing.

Turtle ended up telling Frank that his Great Grandfather had been a King before the white invasion of Australia, and that his kingdom was about the size of Austria, full of 'bush tucker', kangaroos, great fresh water creeks and rivers, fish galore, and it used to take him a full twelve months to go around and meet all the tribes and his wives. He was a man who had a great many children and he provided for them all on each visitation.

Frank was amazed and fascinated by Turtles stories, and the massage fest had brought about relief to symptoms that he had been carrying for years, as well as healing the skin taken off in the sand blast.

Frank wanted Turtle to stay on longer, but he replied in that manner which was so characteristic of Turtle, "Oh man that's a nice offer, but I'm a musician Bro and I've got a whole row of gigs lined up here in the US and then I have my responsibilities back home, and foremost is keeping an eye on my brother".

"Your brother, is he in any trouble?"

"You could say that, but it's nothing serious that he can't fix himself. I'm like his wing man".

"Then I wish you well, and give him my best and if he ever finds his way over here I'll look after him".

Turtle burst out laughing with Frank wanting to know 'what's so funny'

"Sorry about that Frank, but you already know my brother".

"I do?"

"Yes it's Martin. When Martin and I were just kids, we were so close as mates that we made a blood pact as brothers and we cut our wrists and mixed the blood. Now that's forever".

"By the way Frank you're welcome to come over anytime. I'm sure you'd love the place".

"And so you see Sam that's the story of Turtle and Frank, told to me verbatim by Turtle, and they still remain close friends to this day, and Frank has even come out here and stayed with Turtles Mum and in that sense we are all family".

Turtle did look up Harold Schwartz and they got along like a house on fire.

He persuaded Harold to find someone who could tell the President about the Biggs affair and the reason as to why Frank refused to accept the commendation from him.

It followed that Biggs got his come-uppance and that Frank was duly invited to the White House where the President warmly welcomed him and apologised for his actions on misinformation.

"Turtles Mum nursed me back to health with her special brand of TLC, but her expertise was not to dig too deep into the psychological darkness of my mind, she just poured out love and she was still able to tell me from time to time, when I phoned her, 'Martin you're still not well, I can hear it in your voice, I'm going to have to tell Turtle, but that boy is moving too often for his own good.

You've gotta come back to your Mum. I'll look after you until you get better. You'll see!"

What a wonderful lady, but I just felt I needed some discovery time on my own.

When I came back to Sydney, I found this little place where I'm at now, and I rented from this old guy, who was a lonely old fella.

He was Jewish, so I had a bit in common with him, and even though we did not talk too much of history I would drop a few hints now and again and it soon became obvious that I respected him, and so he would open up from time to time, and he told me he had been married and his wife had passed over, and the only daughter he had, left Australia and went to Europe where she married, and communications with her diminished as she had married outside the Jewish faith, to a wealthy Baron, who required her to renounce her Judaism.

Giant heart-break there.

One night on my way home, I came across a kafuffle right outside my front entrance, and to my amazement here was my old friend being trounced by two thugs demanding money and at the same time delivering some nasty blows.

I stepped in just before the poor old guy went down and gave these two the thrashing of their lives, which took about six months for them to recover at Her Majesty's pleasure.

Some weeks later he turns up with a bottle of brandy in hand and seriously asks me to sit down, and in the first instance I thought the poor old guy was in some trouble and needed a hand, which of course I was ready and willing to help.

Instead of that he asks me to get a couple of glasses and proceeds to pour the brandy and then says "I don't want you to get mad at me Martin", he says hesitatingly, and I interposed by saying "cut it out old mate I would never get mad with you".

"You're like a son to me Martin, and sometimes I feel like I'm imposing".

"Never mate, you come any time you feel like it, after all the place is yours you know".

"Well that's what I've come to talk to you about".

And straight away Sam I'm thinking, Oh my God I'm going to get the flick from here.

Oh well I suppose it was meant to happen some day, can't stay here forever I quickly philosophised to myself.

"Martin, he says solemnly, I held my breath as he drew a letter from his pocket, this is the deeds to this place which is now in your name".

He had a twinkle in his eyes as he handed over the deeds, and I said "Sol what are you doing, I'm flabbergasted, what's going on?"

"As I have said to you before on any number of occasions that you are like a son to me in many ways, and I want you to have this before I go, so that you will have something to remember me by".

Chapter 21
Finding The Lock For This Key

At their next session Sam looks at Martin and says, 'In all my years of talking and listening to people Martin I can not recall anyone who comes near to this absolutely incredible history of yours'.

Martin looked a bit sheepish and replied "I have difficulty in believing it my self, and talking to you makes me feel I'm talking about someone else.

But I have a reoccurring theme which keeps running through my brain which does bring me considerable comfort, and I can only deduce that it comes from you".

"What is it Martin?

"It's like a song that I can't recall ever hearing but it's familiar to me. Just weird. And it goes . . .

It's alright, it's OK
Doesn't really matter if you're old and grey,
It's alright, I say it's OK
Listen to what I say".
And it goes on, and on.
I'm blown away".

Sam looked at Martin and marvelled that his 'patient' had picked up already on the subliminal music that had been quietly playing in the background, hardly audible, but Martins brain had taken hold of it and was benefiting from the therapeutic input. He would tell him about it later when he felt Martin would understand.

"Lets start shall we, just relax, relax Martin".

And the subliminal music played on.

After sorting out your relationship with External Affairs, what happened after that, and what happened to your daughter Louise".

"Oh that was a hard call Sam, and you will remember Jackie wanted a divorce, and how little Louise told me she had a new daddy and my subsequent conversation and threats to this microbe.

They did marry and moved into this charlatans house and it was not until sometime later that someone caught up with him for his dodgy dealings and cheating that never goes down too well with the big boys, plus his implications with the Government, whereby he was able to gain access to some highly confidential documents, which he tried to sell on to some foreign interests, in the hope of being able to placate his criminal masters.

His Mercedes was found at a look-out not far from town and it would seem that he killed himself with a pistol shot via the mouth.

Cynics were saying that it was not suicide but a contract job. He had two major groups who needed to silence him. The spooks and the mafia.

Jackie could not handle the shame and also the realisation that she had backed the wrong horse and as well put all her deceptive eggs into the wrong basket.

She attempted suicide herself, with the upshot being that Louise was taken into State Care".

"What did you do?"

"Well Sam that old adage that I have mention before, "The good you do will come back to you" came into play again.

"You remember those two American kids in Vietnam who got blown up, well another boy that I did not mention in that scenario, was an Australian youngster who would occasionally hang out with Johnny and Jethro and I could see he was damaged goods from all his encounters in Vietnam, and I suspected he was being given a 'hit' from the boys from time to time, but they were decent enough to recognise that too much 'smack' for this guy was not a good idea and were to some extent shielding him, and at the same time dropping hints to me, as another Aussie, that all was not well with their mate Steven.

So separately, I started to take him under my wing and got the low-down on what was bugging him, and learnt that his father held a senior position in 'The Department of Family Affairs' and that also he had a brother who was a medical doctor, married but unable to have children.

It seemed to young Steven that he just did not measure up with a highly successful Dad and a doctor brother.

He had a severe case of low self esteem and worth, and had joined up for Vietnam to prove his manhood.

This was made tough because of an ongoing heavy tour of duty, and in a sense Steven was hoping he would be killed in Vietnam so that his family could honour him.

I took the case to Colonel Drake and asked him if he could pull some strings with his Aussie contemporaries and counterparts of the same ranking, and to see if Steven could get an honourable discharged because of battle fatigue.

It's amazing what friends can do if they are in the right places.

I wrote to Steven's Dad and told him of the circumstances, and suggested to him that he organise a 'hero's welcome home' on his return, as a restabilising effect for when he re-entered civilian life.

He returned a letter of thanks and assured me that if I ever needed help, he was my man.

Hence when the Louise and Jackie situation happened I took Stevens dad up on his offer, and suggested that he organise for his doctor son, who was childless to take Louise as a foster child with a possibility of adoption if he and his wife saw fit.

Jackie was in an institution for the mentally insane and some how got hold of some drugs and overdosed.

In total, a very sorry affair.

My own situation was tenuous to say the least and poor little Louise did not know where she stood or who her father was, and it was not within my moral capability to see her get hurt in this manner, and with a sorry heart I gave my consent for her to be adopted to the doctor and his wife, and at last she would have a mummy and daddy who would love her to bits.

My counsel to the doctor was to not confuse her by mentioning that I had been her dad, but instead, if I ever came to visit that I could be introduced as her uncle, and thereby make the relationship of family.

They thought this was a very unselfish act on my part, but in reality I could not have offered Louise the life she deserved.

It was not about me, but about her. She was the darling of my heart.

"My God, every day a bomb goes off with you Martin, how you coped has me baffled". Sam said.

That incident ranks as the very top up there of all the things I have ever had to do in my life. But there are times Sam when one must put others ahead of self, and in particular children.

They are not toys to create for selfish satisfaction and then to be discarded at the first hump in the road of life's journey.

We must make sure they are safe and loved.

That's how I felt when signing over Louise to this family, as I believed that this was the right path, no matter how arduous it may be on me.

'John Jamieson' was a comfort then.

I found it difficult to resettle, and after several job knock-backs I thought of security work, but I soon realised this was not my thing, and just by chance one senior executive who had been going through my CV, bailed me up saying, "I had a look at your background and I thought this could be a go for you.

Have you any experience in tracking people down, like absconders or missing persons".

I had to acknowledge that this was not something that I had done previously, but agreed that it did interest me.

"Well I'm prepared to give it a shot if you are and we will see where it takes us".

"That was the beginning of my present career and I just built on it from there, creating my own style of getting the desired results, and here I am."

Sam enquired, "What are some of the high lights or important incidents in your life during that time which have had an impact on you".

"Well fifteen years spins around fairly quickly and the twins of Vietnam had given birth to two beautiful boys, who incidentally turned out to be some what of a medical miracle, in that they had the same blood type and the same DNA, and were identical.

Charlies father, Darcy, and I had lengthy correspondence during this time on the whole matter of the girls and the boys, and it was finally concluded that they all should take his family name, Sukarian, as it would make a whole lot of things easier, including assimilation and citizenship.

And to this end when the boys were born, I suggested that Charlies name should be entered as the father, on the birth certificate, while not strictly kosher, but he was after all a brother to me, of the same blood type, and his name would be more beneficial to the boys.

I would of course, financially support the family until they were twenty one.

After much to and fro, the matter was finally settled.

Charlies father kept reminding me over the years that the financial support I was giving was too much. But I insisted that no matter what, those two girls and the boys were ultimately my responsibility. I learnt later that he had invested the money and they now had a nice nest-egg waiting for them.

Out of the blue Charlies Dad actually called me on the phone and said the boys were graduating to College and they had expressed a desire for me to come over and be present.

"If monies a problem Martin I'd like to buy your airfare".

"No money was not a problem", I lied, and so off I went to the bank with my Unit Deeds and arranged a loan, just enough to make me look anything but down at heel.

I was determined to travel lightly as the clothes I had in my cupboard were not a great selection, and as I had a fairly low opinion of myself and was hitting the grog too seriously, for clothes to be of any great concern to me.

I was flying economy and I threw my gear into the overhead luggage rack and started to settle in and as I looked out of the window a familiar sound made me brace myself, as out on the tarmac a helicopter was landing and some Army Brass disembarked and marched up a stairway which had been joined to the plane and they obviously entered first class.

This whole scenario, with the sight of a military aircraft, the sound of the rota blades beating, sent an emotion so powerfully through my whole body that I thought I was about to explode.

I put my head down between my knees, as though I was hiding, and let out a bellow as the pain was so intense, that it felt like I was about to expire. Tears ran and sweat ran uncontrollably and I thought this is it, I'm about to have a crack-up, this time I've gone over the edge.

Every memory of Vietnam had flooded back like a tsunami and I was drowning, and nowhere to run.

A gentle hand bought me back to some semblance of calmness, and a soothing voice was asking "are you OK, can I help?

"I don't know I think I'm having a crack-up".

"I'm a doctor, maybe I can help in some way, a glass of water perhaps".

"A double whiskey would probably do the trick".

By this time a couple of air hostesses were in attendance wondering what all the noise was about and my lady friend ordered the double scotch and reassured them that everything was under control.

Seat belts on and we were away. No turning back now. When the seat belt sign went off I turned to the lady next to me and apologised for my behaviour.

"Well we do have about twenty hours flying time ahead of us and if you feel like talking I'm a good listener because that's my job.

She seemed to be looking straight at me and I said "you're a shrink"?

She smiled, revealing the nicest teeth I'd ever seen. They were perfect.

"Not the best description of my job, but yes".

The thought had passed through my head that I would probably never see this woman again so what the hell, it might be just the opportunity I needed to get some of this shit out of my system.

The Vietnam saga poured out of me until I thought I must be boring her witless, but she protested no, "I want to hear this through and I'm beginning to understand your hurt. But just excuse me for a moment".

With that she presses the hostess call button and she is assisted up the isle to the toilets.

When she returned I said "what was that all about?"

"What was that all about . . . I needed to go to the toilet".

"I can see that, but why the hostess"

"Haven't you noticed I'm blind".

"No I had not noticed and I'm so sorry, I've been so wrapped up in my own problems that I just did not see".

"Don't get all cut up about it as I'm pretty good at hiding it, don't you think?"

"Well you certainly had me fooled".

"I'm going to give you the short answer to your problems here Martin.

"You're too keen to beat up on yourself over circumstances beyond your control. In a way you are a bit of a control freak but you're hardest on yourself. Now I'm here to tell you to back off and give Martin O'Leary a chance and stop riding him. He's only human, and subject to the faults of life just like anybody else.

You've got to give him some respect Martin.

Have you ever heard of forgiveness? Of course you have, but it has always been for some one else, not Martin O'Leary.

One of God's greatest gifts to us is forgiveness. But it starts with you first Martin. Because if you can't forgive yourself, you can't forgive others.

To be other wise is a false sense of piety Martin.

Now I know you're probably not religious, but that doesn't detract from this behavioural trait.

Get on with your life Martin it's a valuable asset you have there, encourage it, don't destroy it".

"Boy Oh Boy, you certainly shoot from the shoulder".

"Well I'm like you Martin, I figured that I'll probably never see you again, so I wanted to give it my best shot".

"How in the hell did you know I was thinking that".

"By your attitude, by your voice and your sensitivity, and by the way, I admire that in a man".

"OK now it's my turn. I have a degree in psychology myself, but not like yours, mine's in Industrial psychology.

"I'm impressed".

As she seemed to snuggle up to me I said,

"Now, in your own words tell me how a beautiful and talented young lady like yourself ends up sightless. Don't spare the details, I want to know everything about you".

"I grew up in the mid-west, did fairly well at school and completed my med degree and was at the end of my hospital training and decided to drive home for the week-end as I was missing my folks terribly and of course I caught up with some my old school pals and an old boy friend.

But instead of relaxing and catching up on missed hours of sleep, I let myself be persuaded to join in the fun, and of course over did it and then on the Monday afternoon decided to drive all the way back to the hospital, as I thought of my self as being indispensible, important, and way above my colleagues.

Foolishness finds the tree that a wise person avoids.

Instead of stopping when my eyes started to droop, nope I said, I can do it. I'm needed back at the hospital. Dr Sophia Cornell will be there no matter what.

I found the tree. Next thing I know I'm in the hospital, where I was 'so indispensable', coming out of a month long coma.

I could hear all the familiar noises but I couldn't see anything.

My Dad broke the news to me and I wept uncontrollably for a full day. No one could help. I wanted to die. There's no life for me in the dark, please don't let me live.

My despair went on for at least two months, and apart from the eyes I had several fractures and a broken arm.

That was my operating arm I kept hearing myself say.

Time they say heals all wounds. That might be physically, but my trauma was psychological and time was not doing a great job on that.

Because of my extensive injuries bodily, I had to have a lot of rehabilitation sessions and on one occasion I met a young girl who was twelve and even though I could not see her I thought I could feel her spirit, and her hurt.

She had been diagnosed with terminal cancer and naturally was distressed that her short life was about to end.

Forgetting my own woes I reached out to her with compassion, and in my blindness tried to understand what she was going through, and thus it shrunk my problem into insignificance.

She gave me hope, because this experience led me to believe that I might have calling in this area.

After several months of meeting with this girl and counselling her, encouraging her and giving her hope that in life nothing is impossible, she came running into my ward one day, crying out "Sophia, Sophia, your right nothing is impossible, my tumour is shrinking. The doctor has said 'I don't know what you are doing but keep it up because it's working'.

And I told him it was you".

"This set my flame alight and I thought maybe I can do this.

I immediately enrolled in a course of clinical psychology, told them of my condition, to which they basically said 'no problems' and with the aid of tapes and a very keen final year student who studied with me, I completed the course. She said it helped her too, by reading the papers to me.

We have remained very close friends and she operates a practice in New Hampshire.

Attending seminars was my thing and on one occasion this elderly gentleman was impressed with my abilities and take on the profession. At first I thought he might have been a "dirty old man" looking for some young stuff, but a further revelation came to hand when his wife came and sat down beside me for a chat, and she was also a psychologist.

Eventually she said 'you know my husband is quite taken by you and I must say so am I.

If you could see, you would notice that we are reasonably old, and we want to retire from practice, but we are unable to find someone who could take over and meet our strict requirements for our patients'.

"What makes you feel I'm that person?

As you can see I'm handicapped and not every patient will take to that".

"You're not handicapped Sophia, your beautiful and compassionate, your smile is genuine, and you can see and understand more than most sighted people.

I think you are perfect for our practice. Would you like to consider it?"

"Well here I am a lady of circumstance, not unlike yourself Martin".

We spent the rest of the flight talking on just about anything and basically cuddling up, that on lookers could have reasonably suspected that we were a couple.

LA Airport is a big affair and Sophia invited me to come and stay for a week when I returned from seeing the boys. She gave me her business card, and a car was waiting for her and we bid our good byes in a fairly formal fashion.

Charlies father, Darcy was there to meet me with a big smile, paying me the compliment of saying "you don't look a day older from when I met you in Vietnam".

It's the thing people say to each other, and I returned 'you don't look too bad yourself'.

When I arrived at the house every one was excited and a little bit coy.

The twin girls definitely did not look a day older, it was bazaar and hard to believe.

The boys were really handsome and polite and to some extent shy of me, but they stood tall, and with a firm hand shake said,

"What shall we call you Sir'.

"Well not Sir for starters, I think Martin will do. OK?".

"Charles and Martin, two of the best looking guys I've seen in a while.

Looks like someone's been feeding you well too.

My God you both look like Charlie, and instantly I turned and looked at Grand Dad Darcy, I'm sorry I meant that in the nicest way".

I was so nervous about this family meeting that my foot got to my mouth.

"Don't stand on ceremony here Martin, you're one of the family, as you may not know, we've informally adopted you, and hope that's OK by you."

"I'm honoured Darcy and to you Colleen, Darcy's wife, and to you Mai, Su and Ky's mother, whom I had never really got meet prior to this, as back in Vietnam she kept well out of the action that was going on.

The graduation night was a tremendous success for the boys and they were duly acknowledged as Dux students of the school, and everyone was pleased that their "uncle" could make it all the way from Australia for the occasion.

The "uncle" was pleased too.

Back at Darcy's house for the rest of my time with the family, it seemed to me to be a question and answer time, night and day, and even though I found it mentally exhausting after the trauma event on the aircraft, it was in it's own way therapeutic and cathartic for all concerned, especially the boys as they hung on every word and at the end of my stay they were hanging all over me.

Their Mum's by the way were also graduates and were an inspiration.

A week goes by quickly, and as I'm not one for airport dramas with good by's, we did all that at home, with kisses and hugs, and I convinced Darcy that I would prefer catching the bus back to the LA and it would give me a chance to chill out.

He understood.

"But before I go, I am aware that Charlie was posthumously awarded the Bronze Star Medal, and so was I. I'd like the boys to have mine as well".

I got off the bus and was heading for the nearest cab rank when I heard this commanding voice "O'Leary. Martin O'Leary?"

I stopped in my tracks and watch this figure approaching. It became clear that he was a policeman, as he had the badge and a side arm.

He wore a five gallon cowboy hat and shades, just like they do in the movies, and the next thing he said was "you old bastard, I'd know you anywhere". By this time he had a three day smile on his face as he approached and I was looking but not recognising, and said as I dropped my kit to the ground, "guilty as charged Sheriff".

At this point he removed his glasses and hat, and I nearly fell over as I recognised him as Captain Harrison Young.

William Lowry

Oh he was a sight for sore eyes, as another round of hugs, back slapping, and hand-shakes followed.

Over a cup of brilliant LA coffee I told him of my reasons for being here, and he told me "I'm still a Captain you know, only of the LA Police Department".

"I'm here for about four days as I'm seeing a psychiatrist in Beverley Hills, still need a bit of work on the old brain box".

He nodded knowingly, "Its not easy Martin, and I know where you are coming from, as I have flash backs myself from time to time, but the Department keeps an eye on me".

Harrison was still the straight up and down guy of the past and I drew comfort from that.

We agreed to catch up again before I left to return home and with his card in hand, that had all his direct line contacts, he gave me a salute farewell as I got into a cab headed for Dr. Sophia Cornell.

I was greeted at the door by an all-smiling black lady who introduced herself as Delores, Doctors' personal assistant and right behind her was husband Leroy, who immediately sent hackles up my spine.

I could hear Sophia's voice from up the stairs bidding me welcome, as Leroy offered to take my kit, but I refused and humped it onto my shoulder as usual, and went to greet the good Doctor.

A quick look around revealed to me what seemed to be an excessive number of security cameras, but I put it aside in the excitement of catching up with Sophia again.

She then announced, with a mischievous smile, that Delores and Leroy were going to take a four day vacation, so we'll have the place to ourselves.

Sophia was pleased, but Delores and Leroy definitely showed signs of displeasure.

Their bags were packed and at the door and as I went down to lend a hand, this Leroy turns on me with a veiled threat, "you better watch yourself man or you'll have me to deal with".

All delivered with that too familiar TV ghetto mob style.

I wheeled on him and whacked him up against the wall with a Bruce Lee choke-hold, that fairly had his eye balls popping.

"You ever speak to me again like that and I'll kill you. Make a noise and I'll do it now".

Leroy nearly shit himself and Delores came back to see what was going on and let out a bit of a yelp as I shoved him out the door.

"Everything OK Martin?".

"Yes, just helping Leroy with his bags and telling him not to come back before Tuesday. OK?"

She thought that was funny, and said 'let me show you around'.

We visited the bed rooms with Sophia showing me her room, and there they were again, those bloody security cameras, three in fact, two in the bed room and one in the en suite bath room.

Now I knew there was something fishy going on here.

My old investigative hunches were not out of whack.

Sophia showed me my bed room which was next to hers and with a twinkle in her eye, it was hard to believe she was blind, 'with inter connecting doors'.

"Nice touch".

It was a massive place for one person I questioned, but she said Delores and Leroy had had their own flat out the back.

The counselling office was next, and there again were the ubiquitous cameras.

Down stairs was a gym and a lap pool along with the cameras placed at an angle that minimised their security value. They were spying cameras I concluded.

Sophia said it was Leroy's job to look after security along with being the general rouse about and handy man.

I threw in a few why's and wherefores and said,

"Leroy's office was just before you go outside to their flat?".

"Why are you asking all these questions Martin" she said quizzically.

"It's part of my thing Sophia, I just like to know how things work".

"A man thing I suspect".

"Yeah, probably Sophia".

We ate and enjoyed some beautiful California red wine and Sophia just gently quizzed me on my visit to see the boys and generally how I was travelling. It was all non invasive stuff, and I felt relaxed and enjoyed the ambience of the place and mulled over whether or not she was lonely in a giant place like this, she said it had been owned by a movie star originally and the two old psychologists she taken over from bought it because they felt it would make the "Stars" who came for treatment, feel less intimidated in these surrounds.

She also said that she did not really have a full concept of the size, as being blind it was hard to imagine the extent of the place.

Next morning it was agreed that we would take a dip in the lap pool to start the day off.

She turned on some mood music, and then to my surprise she dropped the gown she was wearing to reveal she was naked.

"You're not embarrassed are you Martin", with a bit of naughtiness in her voice.

"Not at all. I'll help you in".

She was in terrific shape and as we frolicked in the pool I could see the faint traces of the scars that could have nearly taken her life.

"Do you do this often", I asked.

"Yes I love skinny dipping after I've had a work-out".

Out the back of the pool I could see Leroy's "office" and while Sophia did a dry down I went over and had a look, and just as I had suspected this was the control room for the security cameras through out the house.

I found the transmission cable and closed down the system and I thought I'll come back later for a closer inspection.

There was a rub down bench beside the pool that she said Delores used to give her a massage and looking right up the gun barrel was Leroy's camera.

I suggested that I could give her a massage, but Sophia was in the mood for love, and it did not take me more than an instant to feel the same way.

I told her I felt I was taking advantage of her to which she replied, "I need a man like you in my life right now Martin, and unless you feel I'm unacceptable" . . .

"Are you kidding, you're the best thing that has ever happened to me".

She lay back after we had finished and said "life has never been so good, I want to cling to you forever".

"Hey don't get too carried away, I laughed, I'm a damage man, you'd have a non paying patient for the rest of your life".

"Your too cynical Martin".

We fell into another embrace. She was as hungry for this as I was, and too much was not enough.

Oh happy days.

Finally I said I would like to give her a special massage and convinced her I was good at it, as I had got this "magic tuitio" from a friend of mine. I meant Turtle.

"What's so special about this ", she asked.

"You'll see", was my only reply.

I selected a massage oil from her collection which was Emu and Aloe Vera oils with a sensational aroma.

And so began a remarkable journey and as I worked her back, her buttocks, down her legs and feet and back up until I reached her anus, which has tender skin, as you know Sam, just like our lips, and though she bucked at first, I encouraged her to just let it happen and in the end she was saying don't stop, I could see that every sinew in her body was letting go and she was entranced.

I turned her over and stretched her arms, shoulders, hands and fingers, and gently massaged her beasts and she was in ecstasy. Down her legs to her toes, with a reflexology foot massage, and back up to her outer vulva and that completed the total tone up.

"Oh you are good Martin, you are good".

She turn over and I proceeded to follow the spinal cord with a nerve tingling sensation poring right out of my hands, right up until I got to the neck and with thumb and index finger feeling their way, and just as Turtle had said, there was this small bony outcrop just below the skull.

All the while, *'in spirit'*, I had been in contact with Turtle and I had this sensation, that I could actually hear him speak his instructions to me, and as I gently manipulated this area, there was a sudden *'pop'* like experience, as this object moved to it's rightful place.

"My God what was that", Sophia exclaimed.

"Just be still Sophia and relax, and I massaged her again ever so gently, not wanting to disturb anything.

And then as if it was as clear as day I heard Turtle say, "She's OK mate let her sit up".

Sophia sat up and her chin began to tremble and then the tears followed and she hugged me saying, "I can see Martin, I can see".

What a time of rejoicing that was, and Sophia was giddy with excitement.

We talked long into the night, drank champagne, sang a little, and Sophia remained in gob smacked wonderment.

We fell into bed together, as she would not have it any other way.

The next day we just stared at each other like two cats up a tree, not saying much but just taking in the wonderment of it all.

Eventually I had to tell her about Turtle and my connection to him as a blood brother, and try to explain the wonderful powers for good that this man had, even though I did not really have full grasp on it myself.

Sophia sat there listening intently, and I could feel her intellectual mind trying to make sense of what I was telling her.

"Don't try and intellectualise it, I said, just let it sink in and enjoy the knowledge and the result of your experience. I have named this the 7th dimension"

"I'd continue to wear your shades for the moment until you work out how you are going to handle this professionally in your work and the people around you.

Could be a good way to find out who your friends really are.

And for the rest of the day I'm going to check your place out. I do it for all my friends, and you can get used to being a sighted person again.

Life's just great aint it?" I said with a put-on American accent. She smiled back so beautifully.

Just as I had suspected Leroy's den was a full on recording studio with banks of monitors and movie equipment with video capability and stacks of recorded cassettes.

That was enough for me and though I did not want to put a dampener on Sophia's joy, time was critical and I was booked to fly home in a couple of days time.

I sat pondering the situation and Sophia caught on to the fact that something was troubling me.

It was hard, but I felt if I didn't bite the bullet now then the whole situation could fly out of hand all to her detriment.

"OK out with it, what troubling you. I can see you now you know, and it's not a pretty picture. You want to cut and run. Is that it?"

"Sophia, the last thing I want to do is hurt you, but there is something I must tell you but I'm not sure you are up for it".

"For goodness sake Martin, I may have been blind, but I am an adult so out with it!"

This girl had fight in her.

However the information she had to hear took every ounce of adulthood she could muster.

Betrayal and indecent exposure was a double whammy.

We talked through the ramifications of this and I offered a plan that I thought would minimise the damage, and in particular her professional reputation.

I filled her in on Captain Harrison Young and suggested I contact him immediately to get the ball rolling.

"Oh Martin, what would I have done without you".

"If you hadn't taken a chance in inviting me up here, this voyeur would have continued on his sick way and you would not have been the wiser".

"My old man use to say to me "the good you do will come back to you Martin" and I believe that's true".

I called up Harrison and told him I had a very sticky situation to deal with and I needed his help.

He was quick to help, and even though it was his day off, in fifteen minutes he was there.

When he met Sophia he presumed she was blind and in the course of our introductory conversation said to me, "have you heard about old Colonel Frank Drake?, One of your mob from Australia did something to him and he got his sight back. One of our Nam mates told me the other day", he chortled away looking at me.

Sophia removed her glasses and said "so have I".

Well poor old Harrison was staggered and scratched his head in dismay.

We'll tell you all about it down the track mate, but right now I want to show you the evidence, and get your authoritative opinion on how best to handle this.

"All Harrison could say was "the dirty mongrel, I'll lock him and his missus up right away".

"This is an idea I had mate, we have to protect Dr Cornell's position and reputation by what ever means.

My thinking is that if you arrest them, and charge them this is going to go public with a lot of adverse scuttlebutt and innuendo, that could leave the Dr. in an invidious position and having to open shop elsewhere. Not a good scenario I'd have thought".

"Well you seemed to have done all the thinking for us Martin. What's your suggestion"?

"How about we gather these two creatures up and stick them in the pen for as long as you can, show them that you have all the evidence to put them away for what ever time, scare the shit out of them big time, but you will let them go, by the good nature of their previous employer, if they surrender all the cash that they have stolen from her in defrauding the books, sign a statuary statement of some kind, to the effect that if they are ever seen in this state again, or to be in possession of any other material related to this matter, you will lock them up and throw away the key.

And as well, that they are never in a life time to approach the Doctor under any circumstances.

"I think I can handle that Martin, is there anything else you want to tell me about my job.

Just joshing man, you can come and join my team any time".

"Let's have something to drink and maybe something to eat Captain".

Well thank you ma'm you know any friend of Martins is a friend of mine.

Did he tell you about me and him in Nam?", she nodded.

"That was a bad time for Martin, but he looks as if he's got his act together".

Harrison was well and truly enamoured with Sophie, he watched her every move and was attentive to almost the absurd.

Sophia initially thought it was a bit of a giggle, but after I explained to her what a great guy he was, in a responsible position, well respected in the community as man with integrity, so she should take another look at the scene.

Harrison knew of another black lady who could perform the work of Delores, as a receptionist, book keeper, cleaner and companion if she liked, and she came with his high recommendations as she had been looking after him when he was a child.

"You don't need a Leroy, you just call me up and if I can't handle it I know some one who can".

"You're just too much Harrison, no wonder Martin speaks so highly of you".

A further investigation of Leroy's pad revealed a large stash of cash, which he had stolen from Sophia, and so as not to bring attention to himself, he didn't bank it, but kept it in his 'hideaway hole' for the rainy day he thought was coming his way.

Well things were just about stitched up to everyone's satisfaction and I had to be on my way.

"Why do you have to leave Martin, I do love you, you know.

"Sophia I love you too, but I'm not about to inflict myself onto someone as beautiful as you.

I'm too old for you, too complicated, with too much of an itchy foot to settle down. You need a guy like Harrison. He's madly in love with you. He's an American and one of the truest guys I have ever met.

He comes with minimal baggage.

I'd put my life in his hands. Don't let him slip through your fingers".

"Your so wise Martin", and she kissed me good bye.

I heard later from Harrison how he had pursued her and won her heart and they were to get married and would I come.

I respectfully replied that I was unable to make it and wished them both all the success in the world.

Chapter 22

Is This The Last Key?

"So here I am Sam, I've spilt my guts, warts and all, and strangely I feel great about it, even though my reputation with you will no doubt be tarnished with all the shenanigans.

I don't know what it is you did, but what ever it was, you have released all that's been contaminating me for years".

"You have healed yourself Martin. All you needed was someone to hear your story, to be non judgemental and with a few nudges here and there to keep you focused.

And then 'whamo' you pop out the other side like you have been born again.

Your brain is a self healing machine. Marvellous isn't it?

Don't change a thing Martin!

Your reputation with me was never in question, but it has been enhanced by your frankness, honesty and your ever good will to your fellow man.

I don't know of any other person I have met who measures up to your standard, and I probably never will as you have set a high bench mark that others will have difficulty in reaching. You have sacrificed your own chance at happiness by not taking up the offers of so many.

You have liberally given support to those in need, when your own need was so depleted and on the edge, yet you gave unstintingly.

You have cared for your children at great personal and emotional cost, but you did not abandon them.

Well done Martin, I am proud to call you my son and that you are part of my family.

You have taught me more than I could have ever learned in a normal life time.

I now understand why Rossannah worships the ground you walk on. She loves you Martin and I love you.

Martin and Rossannah went on to get married, and as the mysteries of life always unfolds to those who keep an open mind and heart, and a longing to give, rather than take; they had a child, a little girl and they named her Rosie.

Remarkably Sam went on to live until he was ninety nine and remained the patriarch right to the end, and was heard to say, by those who hang on his every word, that no one could give him anything else to add to his life.

In a quiet private time with Martin just before he shrugged off his mortal coil, he took Martin's face in his hands, kissed him good bye, and his last words to Martin were "Don't change a thing my son".

He closed his eyes and went to stand before his Maker.